BAD HABIT

CHARLEIGH ROSE

CHARLEIGH ROSE

Paperback

ISBN-13: 978-1979833561

ISBN-10: 1979833567

Cover Designer: Letitia Hasser, RBA Designs

Editor: Paige Maroney Smith

DEDICATION

For Sara Burch, lover of jerks, collector of alphas.
I hope Asher does you proud.

And for Leigh Shen, & Ella Fox.
This book wouldn't exist without you two.

Second chances are not given to make things right, but are given to prove that we could be better even after we fall.
-Unknown

SOUNDTRACK

"Hoodie"—Hey Violet
"Unholy"—Hey Violet
"Eyes Closed"—Halsey
"Back to You"—Louis Tomlinson ft. Bebe Rexha
"Glycerine"—Bush
"RIP"—Olivia O'Brien
"Once Upon a Dream"—Lana Del Rey
"Ghost"—Halsey
"Haunting"—Halsey
"Do Re Mi"—Blackbear
"New American Classic"—Taking Back Sunday
"The Funeral"—Band of Horses
"The Boy Who Block His Own Shot"—Brand New
"Jesus Christ"—Brand New
"Walk the Line"—Halsey

THREE YEARS AGO...

The first time I laid eyes on Asher Kelley, drunk and bleeding, I decided two things. The first being that he was the most beautiful boy I'd ever seen in my entire life. I was sure of it. And the second thing? He was the kind of boy that I should never, under any circumstances, get involved with. But, even my pre-pubescent self knew on some level that I'd gladly reach inside my own chest and offer him my beating heart if he'd only ask.

What I didn't know then was that would be the first of many nights just like that one. Turned out, Asher's dad was a little bit of a drunk, and a lot of an asshole. If it wasn't his dad, it was some poor soul who decided to cross Asher. He was always looking for trouble, it seemed. Or maybe trouble just knew where to find him.

My brother, Dashiell, was always quick to kick me out of his room on the nights Asher snuck in. It became routine to them. Just another Thursday night. But seeing him tumble through my brother's window never ceased to break my heart and make it beat faster all at once.

Over the past three years, Asher has pretty much become a permanent fixture in our lives. My parents are either oblivious or don't care enough to question why he's always here, or why he occasionally dons a black eye or a split lip. Part of me hates them for it. They've made their feelings on Asher clear. They don't like him hanging around, think he's a *bad influence*. But Dash is stubborn, and loyal to a fault. So, they tolerate Asher at best.

I'm sitting cross-legged on the floor of Dash's room playing Guitar Hero on his Xbox when I hear the tell-tale tapping on the window that signals Asher's arrival, and I'm immediately uneasy. Dash was supposed to meet Asher and their other friend, Adrian, at a party earlier. Alarm bells go off, and I drop the guitar, scurrying over to the window on my knees. I help him slide it open, and he hefts himself over the sill.

"Asher? What happened? Where's Dash?" I reach for the lamp on Dash's bedside table, and when it illuminates his swollen, bloody face and T-shirt, I gasp, my hand flying to my heart.

"Asher!" I run to his side and help him to the bed. He stumbles over the laces of his untied combat boots, almost taking us both down.

"Oh my God, say something!" I panic, warring between getting my dad or calling the police.

"Calm down." He chuckles darkly. "You're going to wake up your pops."

"That's exactly what I'm going to do," I snap, before turning on my heels. Someone needs to do something for once. And being a pretty powerful attorney, my dad is someone who can actually help. I feel a hot hand grip my wrist, and despite the circumstances, my already racing heart quickens at his touch.

"Come on," he says in a hushed, gravelly tone. "It's just a little cut. You should see what he looks like," he tacks on with a hint of a smirk tugging at his full lips.

"Is that supposed to make me feel better?" I ask, trying to jerk my arm out of his grasp, to no avail. "Because it doesn't. Not even a little." Tears start to fill my eyes, and his own soften at the sight.

"I'm okay, Briar," he promises, his voice uncharacteristically soft. "Just hang out with me for a while until Dash gets back." Indecision swirls in my gut, and I bite my lip, contemplating my next move.

"Fine." I sigh. "I'll be right back." I tiptoe out into the kitchen, my bare feet sticking to the hardwood floor. I grab a washcloth and run it under the sink before snagging a bandage out of the cabinet. I'm no nurse, but it's better than nothing. When I come back to the room, Asher is sitting on the bed with his elbows on his knees and his hands fixed on either side of his neck. I drop to my knees in front of his spread ones and gently brush his dark hair off his forehead. His eyes snap up to mine—one green with yellow flecks, and the other a honey brown with flecks of green. He swallows, his throat bobbing with the motion. I avert my eyes and bring the damp washcloth up to dab at the dried blood crusted near his eyebrow. He clenches his jaw, but says nothing as I do my best to clean him up.

"Where's my brother?" I question, if only to distract myself from his close proximity. Up until recently, I'm fairly certain Asher has only ever seen me as an annoying little sister. Lately, things have been… different. Like all the air is sucked out of the room when we're in it. And I can't help but wonder how no one else feels it when it's suffocating me.

We've had a few *almost* moments. I thought he might even kiss me once. I was walking out of the bathroom in my towel, and there he was, waiting on the opposite wall with his arms crossed. His eyes raked down my damp body, my long, blonde hair dripping water onto my pink toes, leaving a puddle at my feet. His nostrils flared. I squeezed my towel tighter, and he moved toward me. He extended his arm, and I could feel the heat of his skin at my hip, even through my towel. I sucked in a breath, closing my eyes. Then… nothing. I opened my eyes to see that aloof smirk back in place, his face mere inches from mine. His hand gripped the doorknob I was standing in front of.

"I need to take a piss," he said, moving past me. I swallowed my embarrassment, rolled my eyes at myself for thinking he might actually kiss me, and scurried back to my room, leaving him chuckling behind me.

"He's at the party," he says, bringing me back from the past. I feel my cheeks heat from the lingering mortification of that day.

"I never made it there," he clarifies. "I just thought I'd chill here for a while." He doesn't elaborate, but I know what he means. Until he cools off. Until the alcohol catches up with his piece of shit dad, and he finally passes out.

Rising on my knees, I blow on the gash above his eyebrow to dry it off a little before applying the Band-Aid. His eyes squeeze shut, and one hand comes up to grip the back of my bare thigh. I freeze, feeling that tightening low in my stomach that only seems to happen when Asher is near.

"It doesn't look that bad now," I say quietly, reaching forward to pluck the Band-Aid off the bed next to him. I feel his thumb rub small circles on the back of my thigh, and I try not to gasp. Crazily, I wonder what that hand would feel like between my legs. I shake that thought from my head and smooth the bandage over his cut with my thumbs.

"Head wounds tend to look a lot worse than they

really are," Asher says, clearing his throat and pulling away. I back up, still dazed, as he stands and reaches behind his neck to pull his blood-speckled white tee off his back before balling it up and tossing it to the floor. I think he's going to take one of Dash's shirts, but he doesn't. He plops back down on the bed, exhaling roughly, running a hand through his hair. I gulp watching the way his forearms flex with the motion, and when he lies back on the bed, displaying the muscles on his stomach, I have to look away.

He's always been magnificent to me, with his onyx hair that hangs in his dark, mismatched eyes. His full lips and slightly pointed nose. The dimples that I didn't even know existed for an entire year into knowing him, because the boy never really smiles. Smirks, yes. Taunting, mocking, sarcastic grins. But a full-blown Asher Kelley smile is rarer than a blue moon. Now that his shoulders are broader, his chest and arms bigger, and his jaw more chiseled...he's a man. And he's perfection. Suddenly, I'm all too aware of my small breasts that visibly harden beneath my tank top and my tiny baby pink sleep shorts. I'm looking every bit of fourteen, feeling so inferior kneeling in front of this young god.

Asher scrubs a hand down his face, and I notice that his knuckles are bloody, too, but the sight is nothing new.

"Do you want ice?" I ask as I stand up, gesturing toward his hands.

"What, this?" he asks, examining his knuckles. "I'm fine."

"Do you want me to go?" I fidget with the hem of my shorts. His eyes follow the movement, then move up my body until his eyes lock on mine.

"No." His tone is firm, but he doesn't elaborate. My stomach flips with nerves, and I nod, biting on the corner of my lip.

"Do you...want to watch a movie?"

A shrug. "Sure."

"What do you want to watch?"

"You pick."

I look around for Dash's remote before finding it underneath a sock and start flipping through the channels. I stand in front of the TV awkwardly, not knowing if I should take my spot on the floor or join him. Asher pats the bed next to him, seeming to sense my hesitation.

"I won't bite, Bry."

I sit next to him and settle on one of my favorite movies. No matter how many times I've seen it, I always have to watch it when it's on.

"Really? *Tombstone*?" Asher cracks a real smile at that.

"Hell yes. It's my favorite."

"I'll be your huckleberry," he says, quoting the movie.

"Shut up." I give a weak smile, still feeling helpless

in this situation, but I toss a pillow at him in an effort to appear unfazed.

"Shit!" he growls, bringing his hands up to his face.

"Oh my God! I'm an idiot! I'm so sorry!" I say, crawling over to his side of the bed, feeling terrible for already forgetting.

"Are you okay?" I ask, prying his hands away, but when I do, he's laughing.

"Jerk," I huff, turning away, but he grasps my wrists and flips me onto my back. His body hovers over mine.

"I'm sorry," he says, not sounding sorry at all. "But you were looking at me like my dog just died. I had to do something to lighten the mood."

He still has my hands pinned above my head, and he's close enough that I can smell his spearmint gum and the faint trace of cigarettes.

"I worry about you," I admit, not making any effort to escape. His eyes clench shut, like it physically pains him to hear those words.

"Don't," he says. "The last thing an angel like you should be doing is worrying about a fuck-up like me."

"You're not a fuck-up. And I'm no angel."

Asher drops his forehead, rolling it against my own.

"You are," he insists, his lips trailing from my cheek down to my ear, leaving goose bumps in their wake. "And this is the last fucking thing I should be doing with you."

"What are you doing with me?" I whisper.

"Touching you," he says, rubbing my wrists with his thumbs. A small noise slips from my mouth, and he lowers his body onto mine. Instinctively, my legs part to make room for him. He groans once he fits his hips between them.

"I need to leave," he says, his voice thick and strained.

I lick my lips, mustering up all the courage I can when I ask, "Can I kiss you?"

He makes a pained noise, but he doesn't deny me. He presses his lips to the skin just beneath my ear, then he trails his lips back across my cheek, down to my chin, and finally, his mouth is on mine. I've kissed a few boys, even though Dashiell, Asher, and Adrian, have done their best to run them off, but this is so much more than just a kiss. At least, for me it is.

Asher licks the seam of my lips before tugging the bottom one into his mouth. He sweeps his tongue inside, and tentatively, mine flicks out to tangle with his. I don't know what I'm doing, but he must like it, because his hips flex, grinding into me. I feel him harden beneath his jeans, and I spread my legs further, wanting *more, more, more*. I pull my hands out of his grasp and bring one to the back of his neck, kissing him harder. The friction between my legs is something I've never experienced, and I don't think anything could stop me from chasing this feeling. I feel it building, much more intense than anything I've ever done alone in the privacy of my bedroom. I wrap my legs around his back and rock into him, uncaring of seeming too eager.

"Fuck. Stop," he rasps. I don't.

"Briar, that's enough," he says, pinning my hands to the bed once again, this time using his demanding tone that brooks no argument. But I don't listen. I tilt my hips up again, and he groans. Before I know what's happening, I'm flipped over onto my stomach, my arms trapped at my sides by his knees as he straddles me.

"You're fucking fourteen, Briar. I'm not even in high school anymore, for fuck's sake."

"I don't care," I say stubbornly. "I'm old enough to know what I want." My hair is in my face, muffling my words. He brings a finger to my cheek and sweeps the strands behind my ear.

"You have no idea what you want," he counters. "What you're asking for."

His condescending tone makes me feel childish and inferior, and if it wasn't for the fact that I could feel his want for me digging into my backside, I'd probably feel hurt, embarrassed, and rejected. In a brazen move, I arch my backside and move against him.

"So, show me," I say, looking over my shoulder at him. His eyes are fixed on my pajama shorts that have ridden up, exposing my cheeks.

"No," he says harshly. I drop my face into the mattress. God, my *brother's* mattress. I'd tell him to take me to my room if I thought for one second he wouldn't come to his senses and put a stop to this—whatever *this* is.

He shoves off me, horrified, and sits as far away from me as Dash's queen bed will allow. "Fuck!" he yells, tugging at his hair. Seeing him like this is enough to make me feel guilty, but not enough to regret anything.

"Why, Asher?" I ask, tears brimming my eyes. "What is *so* wrong with me?"

When he doesn't respond, I turn to leave, but Asher lunges for me, snatching my wrist and pulling me back toward him until I'm straddling his lap.

"Briar," he says, his eyes searching mine, begging me to understand.

"Say what you mean and mean what you say, Ash. I'm not a mind reader."

"You're *fourteen*," he stresses, as if that's reason enough. And I suppose it is. But this thing feels bigger than our ages. He's not some predator. He's just...Asher.

"Not to mention, my best friend's little sister. Do you know what I'd do if someone even *looked* at my little sister sideways?"

"You don't have a sister," I point out. "And it's different," I insist. I'm not like other girls my age, and I want this. My friend Sophie still plays with Barbies—when no one is looking, of course—and loves One

Direction. I like *this*. This feeling with Asher, right here, right now.

"It's not. It makes me sick," he starts, his warm hands smoothing up my back. "It's not right."

I push his shoulders, causing him to fall backward, and boldly, I lean down and press my lips to his. At first, he doesn't react. He simply lies back, allowing me to explore, to kiss and nibble and suck with his hands clenched at his sides. But when he feels my tongue against his lips, seeking entrance, his hands fly to my waist, and he kisses me back. This time it isn't timid or polite. This kiss feels like war. A battle between right and wrong. Moral and corrupt. Honorable and deplorable.

Asher slides his right hand into my hair and positions us so that we're both lying on our sides as he continues his assault on my mouth, on my soul. He shifts his body until his leg is wedged between mine, and I can't help but chase that glorious friction once again. A moan slips free, and I feel him stiffen like he's about to deny me again. I bring my hands to his cheeks to keep his lips on mine and rock into his thigh.

"Please, Ash. Touch me," I beg.

"No."

"Then let me touch you." I reach for the bulge in his jeans, and he smacks my hand away.

"Fuck no. It can't go any further than this."

I could cry tears of disappointment right now.

"Look at me," he orders, hooking a finger under my

chin. "Keep your hands to yourself. If you go for my cock again, I'm gone. Understand?"

I nod eagerly in agreement.

"Goddammit, give me words, Briar."

"I promise. Just make me feel...*that*." I feel my face burn with embarrassment, and the corner of his mouth twitches, like maybe he'd be amused if he weren't on the verge of jumping over a line that should never be crossed.

Asher plants each of my hands on his shoulders and gives me a searing gaze, silently ordering me to keep them there. I swallow and give a sharp nod, and he places his own hands flat on the mattress by his head, purposely not touching. I press my lips to his, and he reluctantly kisses me back. I start rocking into his leg, powerless to this feeling. Once I find my rhythm, he clasps his hands behind his neck, watching my body move. Seeing him lying back like a king while I grind into his thigh is the hottest thing I've ever seen in my life.

"Oh my God." My voice is just above a whisper.

I press myself into him even harder. The new angle has my eyes snapping shut and my head flying back. My movements are becoming sloppy and jerky, and I know I'm close to something epic. Life-changing even. I hear Asher shifting again, but I don't dare open my eyes. I can feel my wetness leak through my shorts, and somewhere in the back of my mind, I wonder if that's normal. But Asher doesn't seem to notice, or if he does, he doesn't mind.

I'm climbing higher, higher, higher, when I feel something hot and slightly damp wrap around my nipple. My eyes shoot open to see Asher drawing the tiny bud into his mouth through my tank top. And just like that, I come apart. He holds me in place through my orgasm as he continues to suck until I'm shuddering and shaking in his arms.

I'm practically panting as he uses his palm to brush the sweaty hair off my face and leans in to kiss the damp skin of my neck.

"Thank you," I say dumbly. Because what else can I say after that?

"I'm going to hell."

"We didn't do anything wrong," I say honestly, laying my head on his shoulder, feeling so content that I could fall asleep and stay here forever.

"You didn't do a damn thing wrong. I did. You don't understand it now. But you will look back at this some day and see it for what it is."

"And what is that, exactly?" I ask, feeling my temper rising.

"A man who just took advantage of a fucking child," he spits, looking up at the vaulted ceiling.

"That's bullshit. Don't do that."

"Do what, Bry? It's the truth."

"Don't act as if I didn't practically throw myself at you. That I'm too young to make my own decisions.

You didn't take advantage of me. You didn't *take* anything. You gave."

"The only thing I gave you is false hope. You know this can't ever leave this room. If Dash knew..."

"Why would I tell my brother about hooking up with *anyone*? I know this doesn't make you my boyfriend. I'm not that naïve. But maybe when I'm eighteen..."

"This shouldn't have happened," Asher says, grabbing me by my hips and lifting me off him. He stands and reaches for one of Dash's T-shirts lying on top of his dresser. "It's wrong," he says once again.

"Yes, Asher, tell me again how wrong I am for you. I don't think you've gotten your point across." I roll my eyes, sarcasm dripping from every word.

He pulls the plain black shirt over his head, and I watch his muscles flex with the movement. I gulp. Asher's growl has my eyes snapping back up to his.

"Stop looking at me like that, Briar," he warns, his voice lethal and low.

"Like what?" I ask, feigning innocence.

"Like you want what I can't give you."

"The only thing I want is for you to stay."

"I have to tell you something," he says, changing the subject.

"What is it?" And why does it feel like he's about to end our nonexistent relationship?

"I got a scholarship," he says, his mouth twitching at the corner in an almost-smile. "A full ride."

"Are you serious?" I squeal, my frustration from a minute ago all but gone. I'm more excited for him than I've been about anything in my entire life. I knew he was applying, but he told me it was impossible for swimmers to get a full ride. "That's amazing, Ash!"

I throw my arms around his neck, but there's nothing sexual about it this time. Just genuine pride and happiness for him. Ash is one of the best people I know, and he deserves an opportunity to live a life as good as he is. I pull back, scanning his face. He's not easily excitable, but I expected more enthusiasm than this.

"What is it? What else aren't you telling me?"

"It's in Georgia."

For the second time tonight, I feel like that time I fell on the playground in the fourth grade and got the wind knocked out of me. "What?"

"I leave in four months."

I nod, caught between two warring emotions. I'm elated for him, but I'm sad for me. He untangles our limbs and sits on the edge of the bed, resting his elbows on his knees, avoiding eye contact.

"Does Dash know?"

"Yes." He looks over at me, and his eyes soften at his admission.

He never even bothered to tell me.

"I'm happy for you," I say, my voice contradicting the words coming out of my mouth. "This is your chance."

He nods, and we sit in strained silence, unsure of where to go from here.

I try to hold back the tears. To be a good friend and be happy for him, but my chin starts to wobble, and one, single tear runs down my cheek. Asher is in front of me in an instant, gripping my face with both hands, forcing me to look into his eyes.

"Don't waste one fucking tear on me."

I sniff and look away.

"Dash is losing his best friend. And so will I."

"I'm not leaving tomorrow, or next week. We have time."

"Promise me something."

"What's that?"

"Promise me you won't leave without saying good-bye. Promise me I won't be blindsided."

"I promise," he swears.

I nod, feeling slightly pacified. I want nothing more than for Asher to get the hell out of there, but selfishly, right now I can only think about losing him.

"When you leave..."

Asher watches me, waiting. "Yeah?"

"It won't be forever, right?"

"I can't promise you that."

"You really need to work on this whole 'comforting someone' thing. You're really bad at it," I say, pulling back to look up at him. Ash is at least six feet tall, and I have to strain my neck to make eye contact when we're this close.

"I've never had to do it before."

"Why does it feel like we're saying hello and goodbye all at the same time?" After years of tugging at his sleeve and following him like a lost puppy, I've finally gotten Asher's attention in the way I've always wanted. But I'm not naïve enough to think that this could end well.

"Because once I leave, you're going to forget this night ever happened."

I lick my lips, and his eyes follow the movement.

"But you're still here now, so..." I rise onto my tiptoes, circling my arms around his neck. Asher grips my waist and lifts. My legs automatically wrap around him.

"For once in my goddamn life, I'm trying to be the good guy, and you're not making it easy."

"I like you better when you're bad."

Something not unlike a growl is all I hear in response before his lips are on mine once again. Ash walks us over to the wall next to the window, still holding me by my ass. When my back hits the wall, his hands are free to roam. He smooths them up the outsides of my thighs and then either side of my waist. I hold on to his shoulders to keep from melting into a puddle at his feet as I feel it building again, and my hips shift in search of the friction I need, when I hear it.

Giggling. Feminine, *annoying* giggling.

"Shut the fuck up! You're going to wake my parents," says a familiar, albeit irritated voice.

"Fuck," Ash whispers, dropping me like a sack of potatoes, right before Whitley, Asher's ex, appears in the window. She lands in a pile at my feet, and she smells like alcohol and cheap perfume. When she notices me, her face morphs into one of total and utter disdain.

Dash climbs through after her—his preferred method of entry when he has a girl with him—and looks between us. It's not exactly suspicion I detect on his face, but confusion. I feel the need to straighten my shirt or tame my hair, but I'm frozen, afraid of doing anything that will display my guilt.

"What's going on?" he asks, concern coating his tone.

"A little help here!" Whitley slurs in her high-pitched, dolphin sonar voice. Dash rolls his eyes, reaching down to help her to her feet.

"She was looking for you. Wouldn't take no for an answer," Dash explains. "Figured you'd be here when we didn't see your truck at yours."

"I was just, uh, helping Asher with something," I say. Dash reads the meaning of my words, and his head jerks toward Ash, assessing.

"You okay, man?" he asks, keeping it vague since Whitley is here.

"I'm good," is all he says, and the two share a look that even I can't decode.

"What the fuck are you doing here, Whit?" His tone is harsh, but hearing him call her by her nickname reminds me of the fact that they were close once.

"We need to talk," she says, crossing her arms over her chest.

"The fuck we do," Asher snaps. "Go home."

"I can't!" she protests, and I fight the urge to cover my ears. She's always so *loud*. "I didn't drive."

"Jesus Christ," Asher says, scrubbing a hand down his face. "Go wait for me in my truck. I'll take you home." Whitley wastes no time, probably knowing that he'd rescind the offer if she pushed her luck.

"Which is it this time? You pick a fight with some random asshole, or is your dad drunk again?" Dash asks once we hear the car door slam shut.

"The latter."

"Does he look like you?" He gestures to his bloody appearance.

A devious smirk lifts the corner of his lips. "Worse."

"Good," Dash says solemnly. He hates this just as much as I do. It's the most helpless feeling in the world, standing by and watching something so awful happen to someone you care deeply for, and not being able to do a damn thing about it. As much as I hate the thought of him leaving, I feel so much relief in knowing that there's now an end in sight. "Call me tomorrow. I gotta take a piss."

The moment my brother is out the door, Asher's

guilt-ridden eyes dart over to mine. "This was a mistake."

"Bullshit," I argue, moving toward him.

"Don't," he says, backing away, and I die inside, just a little.

And before I can pick my stupid, naïve heart up off the floor and form a response, he's gone.

CHAPTER 1

BRIAR

"**A**re you sure this is a good idea, Briar? Maybe you should just come with us." Mom tries for the tenth time today as she checks her lipstick in the hall mirror. I roll my eyes.

"I'll be fine, Mom. You guys are moving to California, not Egypt." Dad decided to merge with some new hotshot firm in Southern California. Vale and Associates is now The Law Offices of Vale and Pierce. I talked them into letting me stay here with Dash. Not without monthly visits and weekly FaceTime sessions, of course. Dash is a year away from getting his bachelor's degree from The University of Arizona instead of Harvard next year, much to our father's dismay. He agreed to come home and stay with me for the summer instead of staying in Tucson, contingent on my parents not being there.

"I'm serious. You call me the second you change your mind. Do you hear me?"

"Yes, Mother." My relationship with my parents is a weird one. We love each other, but we've never been particularly close. My brother's relationship with them is another story. It's much more strained than mine. It's always been Dash and me against the world. He's always my best friend, brother, and protector all rolled into one. After he left for college, we inevitably drifted apart, but whenever he visited, it was as if no time had passed.

Mom moves on to lecture Dash about the weight of his responsibilities, and I walk outside to say goodbye to my dad. He doesn't do emotions, so I run up to the driver's side of his brand-new Range Rover and pop a quick kiss on his cheek.

"Good luck out there, Dad. Drive safely."

He grunts, but his eyes are soft. "Ditto."

After Mom is settled in the car, Dash comes up to stand next to me on the sidewalk, resting his elbow on top of my head. We stay and watch until their taillights fade into the distance, and then we make our way back inside.

"Did that really happen?" I laugh. My parents are control freaks. They're distant and uninterested, but control freaks nonetheless. My mom is probably more nervous about what might happen to her house without her here, rather than her kids.

"You're definitely the favorite. There's no fucking way they would have let me stay behind when I was seventeen."

"That's because they know you'd have had the cops called in two point five seconds and would live off nothing but beer and pizza." Twenty-one-year-old Dashiell can get a little rowdy, but seventeen-year-old Dash? Let's just say that being young and having an unlimited supply of money was not a good combination for someone like him.

"Touché. So, what are you doing tonight?"

I shrug. "Nat wants to hang out with some friends. Some end-of-the-year party." Natalia Rossi is one of the best people I know. She's hilarious, outspoken, ridiculously beautiful, and fiercely loyal. I met her in dance class on the first day of sophomore year when she was horrified to learn that she'd been given the elective. She annoyed the dance instructor until she let her withdraw, claiming there must have been some mistake. She ended up switching electives, but when I saw that I had her in my next class, I decided we needed to be friends, and the rest is history.

"All right, I'm heading out, too. Lock up when you leave. Don't call me unless you're dying."

Rumors of my brother's sexual proclivities are widely known, but I've managed to stay ignorant to the details. But it's his first weekend back from college, so it's not hard to figure out what he'll be up to tonight.

"Noted."

I run upstairs to hop into the shower. I throw my hair into a messy bun on the top of my head to keep it dry, then run a razor over my legs and quickly wash up. When I walk back into my bedroom, I'm not even a little surprised to see Nat. She's making herself at home, sitting cross-legged on my floor, using my makeup in front of the full-length mirror that hangs off the back of one of my closet doors.

"Get dressed, bitch. We're going to The Tracks," she says, waggling her brows before applying another coat of mascara. My heart jumps in my chest, both scared and excited. The old trotting track was abandoned in the 1960s and hasn't been touched since. It's said to be haunted, so, naturally, that's where you can find the cool kids on any given Friday night. A frisson of both fear and excitement sweeps through me at the thought of being there. I've never ventured inside, but Asher brought me there once.

"Can you take me somewhere?" I asked on the verge of tears. Everyone was fighting. Dashiell was fighting with my parents, and my parents were fighting with each other. I was so sick of the yelling. Asher had been here when the argument about Dash's choice of college started, once again, and we were both hiding upstairs, avoiding them like the plague.

"You know I can't do that," he said, looking up at me from his spot at my brother's desk as he looked up music videos online. "Your parents already hate me."

"I don't care," I stressed. "I just need to get out of here. Anywhere. Where do you go when you need to get away?"

His eyes lock onto mine. "Here."

"That's helpful," I said, fighting an eye roll.

"There is one other place," he admitted. "But I don't know if it's your kind of place."

"Anywhere but here is my kind of place," I said, grabbing my phone and making my way over to climb out of the window. I wasn't normally rebellious, but I knew my parents wouldn't notice I was gone. They'd argue with Dash until they were blue in the face, then they'd have a cocktail and stay in their room for the rest of the night, like every other time they had this fight.

"Wait," Ash said, pulling me back inside, and at first, I thought he was going to stop me. Instead, he surprised me by saying, "Let me go first."

He jumped down and held his arms out to help me down after him. It wasn't a far jump, being a single-story house, but I landed on a rock and rolled my ankle. He caught me under the arms before I went down, and we both stood there awkwardly for a minute or ten, our chests touching, neither one wanting to pull away. Ash swiped a thumb underneath my eye to wipe away a stray tear, and my eyes fluttered shut, loving the feeling of his skin on mine.

Finally, Ash cleared his throat and backed away. I smothered my smile and followed him to the old, beat-up GMC Sierra that he spent his entire summer last year working to buy. It was older than me. Red with a thick, white stripe. The interior was this ridiculous red velvet, and it smelled like cigarettes, but I loved it. And so did he.

We sat in silence as he drove. I didn't know where we were going, but I was just happy to be anywhere with him. When we pulled up to our destination, I was just as clueless. It was this massive building in the middle of nowhere. It was pitch-black, and I couldn't make out any distinguishing characteristics that gave away what it was. Asher drove right up to the fence and cut the engine.

"Where are we?" I asked, leaning on the dash and scanning the foreboding building in front of us.

"The Tracks," he explained. "Horse racing. It's been closed down for years."

"Are we going in?" I asked, gripping the metal door handle. It screeched as I pulled, but Asher grabbed my left hand that sat on the bench seat, stopping me.

"No. It's not safe inside."

"But you go inside?"

"That's different. We can sit on the hood if you want."

I bit my lip and nodded. What started as an escape now sort of felt like a first date. I mean, I'd never been on a date before, but it felt a whole lot like what I'd imagined it would, even down to the boy I'd imagined it being with.

Asher effortlessly hopped onto the hood while I climbed up, using the bumper. I sat next to him, hugging my knees while he opted to lie back against the windshield with one arm behind his head.

"You can't see the stars in the city," he said quietly. I lay back next to him and gazed up into the star-filled sky.

"You're right," I said, lying stock-still next to him. The hood of the truck was hot on my exposed thighs. Our hands were just centimeters from each other, not quite touching.

My phone buzzed with a text, and I checked it on the off chance it was Dash or my mom wondering where I was. It ended up being a text from a girl from school, so I ignored it, setting the phone on my stomach.

Ash reached over, and I held my breath as his fingers brushed against the thin material of my tank top to grab my phone. My entire body prickled with goose bumps, and I hoped he couldn't see my nipples harden beneath my shirt.

"What are you doing?" I asked, breathless.

"We need music," he answered simply. After a few clicks, it started. A haunting song about love and dysfunction and heartbreak. A song about the right love at the wrong time. I decided right then and there, it was my new favorite.

"What is this song called?"

"'Glycerine' by Bush. It's the one song I'll never get sick of."

"I love it," I whispered. It was raw, beautiful.

After asking him to play it for me again, we lay in comfortable silence once more. Halfway through the third time, I felt his pinky finger graze mine. My pulse sped up, and I tried not to move while I wondered if it was on purpose. As casually as I could, I turned my palm skyward, waiting to see what he'd do. I couldn't breathe as Asher laced his much-larger fingers with mine.

I didn't know what to say. What to do. I was too afraid to move in fear of ruining this moment. His thumb rubbed against mine, and I squeezed a little bit tighter.

"What does your name mean?" he asked out of nowhere. Ash wasn't one for small talk, so the question took me by surprise.

"It's a type of bush," I said anticlimactically, and he rubbed at his mouth with his other hand to hide his smile. "But my name is from Sleeping Beauty," I explained. "Princess Aurora's real name is Briar Rose."

"Your parents don't strike me as Disney fans," he deadpanned, and I laughed because it was true.

"I guess my mom was once upon a time."

"But you do look like a princess," he teased.

"Tell me about your mom?" I asked after a beat of silence. He inhaled deeply, returning his gaze to the stars. "Her name was Isabel. She came from a wealthy family, but she met my dad and got pregnant with me shortly after. She was beautiful. And she gave good hugs. She beat me at every video game we ever played."

I laughed, never having expected that.

"She died saving me," he explained, wiping the lingering smile clear off my face. "I had been working on a ramp for my bike all day. I decided to try it out in front of my house. We never had a lot of traffic, so I didn't think anything of it."

I held my breath, knowing where the story was going.

"My mom pulled into the driveway with a trunk full of groceries. She waved and smiled at me, but I didn't smile back. I was frustrated because I couldn't land this trick. I tried over and over, with my headphones blasting in my ears. Each time, I got sloppier and hit the jump harder. On the last try, I don't know what happened, but it sent me flying. I landed right in the middle of the street. I didn't hear it coming, but I saw the car, a big, white Dodge Durango. I couldn't move quickly enough. I hurt my leg so I couldn't stand up. I saw the car try to swerve, and then I saw my mom rushing toward me. I remember her dark hair blowing behind her as she ran. For some reason, that's what stood out the most. She was able to push me out of the way in time, but the car hit her instead."

"I'm sorry," I said quietly, brushing a tear away. Because what else could you say to something like that? That's a kid's worst nightmare.

"My dad blamed me. I blamed me. And that's when everything changed."

"You were just a kid, Ash. It wasn't your fault."

"Yeah," he said noncommittally, and I knew he didn't believe it.

"I think I would have liked her," I said, referring to his mom. "She sounds like the opposite of mine."

"She would've loved you."

One green eye and one brown with flecks of gold met my blues, and something passed between us that I didn't understand, but I felt it nonetheless. I licked my lips, and his gaze followed the movement. I thought, once again, that he might just kiss me. My phone buzzed violently against the metal hood, making me jump. Asher blew out a breath and ran a hand through his hair.

"We need to go," he said, jumping down and climbing back in the driver's side.

"Yeah," I said and cleared the lust from my voice. "I should get back."

And the moment was gone.

"Sooo, are you in? Bry?" Nat asks, snapping me back to the present. That night was just weeks before the night he told me about his scholarship. The night he left for good.

"Who's all going?" I interrupt her primping when I open one of the French doors to my closet that she's sitting in front of and slip inside. Dropping my towel, I snag my H&M black cropped top off the hanger, a pair of frayed jean shorts, and my plain black combat boots. I quickly dress as I listen to Nat's never-ending list of attendees.

"Jay for sure. I think Steven and his girlfriend with bad eyebrows... What's her name? Melissa? Anyway, Thomas, Trey, Lexi... Oh, and Jackson will be there, too."

"Seriously?" I ask, cutting my eyes to hers. Jackson Price is arguably the hottest guy in school. The *only* guy to pique my interest even moderately, other than Asher Kelley. And the only guy I've ever slept with. I've hooked up with plenty of guys, but as soon as it moved from anything more than heavy petting, it was like a record screeched, and it wasn't fun anymore. I had a change of heart, mid-hookup, every single time.

Jackson happened a couple of months ago, and Nat dragged me to a party at his house. Part of me was still holding on to my childish delusions of being with Ash someday, when Whitley came bouncing in, blowing that to pieces.

She was standing there all tall and dark and edgy, the complete opposite of everything I am, bragging about sleeping with Asher over the weekend. Of course, she wasn't telling me. She was talking to a girl named Marjorie—loudly, for my benefit, no doubt—with no shortage of crude gestures and the hickies to back it up.

I remember exactly how I felt in that moment. The way the beer turned sour in my stomach. The way my chest ached and the way my face heated with anger, embarrassment, and jealousy. I remember how I let Jackson, whom I barely knew, lead me upstairs and take my virginity. I remember how I wanted to give it to him, if only to spite Asher. I remember his practiced movements and the pain he caused, even as he tried to be gentle. I remember how even though I hated myself for it, I could almost pretend it was Asher if I kept my eyes squeezed tight. But mostly, I remember how I felt the next morning. Empty and completely alone, even with Jackson's arm curled around me, and every bit the child that Asher always accused me of being.

I'm *that girl*, the one who got drunk at a party and gave it up to the first boy who came along. And I've avoided him ever since. What would Asher think of me now? Even thinking his name is enough to cause physical pain, but I bury it. It's been three years. Three years since he walked out of my house and never came back. Three years since I've so much as heard his voice.

Three years since I've been pining for a boy who was never even mine. This is bordering on pathetic.

"He wants you, Bry. I don't know how he could make it any clearer." Nat fluffs her dark hair and stands, giving herself a once-over in the mirror. "I'd fuck me," she says with a nod of approval. I roll my eyes, but a laugh slips out.

"Why, though?" I muse aloud. There is no shortage of high school girls who want to hook up with Jackson Price. Or college girls, for that matter. He set his sights on me, seemingly out of nowhere last year. He's gorgeous, funny, charismatic, but...a bit of a whore.

"Besides that whole innocent, blonde, blow-up doll look you've got going on?" She circles a finger in my direction and grins when I flip her off. With my freakishly big eyes and pouty mouth, it's not the first time I've heard that comparison. She knows I hate it. "Give him a chance. You don't have to marry the dude. Just... have fun. *With his penis.*"

"You're an idiot." I laugh. She has a point, though. I need to put Asher out of my mind for good.

Twenty minutes later, we're pulling off the I-10 in my little black Jetta. We're only about twenty miles from my house, but it's like a different world out here. No streetlights, no noise, no gas stations on every corner. Just a long, eerie, dirt road that leads to the old trotting park.

"You're quiet."

"I'm driving." I shrug.

"You're nervous," she accuses.

"You wish."

I pull up next to a few other cars and trucks I don't recognize and kill the engine. Without so much as a word, Nat hands me the chapstick she just used at the same time I hand her some gum from my purse after popping a piece into my mouth. I rub my lips together and hand her the tube when a loud banging on my window causes me to jolt.

"Jesus!" Nat yells—while I make some noise that comes out as more of a squeak than anything—and cackling from outside my car follows. I open the car door to see Brett and Jackson standing there with shit-eating grins plastered to their faces, beers in hand.

"For you, Briar, my lady," Jackson says, offering me a can with a dramatic bow. I'm still catching my breath and trying to calm my frantic heart, but I take the beer anyway as I glare at him.

"You guys are dicks," Nat mumbles, accepting her own beer from Brett.

"Who do all these cars belong to?" I stuff my phone into my back pocket and leave my keys in the ignition in case we need to make a quick getaway. Local cops are starting to catch onto the growing fascination with this place, and I heard they've been patrolling the area more than they usually do.

"A couple belong to our group, but I'm not sure about the rest. Guess we had the same idea."

"No better way to celebrate the end of school than

to hang out in an old, decrepit building. Yay," I say, weakly pumping a fist into the air, sarcasm dripping from every word. I'm surprised Jackson deigned this place an acceptable hangout. I wouldn't think he'd be caught dead here.

Nat saunters over to me and hooks an arm though mine as we start to walk toward The Tracks. "Don't be a pussy."

As we get closer, I notice a huge gate surrounding the perimeter of the building. I reach the entrance and tug on the padlock.

"Guess they're cracking down."

"That's always locked. This way, amateur," Jackson says, peeling back a break in the chain link fence. "Everyone else is already inside. We just came out to get you guys."

Nat giggles, totally getting off on this creepy shit, skips over to where he's crouched, and slips through the hole. I hand my beer to Brett and follow her, but my belt loop gets stuck on a rogue piece of metal protruding from the fence. A warm hand lands on the small of my back, and my head snaps around.

"You're stuck," Jackson smirks and gives an innocent shrug. I'm on my knees, halfway through the fence with my ass on display, but Jackson holds my gaze as he reaches to free my belt loop with his fingertip. I wonder if he's thinking of that night. Does he regret it? Does he know I do? Not that it was his fault. I was on a mission to self-destruct that night, and I was lucky I ended up with someone halfway decent.

"Thanks." I'm not really sure what to say, or how to feel. I have a tendency to overanalyze things, so it's probably best that I don't try to decipher anything just yet. I stand up and brush the dirt off my knees and tighten the mess on my head. Brett passes me my beer and shoves his way through while Jackson opts to scale the fence like a fucking ninja. He lands in front of my feet, looking smug as hell, and I arch a brow in return.

"Am I supposed to be impressed or something?"

"Only if you don't want to wound my precious ego," Jackson says, clapping a hand to his heart dramatically. He really is gorgeous—in that all-American, golden boy way—with his light brown hair, high cheekbones, and strong jaw. He's tall and broad and clearly doesn't take himself too seriously. Maybe I misjudged him.

As we all approach the massive, formidable building, nerves and excitement tangle in my stomach, and the baby hairs stand up on the back of my neck. The hot August air is suffocating, and a bead of sweat rolls down the small of my back. I head for the rusty, decayed turnstile, but stop short when I notice the razor wire coiled in the old entrance. Jackson hooks an arm around my shoulders and jerks his head to the right with that Ken-doll smile. He leads us to a different gate, this one with vertical bars. At first, I'm confused as to why we're going this way, but then I notice that one of the bars has been pried apart, leaving enough room to squeeze through. Razor wire and double fences...makes you wonder what happened here and why they're so determined to keep people out.

Before I can ask how we're getting inside the building, Brett darts toward a ditch with steep walls. He skids down the sides like he's surfing on concrete, and Nat—never one to give a shit about consequences— downs her beer, then slides down on her butt after him.

"Nuh-uh." I shake my head when Jackson looks to me expectantly.

"Mhm." He grins.

"Nope. No fucking way. I'm wearing shorts!"

"I guess I'll just have to carry you then."

"You wouldn't." I call his bluff, backing away slowly.

Nat yells something along the lines of, "Just do it, you stupid jock!" before slipping through the gap and disappearing into the abandoned building.

Jackson charges for me and I screech, losing my grip on my beer when he drops a shoulder and scoops me up over it. One arm bands around the back of my thighs, and he chuckles when I grip his waist for dear life. I know what's coming next. Jackson effortlessly skids down the side of the ditch, his white Nikes crunching over the loose dirt and gravel.

"Don't mess up your pretty shoes, golden boy."

"Brave words from a girl who's at my mercy."

Instead of putting me down, he carries me inside the narrow opening. I'm hanging upside down, and that, coupled with the fact that it's dark as hell, makes it hard to see much except beer cans littering the concrete floor and an endless amount of graffiti splashed on every surface. I hear muffled voices and laughter, so I know we're getting closer.

"You can put me down now," I say, using my hands against his lower back as leverage to swing myself upwards. But Jackson's grip on my thighs only tightens.

"Why would I do that when I have such a nice view?" He smacks my ass, and a laugh tumbles from my lips. I don't even know if I like Jackson, but it feels... liberating. Like I'm finally starting to break free of the curse Asher unknowingly cast upon me the day he left. Or maybe it was the day he landed at my feet on my brother's bedroom floor. But my freedom is short-lived, because mid-laugh, I hear an all-too familiar voice.

"What the *fuck*."

Dash. He's here? Jackson finally sets me on my feet, and I right myself just in time to see my brother storming toward us, looking positively murderous.

"What are you doing here?" I ask, tucking my hair behind my ear, aiming for casual.

"You wanna tell me why you just had your hands all over my baby sister's ass?" Dash asks, ignoring my question, shooting daggers at Jackson over my head.

"Whoa, dude. You have a sister?" Jackson throws his hands up in surrender. "I swear I didn't know."

I scrunch my nose at that. Everyone knows Dash, and I mean *everyone*. In fact, I'm known as "Dash's little sister" to most people. But why would he lie?

"You didn't *know*, or you didn't realize I'd be here?"

Jackson's jaw clenches, but he doesn't answer. I feel like I'm in the twilight zone. Dash is protective, in the way that every big brother is, but this? This reaction is completely foreign to me.

"Dash, I told you I was going out with friends. What's the problem?"

"The problem is that you didn't mention *him*."

"We're just hanging out," Jackson tries, but Dash cuts his eyes to his, and Jackson wisely shuts up.

"You. Keep your hands to yourself. And you," Dash says, turning his attention to me, "be smart."

Dash turns and heads back to his group of friends on the other side of the dark, dank basement. The air seems to shift, and I hold my breath, somehow aware that something big is about to happen. My eyes follow Dash in slow motion, and my heart sinks like a ton of bricks when I lock eyes with *him*. Asher fucking Kelley.

Asher stands there, unmoving. Adrian and their friends are laughing and talking all around him, but he's zeroed in on me. I hear Jackson whisper-yelling at Brett for not warning him that my brother would be here, but it's all that I can do to focus on the important stuff, like standing upright and breathing. I can barely make out his face in the dark, with only glow sticks haphazardly tossed around for light, but I know it's him. I can feel it. I can feel *him*. And more than that, I can feel the rage floating off him in waves. But what does he have to be angry about? He's the one who *left me*. Lovesick and lonesome. If anyone's allowed to be upset here, it's *me*.

I force myself to turn my back on him, already feeling the loss. I don't want him to know he can still get to me. I don't even know if he *remembers* that night. Asher pretty much *stayed* drunk back then, and I can't help but wonder if that's changed.

Nat's face is suddenly in my line of vision, and I do my best to blink away thoughts of Asher.

"I think I just came," she breathes, fanning herself. "When did your brother get all hot and...growly?"

"Apparently, it's a new development," I say bitterly. Jackson and Brett finish their little lover's quarrel and come stand next to us.

"I'm sorry," I start. "I have no idea why he's even here."

"It's all good," Jackson says, running a hand through his perfect teen-heartthrob hair, flashing a cocky grin.

"I don't know what his deal is," I admit distractedly, because my brain is still stuck on Asher. *Why is he here? Where did he go? What happened? Why is he looking at me like that?* I lost my first love and my best friend that night. I never thought I'd see him again, and now he's here, hanging out with my brother like nothing ever happened. His dad served time soon after he left, but he got out after less than a year, and he's been rotting in that god-forsaken house ever since.

"Earth to Briar?" Nat pulls me from my chaotic thoughts once again. "Okay, I sent the boys to get us drinks. Spill." I take a quick glance around and confirm that Jackson and Brett are, in fact, nowhere to be seen.

"What do you mean?" I usually tell Nat everything. And I mean *everything*. But I can't have this conversation. Not here, and not now.

"I'm going to pretend you didn't just try to play dumb. I know something is bothering you, and I have a feeling it's not the fact that your brother just cockblocked you."

"He's here," I say, widening my eyes for emphasis.

"Who?" Nat immediately scans the building, her eyebrows pinched together in confusion.

"*Him.*"

"Asher?!" she whisper-yells, and I send a pointy elbow into her side. "Ow! He's not fucking Voldemort. You can say his name."

"Say it a little louder. Please," I deadpan. Jackson and Brett are walking toward us now, a six pack of beer in tow. "Okay, they're back. Don't say anything. And don't make this weird. Please." Nat makes the "cross my heart" gesture before turning her attention to the guys. *Super reassuring.*

"Try holding on to this one this time, butterfingers," Jackson quips, and I accept the beer, downing the entire thing in one gulp.

Jackson whistles and a few people cheer, while Nat gives me the *"Oh, honey..."* look. I glance up to see Dash making his way over, concern tugging at his expression. Asher's face becomes visible as he steps out of the shadows, but he does nothing but glare as he walks toward me. This is literally the last thing I need in my life right now. Asher, Dash, and I in the same room for the first time in three years. Dash still has no idea what happened that night, and even though I'm dying to confront Asher, it has to stay that way. For everyone's sake.

I look to Nat, wordlessly pleading with my eyes for her to do something, *anything* to break the tension. She gives me an almost imperceptible nod, letting me know she understands.

God, I love her.

"Soooo," she singsongs, climbing onto an old upside-down paint bucket with a devious look in her eyes. "Who wants to go exploring?"

Phones and flashlights are whipped out, and Adrian and Dash take the lead, Natalia hot on their heels. Asher hangs back, not making a move, as everyone else follows suit. Our eyes connect, and I wait for him to reveal some hint of the boy I grew up with, but there's nothing. Nothing except contempt, and maybe even disgust. I rub my arms, suddenly feeling cold and insecure under his icy glare, even in the stifling heat.

I turn my back on him and catch up to our group, digging my phone out of my back pocket to use for light, but my battery is at five percent. *Shit*. I tuck my phone back into my jeans. I'll have to make sure to stick close to everyone without my own light.

This place is seriously creepy. Graffiti covers every surface, and everything is in shambles. We pass what must have been the bathroom, full of crushed porcelain and crumbling concrete before entering another big, open room.

"Look," I say, snagging Nat's phone from her hand and shining it above us to illuminate what's left of the signage. "Pot pie, Salisbury steak, burgers, and coleslaw... We must be in the old kitchen." We were standing where the food lines were, and each one had a different sign. It's fascinating to me that this place is in ruins, but some things, like the menus and even some old light fixtures, have been well-preserved.

"Guys, over here," Dash says, sounding far away. I follow his voice and find him standing on the old grandstand that overlooks the dirt area where the track once was. As I get closer, I hear crunching with every step and look down to find—

"Is that...?" I ask, lifting a foot.

"Bird shit."

I jerk my head at the sound of Asher's voice. It's deeper than I remember, and it cuts right through me. I don't know whether to laugh or cry at the fact that I've been missing that voice for three years, and the first words he says to me are *bird shit*. I shake my head and trek through the piles of mummified poop and stand in the open air, trying to make out the stables through the glassless windows, to no avail.

"I wonder what happened to the windows," I muse aloud. They run the entire length of the grandstand, and every single frame is empty.

"They blew them up in that Charlie Sheen movie," my brother offers. "I saw it on YouTube."

"Yeah, and killed thousands of pigeons in the process. Pissed PETA off real good," Asher adds. I feel my eyebrows pull together as I try to decipher his tone. He isn't amused, nor does he seem particularly saddened by the fact. Just...cold ambivalence.

"That's disgusting," Nat says, tiptoeing toward us—like that's somehow going to help her avoid the droppings—with her nose scrunched up like she just smelled something foul.

"That's *sad*," I argue.

"Why, because you weren't there to give them a funeral?" Asher says snidely.

When I was eleven, I found a dead pigeon on our lawn. The bright, crimson blood coming out of its eye a stark contrast to the light gray feathers. We were coming home from Dash and Asher's swim meet, and I cried and begged my mom to let me give it a proper burial. She screamed about it being full of diseases, ordered me to stay away, and called my dad to dispose of it. By the time my dad got home, he said the bird was gone. Later that night, when Asher snuck into my brother's window, he whispered into my ear not to worry. He'd buried it near a bush in our yard. Sure enough, the next day I saw the little mound of dirt and expressed my gratitude, but still thought something was missing. It was so plain. So sad. *Everyone deserves to be buried by something pretty*, I'd told him. Even a stupid pigeon. He laughed, the way he always did when he thought I was being a bleeding heart, and plucked a big, purple succulent, also known as a desert rose. The colors were beautiful. The middle was made up of a vibrant purple and faded into a lighter shade. Succulents weren't your typical funeral flower, but I couldn't have loved them more. "Is that better?" he said as he squatted down to place the flower atop the dirt, ever so carefully. Almost tenderly.

I remember thinking how surprising it was to see this gorgeous, rough-around-the-edges bad boy doing anything with such care, much less tending to a flying rat. Correction: a *dead* flying rat. That was one of the first things that drew me to him. I knew it was just a bird, but I cried all night thinking about it, unable to get the image of its bloody eye out of my head. And Asher... He knew it bothered me. He'd listened. And he'd fixed it. Clearly, that Asher is not here today.

Dashiell's eyes dart between the two of us, no doubt wondering what could've possibly caused tension between us already. I look down, afraid my guilty eyes will give us away. Asher scoffs and walks off. Dash shoots a look to Nat, and she holds her hands up in mock confusion before following suit.

"He's been through some shit, Bry."

I shrug, feigning indifference. "Okay."

"He'll come around."

"If you say so. When did he get back?" I can't help myself from asking.

"Couple of weeks ago?" he guesses, running a hand over the top of his sandy blond hair.

"Oh."

I don't know why that feels like a punch straight to my gut, but it does. He's been here for weeks—*plural*—and he hasn't come to see me. Not once.

"Why are you guys here, anyway?" I ask. I know they didn't come to hang out with a bunch of high school kids.

"I really don't know. Asher asked me to meet him here, and then your friends showed up."

He had plans with Ash, and he kept them from me.

"I would've told you sooner..." he trails off, looking uncomfortable, and I know more is coming.

"But?"

"*But*, he asked me not to tell you."

Okay. Ouch. That hurts more than it should. I feel tears starting to well up, and I hate that I'm still affected. I've shed enough tears for Asher Kelley over the years. I vow to myself, right here and right now, that these are the last ones.

"Look, I know you guys were close, too. He was like a brother to you."

I cringe at his word choice. I've felt a lot of things toward Asher, but sibling love was never one of them.

"I just don't get why he wouldn't want me to know." The night he left was perfect...until it wasn't. It was as if a switch went off, and I have no idea what tripped it.

"I don't think he wanted anyone to know, really." Dash shrugs. "He hasn't told me much, but I know the past three years weren't exactly fun."

My chest aches at the thought of anything bad touching Asher. He's had too much of it in his life. Throughout the years, whenever he got a raw deal—whether it was a misunderstanding or plain old shitty luck—he never complained. Not once. He simply accepted every negative thing life threw at him. More than accepted it, he expected it. Like he thought he *deserved* it. And it broke my heart.

"Come on. Let's get back."

I nod, not trusting my voice to hide the hurt, and we head back to our friends. Nat curls her fingers around my hand and gives it a squeeze without saying a word, and we all explore some more. When we come up to a decrepit escalator, I have to stop and stare. It's the creepiest, most fascinating thing I've ever seen. No one realizes I've stopped, so they keep moving, but there's something about this escalator that has me rooted to this spot.

I pull out my phone. Four percent battery. If I'm lucky, I can get a picture or two before it dies. I back up, taking in the missing stairs and gutted handrails with metal protruding like curled ribbons. I lean over the ledge, just a little, to get a better angle, and snap a photo. I survey the picture, and it's too dark to make out. I lean a little further, hoping for enough battery life to use the flash one more time, and snap another.

"Don't fall."

I jerk at the cold, taunting words rumbled near my ear and pitch forward. Instead of falling to my death, I'm yanked back by a fist closed around the back of my shirt. I stumble before righting myself, and I attempt to calm my erratic heart. My chest heaves, and Asher's eyes follow the movement for a fraction of a second before the apathetic mask falls back into place. Those green and brown eyes appear even darker, and the shadows cling to his features, making him look like some sort of otherworldly creature.

For long moments, we stare. Him with his hands in his pockets, me with one hand on my chest, still catching my breath, but both of us unspeaking. I open my mouth to say something, *anything*, like maybe *why the hell did you just almost kill me?* Or *why did you leave us?* But the words are stuck in my throat. Realizing that I'm not going to be the one to break the silence, Asher gives me a derisive laugh before shaking his head and prowling off. *I really hate the sight of his back walking away from me.*

"Okay, so tell me about that night again. Don't leave anything out," Nat says from the driver's seat of my car. After my encounter with Asher, I practically dragged her out of the building, leaving Jackson and Brett's drunken protests behind us. I was feeling a little lightheaded myself—from chugging that beer, or being near Asher again, I still don't know—so I asked Nat to drive.

"I've told you this a million times." I sigh, reclining my seat all the way back. I stick my hand out of the backseat window, feeling the hot, summer wind whip against it. "I threw myself at him. He was into it for a minute. Then, Dash and Whitley showed up before anything else could happen." Not that it would've happened anyway, much to my fourteen-year-old self's dismay. "He basically told me we made a mistake, gave Whitley a ride home, and I never saw him or heard from him again. Until now. He didn't even end up taking the scholarship. I checked."

"Hmm," Nat says thoughtfully, tapping her fingers against the leather steering wheel. "I mean, obviously, he was running away from whatever he was feeling for you. But to disappear for three years? That's a little extreme, even for him."

I snort at that. There's no way I had anything to do with his vanishing act. I'd have to mean something to him for that to happen, and the past three years have proven otherwise.

"There's no point attempting to figure Asher out. You'll only hurt your brain trying." I would know. Asher's always played his cards close to his chest, never letting anyone in on the thoughts and feelings within.

We pull into the long driveway leading up to our ranch-style house, then Nat throws the car into park.

"All right, I'm out. I have to help my mom set up for an event tomorrow, so I promised I'd be home early."

"Boo. Call me after."

After Nat takes off in her little red sports car, I make my way toward the house, then tiredly stab the code into the keypad at our front door. Too lazy to go to my room on the other side of the house, I steal Dash's charger from the kitchen counter and plant myself onto the couch in the media room. It's fluffy and huge and could sleep ten people at least. This is my preferred room in the house. I throw in my favorite movie—the one I love to hate and hate to love since it reminds me of that night. *Tombstone.*

I can't focus on the screen. The events of tonight and the ones of three years ago play in my head on repeat, searching for something, anything, that will fill in the missing pieces. I keep coming back to the same two questions. *What made him leave? And what brought him back?*

Before long, I drift to sleep with images of Asher's hardened expression in my mind.

"Don't fall…"

Someone should've warned me not to fall years ago.

CHAPTER 2

ASHER

"**A**re you sure, man?" I ask for the third time since Dash insisted I stay with him as we walk into his house. Being here again is the *last* thing I thought would happen tonight. Ever since I got back into town, I've managed to avoid this place like the fucking plague. This house and the people in it were the only good part about my life growing up. But after the younger Vale sibling betrayed me in the worst way, I lost that, too.

I stopped by my old house exactly once. I was greeted by my father in an alcohol-induced slumber in his old, tattered recliner. A cigarette dangled from his fingertips, dangerously close to burning the house down. I walked out before he even knew I was there.

"I told you, my parents are living in SoCal now. It's just Briar and me, and you know she won't mind."

I wouldn't be so sure about that.

I'm a bastard for what I did that night—for what I thought about doing every night for months before then. I know this. But I also don't plan to come clean any time soon. Briar fucked me over real good. Maybe that's what I deserved for hooking up with my best friend's little sister, but either way, I'll never make that mistake again. And as far as I'm concerned, Briar Vale is nothing more than a bad memory.

I shouldn't fucking stay here. I should keep paying eighty-eight bucks at the roach-infested motel down the street. I should go kick my pops' old dying ass out of the house and stay there. I should do anything but stay in this house again. Yet, here I am, sharing space with my old best friend and his little backstabbing sister. Because I'm a goddamn masochist.

After digging myself out of the mess Briar got me into, I made a life for myself. I met some good people— a guy named Dare who took me under his wing. I worked on roofs with him during the summer and did snow removal in the winter. Eventually, he finally took the plunge and opened up the tattoo shop he'd been talking about for years, so I unofficially took over the roofing business. I'd put Cactus Heights—and everyone in it—behind me in exchange for four seasons and hard work.

I swore I'd never come back. There was nothing

left for me here, with a deceased mother and a father who only saw me as the reason she died. Then, I got the call that my dad was in the hospital. Liver failure. I didn't know what I expected to feel. Maybe nothing at all. Surprisingly, I felt a twinge of...*something*. Something I still haven't identified. Guilt? Fuck that. I'm not the one who drank to the point of trying to provoke my kid into a fistfight and blacking out—in that order— night after night. Obligation? Probably.

I'm stuck in my own thoughts as I follow Dash down the lit pathway leading up to the house, when something colorful catches my eye. The sight of those damn succulents—the one with the fleshy purple and bluish leaves—has a bitter laugh slipping out of my mouth. If I'd only known how alike Briar and those pointy-tipped succulents were back then. Both deceptively beautiful and innocent, but full of hidden, dangerous needles when given a closer look.

Once we're inside the house, the smell hits me like a ton of bricks—like cinnamon and fresh laundry—and I pinch the bridge of my nose to fight off the onslaught of buried memories that rush to the surface. Memories of a young Briar tending to my wounds with her usually plump lips flattened into a hard line and her eyebrows creased with concern. Memories of stealing her first kiss in Dash's room and hating myself for it afterward. Memories of having dinner with the whole family and staring at a piece of corn on the cob like it was from another planet. My family had corn out of a can. I didn't know what to do with that shit. Briar noticed my hesitation, reached over and grabbed the corn, breaking off the leaves and silky strands. She disposed of them before handing my plate back with a soft smile. She didn't make a big production out of it, and I doubt anyone else even noticed. But that was Briar for you. A tiny little girl with a heart too goddamn big for her body. But then she grew up to be just like the rest of the entitled assholes of Cactus Heights, Arizona.

"You can take the media room. I'd offer you my parents' bed, but, that's fucking gross," Dash says, shuddering. "And the guest rooms are more of an office and an exercise room, so they don't have any furniture."

"That's cool with me. Anything's better than the bed at the motel." I didn't come from a life of luxury. I don't need the finer things in life, but that shit was grimy as hell and I had at least six springs jabbing into me at any given time during the night. I'd gladly take their cushy couch. If it was the same one from when I was around, it's more comfortable than anything I've ever owned.

We toss a few back in the kitchen, catching up, but not really going into detail of the past couple of years. It's the elephant in the room, but I'm not ready for that talk. *He's* not ready. Not for the reality of what happened and where I went. Not for finding out that his precious baby sister was the reason for it all.

I didn't say a word when I left, not to Briar and not to Dash. At first, I wasn't sure if he was in on it, too. Once I was able to think rationally, I realized that Dash probably had nothing to do with it. He would've tried to fight me if he knew about Briar and me.

Briar was like this little naïve angel. Always trying to help everyone and fix everything. She felt everyone's pain as if it were her own. I couldn't fault her for that, even if I didn't understand it. In fact, I envied her ability to *feel* so much, when I could barely feel at all. *Not unless she was around, anyway.* Briar loved with her whole heart. And somehow, she thought someone like me was worthy of being on the receiving end of that love. I don't mean romantic love. She was just a kid. But in the way you love your family, or a stray dog, more accurately in my case.

But for what she did that night? All because she had a bruised ego? That, I could fault her for. And I'll continue to do so.

It all happened because of a kiss...

"I can see your wheels spinning, Kelley. I don't know what the fuck happened, and I'm not gonna lie and say that I wasn't pissed that you left without saying shit. You crushed my sister," Dash starts, and my eyes snap to his. *What the fuck?*

"You were like another brother to her," he continues, and I exhale in relief as I realize he still doesn't know anything. "When I was too busy fucking off and getting laid, you were here, hanging out with her. She didn't handle it well when you left. She cried for weeks, man. *Weeks*."

I can feel my anger rising with every word. *She* is the victim in all of this? Give me a fucking break. If anything, it was her guilt keeping her awake. Not my absence. I squeeze the bottle of IPA so tightly that my knuckles turn white. But I don't say a word.

"Anyway, my point is, I know some shit went down. But you're my brother. You're always welcome here. And once you're ready to talk about where you went, I'm here."

I give a short nod, acknowledging him, and down the rest of my beer.

"Appreciate it." And I do. But I don't have anything else to say right now.

"All right, I said my piece." Dash tosses his empty bottle into the trash, and it clanks against the others. "I'm going to pass out. You remember where everything is?"

I tell him that I do—I practically lived here before —and he doesn't waste any time going to his room. I sit for another minute, collecting my thoughts, trying to figure out exactly how I got here. I press the heel of my palms into my eyes, suddenly exhausted.

I head toward the opposite side of the house and grab a throw blanket out of the closet on the way. I pass Briar's door and pause. She's in there, right now. Oblivious to my presence. I have the urge to take a peek. Just one, little peek. But I shake my head and continue to my temporary living quarters. Once I get closer, I see the TV flickering, casting a light show on the walls. The door is open, and right before I throw my blanket onto the couch, I see it. A tiny blonde form curled up into a ball on her side.

Briar.

She's still in her clothes from earlier. Her shorts have ridden up even further, exposing her long, tanned legs. Her cheek is all smushed from resting on her palm, making her look even younger, and her pouty lips are parted slightly. She still looks like a goddamn angel—even in sleep—but she's the devil in disguise.

I didn't expect to see her at The Tracks tonight. I used to go there when I needed to be alone or to drink myself into oblivion. That's what I planned to do tonight. In a moment of temporary insanity, I called Dash to meet me. He knew I was back and had been asking to hang out, but I kept blowing him off. I figured The Tracks were neutral ground. I just didn't know it had turned into the chill spot for the whole damn high school.

When that douchebag walked in with Briar slung over his shoulder and his hand gripping her ass, I saw red. I don't want her, but that doesn't mean I want anyone else to have her, either. I've never been very good at sharing. Chalk it up to being an only child.

I watched her for a few minutes before she noticed me. She was laughing and talking with her friends. There was a sadness in her eyes that never used to be there, and I wondered if that had anything to do with me.

Three years doesn't seem like a long time, but it made a world of difference for Briar. She has tits now, for one. Nice, perky handfuls and an hourglass figure to match. She's always been beautiful, but grown-up Briar is straight-up lethal.

For some reason that I don't even pretend to understand, I take a seat on the opposite end of the L-shaped couch. I have a perfect view of her from where I sit. I glance at the TV, and I almost laugh when I see what she was watching. *Tombstone.* How this movie is anyone's favorite, let alone a teenage girl's, I'll never know.

I reach for the remote on the coffee table and start the DVD over again. I don't really watch the movie. I mostly watch her. She sleeps so peacefully. Her chest rising and falling in a soothing rhythm, softly snoring, and I realize that I hate her in this moment. Why should she get to sleep so soundly after what she did? I've had three years of sleepless nights.

I'm still sitting here stewing in my resentment when she starts to stir. She hitches a leg up, exposing the bottom of her ass cheek, and stretches her arms out with a yawn. I don't make a move, blending into the darkness. She sits up and blindly feels around for her phone. She glances at it and sets it back down onto the table. She stands, her fingers going to her shorts, unbuttoning them and letting them drop to the floor. The light from her phone illuminates her, and I can make out the curve of her ass in a dark-colored thong. She tugs her long, blonde hair out of her hair tie and it spills down to the middle of her back in waves.

I want to wrap that golden hair around my fist and smash my lips into hers. Make her pay for what she did as I fuck her punishingly from behind.

"My, my. You sure have grown."

BRIAR

I wake up groggy and disoriented. The movie is playing, and I think to myself how weird it is that it's still going. I know I was past this part, and I feel like I've been sleeping for a while. I check the time. Two A.M.

Suddenly, I'm all too aware of my too-tight shorts cutting into my hip. I stand up and wrench them down, then let my heavy hair free from my ponytail, fully intending on passing back out in here. But then a sense of awareness prickles over my body from head to toe. Like I'm being watched. It's the same way I used to feel when I fantasized about Asher watching me in bed or in the shower, even when I was too young to have those kinds of thoughts. I shrug the feeling off. Asher just got back, and he's already fucking with my head. That's all it is.

"My, my. You sure have grown."

I yelp, just as a hand covers my mouth to muffle my screams.

"Shut the fuck up. You're going to wake your brother," the voice that I now realize belongs to Asher says in a low growl.

"Good! What the hell are you doing here?" My traitorous heart is slamming against my ribs as if trying to throw itself at Asher. Like it knows it belongs to him. *Not anymore.* I take a step away from his shadowed figure.

"Haven't you heard? I'm your new roommate, baby girl."

No. No. What?

I'm already shaking my head. This isn't possible. He doesn't just get to show back up after three years and invade my space. I've waited for this day. God, I've fucking *died* waiting for this day to come. But this isn't how I imagined it. Not even a little bit. And, I'm not a lovesick kid anymore. At least that's what I tell myself.

Asher's eyes drift down to my legs, and a smirk tugs at his lips, reminding me that I'm standing here without pants. I sit down on the couch, quickly snatching the blanket and pulling it over my lap.

"A little privacy?" I snap.

"Oh, look who grew a backbone along with those other...assets." He makes a show of scanning my body from head to toe, and my face heats with embarrassment. I know why I'm bitter and angry, but where is *his* anger coming from? Asher has always used his sharp tongue as a weapon, but I wasn't ever on the receiving end of it. In fact, I always got the impression that he purposely shielded me from that side of him.

Guess the kid gloves are off.

"What happened to you?" I say it more to myself, but he hears it, because he balls his fists at his side and his eyes narrow.

"I don't know, Briar. What do you *think* happened?"

"I don't know! That's why I'm asking!" I whisper-yell, bending over to retrieve my discarded shorts and pulling them back over my legs under the covers.

Asher shakes his head, and I get the feeling that I've disappointed him. But that's impossible. He's been back for three whole seconds. I haven't had a chance to let him down.

"It's late," he finally says, his wall slamming back in place, more impenetrable than Fort Knox. He plops down on the couch and crosses his arms behind his head, like he owns the place. "Do you mind?"

"Unbelievable." I bunch my blanket up in my arms with a huff and grab the rest of my stuff. Too drained and confused to keep arguing, I take one last searching look into those soulless eyes before turning around and leaving without another word.

The sun beats down on me through my window, and I smother my face with a pillow, making a mental note to buy blackout curtains. I don't think I slept for more than a few minutes at a time. I tossed and turned all night, alternating between irritation and concern for Asher. Once the initial anger cooled, I started wondering what could've happened to cause the chill in his demeanor.

Dash's words from last night about Asher belatedly echo in my head. Maybe I should've been more understanding. I still can't believe he's here. In my house. Like nothing ever happened. But he's not Ash. Not the one I used to know.

My phone buzzes from my nightstand, and I pick it up to see a text from my brother.

Dash: Asher's staying here for a while. Just a heads-up.

A little late for that.

Me: Do Mom and Dad know?

Dash: No. And we're going to keep it that way.

Me: Don't I get a say in this?

Dash: No. He's family. He needs us, whether he wants to admit it or not.

I sigh and roll out of bed, needing to at least make a coffee run before I can have this conversation, but I decide that a shower is more important. Shower first. Coffee later.

After stripping down, I snag the towel off the hook on the back of my door, wrap it around me, and stumble my way down the hall. I'm rubbing the sleep out of my eye with the palm of my hand when I twist the knob to the bathroom door. It takes a second for my vision to adjust, but when it does, I see Asher. Naked. Standing over the toilet with his left hand braced against the wall, and his right hand... His right hand is wrapped around his length.

I can't look away. God, he looks so different now. He's broader, taller, more muscular. If I thought he looked like a man three years ago, he's a god now. My eyes are glued to the way he works himself, the veins in his arms, the thickness of him. Something shiny catches my eye, and I gulp when I realize it's a piercing.

"Don't you know it's rude to stare?"

My wide eyes snap up to his, and I feel my ears heat with shame. His challenging stare matches the unapologetic tone of his voice, and he continues to pump his length. I can't apologize. I can't even form a response. I'm unable to do anything but gawk at the sight before me. My teeth bite into my bottom lip, and I feel my nipples harden against my towel. Asher grunts, bringing my attention back to his face, and he's staring right at my mouth.

"If you're going to watch, lose the towel."

Without thinking twice, I step inside the door and close it behind me. His eyes widen, just a little, as if surprised that I'm playing along to his game instead of running away. He's not the only one. I don't know why I'm still standing here.

We're both in some kind of trance. The only sounds are those of our quickening breaths and the wet noises coming from his palm. I smell a familiar scent of vanilla and fruit right before I spot my Pink Sugar Plum conditioner on the granite sink next to him. His fist moves faster when he sees that I notice.

"You're going to smell like me." I don't know why those are the first words that come to mind. Why does the thought of him using my conditioner set a fire inside me? *I'm not normal.* I've never felt like this before. I've never experienced such an erotic moment, and he hasn't even touched me. I want to drop my towel and beg him to give me more of that feeling I only ever got a taste of. The feeling that only he's ever been able to give me. But I won't. I threw myself at him once, and I still haven't recovered from the fall. I refuse to be that girl, content to survive on whatever scraps of attention he throws my way when it suits him.

Still, I can't bring myself to look away—to *walk* away. I feel like he's daring me to see this through, and I have some need to prove to him that I'm not a little girl anymore. The naïve Briar with stars in her eyes is long gone. He made sure of that.

I try to discreetly press my legs together to smother the throbbing between my thighs, but Asher notices. Of course, he does. His head falls back slightly, like it's too much effort to hold it up, but his eyes are still locked on mine. Mine, however, start to wander. To his full lips and sharp jaw, his chest that's damp with sweat, the cut lines of his lower stomach, and finally, to what's in his hand, looking angry and impossibly hard. I notice his piercing again, and ever the petulant child, wonder when he got it and how many other girls have seen it. I hate all of them.

"Stop giving me that look before I give you something to pout about."

I reach behind me to open the door and leave. I shouldn't be here. This shouldn't be happening, especially not with my brother somewhere in the house. But Asher shakes his head, pinning me in place. I immediately obey his unspoken request without a second thought, and I mentally kick myself for it.

Asher must literally get off on his control over me, because then he's coming in thick, white spurts into the toilet. His muscles tighten and his body tenses, but he looks at me, still taunting, still daring me to look away with his bored stare.

I swallow hard, but instead of leaving, I put one shaky leg in front of the other and force myself to walk right past him to the shower. Like what happened was no big deal. Like I didn't just watch Asher Kelley jerk himself off. Like it wasn't the most glorious thing I've ever witnessed.

Once I'm in, I toss my towel over the frosty glass door and turn the shower on. The hot water beats down on my chest, only intensifying the ache between my legs. I squeeze my eyes shut, waiting for Asher to make his move. Long seconds pass, and it feels more like hours, but then I hear the toilet flush, and the door slams shut a moment later.

What the hell just happened?

~

My stomach growls as I pretend to be doing something super important on my laptop at Starbucks, reminding me that I didn't have time to scarf anything down earlier in my haste to get out of there. I'm hiding out, because Natalia probably hasn't even rolled out of bed yet, and I needed to be somewhere other than my house.

After relieving the ache that Asher created in the shower, I threw on a pair of holey jeans and a white tank top and slapped on some makeup, all the while nervous that Asher was going to show his face again. He didn't thankfully, but I was still unnerved by what transpired in the bathroom. I couldn't focus on anything knowing he could be lurking around every corner of the house, but he was nowhere to be found.

Even when my favorite barista, Matt, tried to make small talk, I was still unable to focus on anything but the sight of naked Asher pleasuring himself with my conditioner. And the way he looked at me, completely unaffected and unapologetic.

Tossing my empty cup, I make my way toward the

parking lot, skidding to a stop when someone blocks my path, only to find Jackson smiling down on me.

"Hey, what's up? I didn't get to say goodbye to you last night, and I tried to call, but your phone went straight to voicemail."

Oh my God. I forgot about Jackson. And I don't mean about last night... I mean, I literally forgot he existed. Ash's been back in my life for less than twenty-four hours, and, like a solar eclipse, he's already casting his shadow upon everything and everyone else. It's exciting at first. You feel like you're a part of something that doesn't happen every day. And maybe you're tempted to stay in the shadows. But then you realize that you need the sun. You can't survive in darkness alone.

"Briar?" Jackson's concerned hazel eyes assess me.

"Huh? Oh, yeah, my phone died. Sorry."

"It's cool."

I give him a polite smile and move to step around him, but he stops me with a hand on my shoulder.

"Hey, so wait," he says, dropping his hand and stuffing both into the pockets of his jeans. "Let's go out. Like, just the two of us."

"You mean, like a date?" I ask dumbly. *No, Einstein, he wants to take you to Bible study. Of course, he means a date.*

"Yeah, like a date," he says with a cocky smile, probably mistaking my preoccupation with Asher for shyness.

My gut instinct is to say no. But then, I realize that would be falling into old patterns and letting Asher influence every decision I make. *Not this time.* And I do like Jackson. I was even semi-interested before Ash came back. There's no reason I shouldn't give him a chance. He's fun and sweet and hot as hell. What's not to like? Plus, Asher has made it clear that there will never be anything between us. Why shouldn't I move on?

"Okay." I shrug.

"Okay?" he asks, thrown off by my short response.

"Okay," I say, firmer this time, and go to leave again. My stomach is growling, and I need to call Natalia.

"When?" he shouts after me.

"Whenever!"

"I'll pick you up tonight then. Six o'clock."

Before I can open my mouth to object, or at least let him know that I'd drive separately and meet him somewhere, he gives me one of his signature smirks and saunters off.

I guess I have a date.

❦

I pull into my driveway after a long day of avoiding home. Nat was working for her mom at her boutique, Lush, today, so I hung out there for a while. We tried to talk, but it was an abnormally busy day, so I walked around the other shops to kill some time.

My stomach does a flip when I see that Asher's big, black truck is still in the driveway. There's a ladder on top of it, leading me to believe it's a work truck, but it's nice. Really nice. He must be doing well for himself.

I'm immediately aware of his presence before I see him. I give a quick wave to my brother—who's sitting with Asher on the couch, drinking a beer—and drop my keys onto the counter. I'm starving, so I walk straight to the freezer to grab my favorite pizza.

I prop a hand on my hip and whirl around to find the two laughing like idiots.

"I told you she'd notice, man," Dash says, hiding his smile behind his beer bottle.

"Sorry," Asher deadpans in a way that says *I'm not even a little sorry.* His dark hair is mussed up in that perfectly disheveled way only he can pull off, and his full lips are coated in pizza grease. "I was hungry, and your pizza was the only thing that sounded good."

He narrows his eyes at me, challenging me somehow, and licks his lips.

God, why does everything he says sound suggestive to me?

"It's fine." I shrug, feigning ambivalence. "I have a date tonight, so I probably shouldn't eat so close to dinnertime, anyway." I swing open the stainless steel fridge door, grab a yogurt instead, and walk off without daring to look for his reaction, or lack thereof.

I don't know why I said that. Just like in the bathroom this morning, I guess I just wanted him to know that I'm not still pining after him. That life moved on without him, and I'm all grown up now.

After hiding out in my room for a couple of hours and calling Nat to fill her in on everything, I finally decide to get ready for my "date". I have no idea where Jackson might be taking me, so I opt for a black jersey dress. It has thin straps and dips low in the back, but it's still casual enough to wear with sneakers. I throw on a pair of black Vans and a choker that my mom hates because she insists that it looks like something out of a fifty-cent machine. I leave my hair down, and it falls in thick waves to my waist.

Checking my phone, I see a missed text from Jackson.

Pulling up to your house.

I check the time stamp on the text and realize that it was sent over five minutes ago. I bounce down the steps and freeze when I see Jackson at my opened door with Dash blocking his entrance with a wide stance and crossed arms. I hear a chuckle, and my eyes snap over to Asher who is still sitting at the couch, leaned back, with his long legs stretched out, looking more than a little amused.

"You can stop now, Dashiell," I say, rolling my eyes and coming to a stop in front of them. Asher's laugh morphs into a choking sound, and all three of us turn to look at him with furrowed brows.

"Went down the wrong pipe," he coughs, gesturing to his throat.

"Karma." I laugh.

"Desperate much?" he asks, pointing his beer bottle in my direction.

"What?" I snap.

"Your dress. It's so short that I can practically see your asshole," Asher says, crude as always.

"Well, then, it should make it easier for you to kiss it."

"Whatever you say, Sugar Plum," he taunts, referring to my conditioner.

"We're leaving," I bite out, as heat crawls up my neck. I grab Jackson's arm and shut the door with more force than necessary before giving him an apologetic smile. He waves me off, tells me I look pretty, and leads me to his sleek charcoal gray Mercedes. And then we're gone.

CHAPTER 3

ASHER

I flip my phone over on top of my thigh, checking the clock for what feels like the fiftieth time in the past three minutes. Eleven twenty-eight. Briar's been gone for over five hours. What the fuck kind of dinner takes five hours? When she first mentioned her plans, I almost laughed. She wanted a reaction, so of course, I didn't give her one. Her attempt at making me jealous was comical.

But then the douchebag from last night showed up. I thought after Dash's warning, she'd stay away from him. He's a couple of years younger than us, but his older brother was in our grade. He was on the swim team, and he had this *list*. It was more of a points system. Every girl was rated from one to one hundred. The harder to get with, the bigger the score. I never took part, never felt the need to brag when I got my dick wet. But the rumor is that Jackson is carrying on big brother's tradition and bringing it back. And now, he's out with Briar.

What I figured would take two hours tops turned into three, then four, then five. I couldn't exactly voice my concerns. I'd already fucked up earlier by commenting on her choice of clothing, or lack thereof.

When I saw her come down those stairs, looking good enough to eat, I choked on my fucking beer. Between that, my sudden shitty mood, and my brand-new phone-checking compulsion, Dash had been eyeing me suspiciously all damn night. What was I supposed to say? *Sorry, man. Your baby sister begged me to fuck her in your bed, then I left her. Oh yeah, and then she ruined my fucking life.*

Eventually, I told Dash I was going to sleep because I needed to look for work in the morning. It's not entirely untrue. I do need to do that, if I plan to stay in town. But the real reason was that I needed time to dissect my thoughts.

I've only been back for one day, and already, things are starting to blur. The hatred was starting to wane. With her wide, innocent eyes and angelic appearance, it's hard to imagine that she's capable of being vindictive. I need to stay away from her. I look down to her fluffy, pale pink comforter and ball it in my fist, messing up her perfectly made bed.

Tomorrow. Starting tomorrow, I'll stay away from her.

The quiet snick of the front door closing alerts me to her arrival. About fucking time. I flatten myself against the wall behind her door right before she opens it then gently nudges it shut with the back of her foot. She kicks off her shoes and starts to pull her dress up to take it off. Standing with her back to me in front of the moonlit window, I can make out her brand-new curves. Her tight, round ass. The dimples on the small of her back. Her dress is just past her hips when I speak.

"Have fun tonight?"

Briar yelps and drops her dress back in place before spinning around.

"I was until I had some perv spy on me for the second time in as many days."

"Oh, I'm the pervert?" I taunt, moving closer. She wants to back away, but she doesn't. She stands her ground, and it only spurs me on. "Correct me if I'm wrong, but I believe it was *you* who watched me jack off this morning."

I'm almost sad the lights aren't on to see her inevitable blush. I'm standing over her tiny form, and she has to crane her neck to look up at me.

"Momentary lapse in sanity." She shrugs. "It's nothing I haven't seen before."

Those words kick around in my head for a second before I practically tackle her onto her bed. She lands on her back, mouth parted in shock, with her legs spread and her dress ridden up. My hips fill the spot between her thighs, and I pin her hands to the bed.

Fuck, this was a bad idea. She smells good—sweet, like her conditioner—and she feels even better. I have to fight the urge to grind into her.

"Nothing you haven't seen before, huh?"

"No," she says between clenched teeth.

"Who was it?" I demand. "Was it the little golden boy from tonight?"

"None of your business."

"Tell me, Briar," I whisper, getting closer to her ear. "Did he make you come from a kiss like I did? Does he know what you sound like as you do? Because I can still hear you. I can still *see* you."

If her sharp intake of breath didn't let me know she was affected, the way she rocked into my jean-covered cock does. I stay stock-still, still braced above her with my hands around her wrists.

"Does he know that I was the first one to make this little body come before you even knew how to do it yourself?" I bring her wrists closer together so I can grip them both with one hand, and I trail my index finger from her sternum all the way down to her underwear.

A moan slips free, and her hips chase the friction once more.

"No," she whispers.

"No, what?"

"No to all of it."

Briar manages to wiggle a hand free, and she uses it to pull me to her, chest to chest. I can feel her perky little tits against me, and I want so fucking badly to do what we couldn't do three years ago. To feel her from the inside. But then I remember what else happened the last night we were together like this. And everything that unfolded afterward.

"Good," I say simply, lifting myself off her before I do something I'll regret...like fuck the enemy.

Briar scrambles to clamp her legs shut and pull her dress back down her thighs with an incredulous look plastered to that pretty face.

"Keep it that way." I turn to leave, now that I have the upper hand, but then that smart mouth of hers strikes again.

"Fuck you, Asher," she spits, voice full of venom.

I grip the doorknob so hard I almost expect it to shatter in my hand.

"Fuck *me*?" I laugh bitterly. "You already fucked me, baby girl. And I never even saw it coming."

BRIAR

"I'm a zombie. It's official," I complain to Nat, who's gotten the tips of her toes perched on the edge of the pool deck as she paints them a cherry red, while I float on an oversized raft.

Nat snorts. "Maybe you should stop diddling your skittle to thoughts of Asher all night."

I kick my foot out to splash her, and she cusses when she flinches away and paints her skin on accident.

If she only knew how right she was. Except it's not just thoughts of Asher keeping me up; it's Asher himself. I haven't seen him once today. I tossed and turned all night long, playing his words back in my head until it was time to wake up for school. *"You already fucked me, baby girl."* I was too preoccupied with the fact that Ash had just been between my legs to make sense of the words at first, but now, it's all I can think about. What did that even mean? He's the one who left. I'm the one who was wrecked.

When I finally accepted the fact that sleep wasn't happening, I walked around on eggshells while getting ready, afraid to run into Asher or Dash. Asher, for obvious reasons. Dash, because he can read me better than anyone else in this world, and I him. But, neither seemed to be awake.

The past few days must have caught up with me, because all the coffee in the world couldn't help me this morning, and it can't help me now. As soon as Nat got here, I changed into my suit and threw my hair into a high ponytail. That was a couple of hours ago, and now the sun is starting to set.

"So, are you going to tell me how your date with

Jackson went?" Nat asks, snapping me out of my thoughts.

"Meh." I shrug, shifting my legs that stick to the plastic raft.

"Meh?" She stops painting her toes and props her chin on her knee to look over at me. "That good, huh?"

"No, it wasn't *bad*. It was good. He was nice."

"Whoa, watch out. Good *and* nice? You better put a ring on it with those adjectives."

I roll my eyes. "Shut up. It was actually really fun." Jackson took me to this fondue restaurant. There was chocolate involved, so I can't complain. Afterward, he took me to see the Thor movie, which I also can't complain about. *Because Thor.* I had a better time than I thought I would, to be honest. He was witty and charming and polite.

"Are you going to see him again?" Nat asks skeptically.

"I'm not sure. If he asks." Another shrug.

"And you don't think the return of he who shall not be named has anything at all to do with your indifference?"

"I have no idea what you're talking about," I say, inspecting my nail beds to avoid eye contact.

"Lying liar who lies."

We both laugh, but we're interrupted when Asher and Adrian, my brother's other best friend, come barreling out the patio door.

"Well, well, speak of the devil," Nat drawls out in

the worst fake Southern accent I've ever heard in my life.

"Where's my brother?" I ask, cutting a warning glare in Nat's direction to keep her mouth shut.

"Inside making food. Why? You need someone to rub you down with some sunblock?" Adrian asks, taking a step in my direction, but Asher blocks him with a stiff arm across the chest.

"What, bro?" he asks, feigning innocence. Returning his attention toward me, he adds, "I'm just looking out for the baby sister. We don't want that pretty porcelain skin to burn, do we?"

"I'm good." I laugh, shaking my head.

Adrian makes a lot of noise, but he's generally harmless. Growing up, it was always my brother, Asher, and Adrian. The three drunken amigos who basically owned the school and everyone in it. Dash and Adrian are the charmers—the rich boys who fucked shit up with a smile on their faces—while Asher ruled with a quiet authority. They may not be in high school anymore, but they still run this town.

Adrian is Mexican-American, or as he likes to call himself, a *sexy Mexi*. He's tall and gorgeous, with golden eyes and dimples for days. Everyone loves him. It's impossible not to.

"But really." Adrian lowers his voice, smacking Ash's hand away from his chest. "I needed to talk to you guys about Saturday."

Saturday is Dash's birthday, and every year on the

day before, we usually have dinner with our parents at some fancy restaurant in which they end up arguing before dessert. Then Dash and I bail and binge-watch movies all night, with every type of junk food imaginable. His actual birthday, though, belongs to friends. This year, my parents can't make it, with my dad being too busy with the merger. They offered to fly us out, but Dash insisted on staying, using work as an excuse, when really, he just doesn't want to go. Thank God, because neither do I.

"What's up?" I slide my peach-colored, oversized sunglasses onto the top of my head.

"We're taking the pontoon and the Jet Skis out to the lake. It's nothing big, just a few of us hanging out, but it's a surprise. You girls in?"

"I'm out," Nat says dejectedly.

"What, why?" I ask, using my arm to paddle myself closer to the steps. She loves going out on the lake, and we haven't been in a long time.

"Uh, work," she says, like the answer should have been obvious.

She acts like work is a burden sometimes, but, I think she secretly loves it. She spends the majority of her time there, and when she's *not* there, she's talking about it, dreaming up ways to improve it, or hunting for new trends.

"Boo," I pout, stepping out of the pool. My eyes drift to Asher, who's still silent, standing with his arms crossed, as I grab my towel off the lounge chair.

He makes a show out of looking me up and down from my head to my toes before turning and prowling back inside.

Adrian just shrugs. "He probably needs food. You know he gets cranky when he's hungry."

Yeah, and also when he's awake, or, you know, breathing.

"See you in a couple of days?" he asks, one hand on the sliding door.

Before I can answer, Ash's arm darts out and jerks him back into the house by his T-shirt, Adrian's laughter trailing behind them.

"So, we're going to act like this isn't a thing?" Nat asks, looking at me from beneath her sunglasses.

"Yep."

"Just checking."

CHAPTER 4

BRIAR

Saturday morning comes fast, and I haven't seen Ash since the day at the pool. He's been making himself scarce lately, and I don't know what to make of it. Last night when Dash and I had our usual birthday celebration, it took all I had in me not to press for answers. Answers to where he's been and what he's been up to. I have three years of questions I need answered. But, I managed to keep my mouth shut, not even mentioning him once. We video chatted with the parental units—well, with my mom, as Dad was too busy on a business call—watched movies, and ordered from his favorite pizza joint, before I finally called it a night.

I told myself to put Asher out of my mind. Things are different now, but somehow not different at all.

Because even though I'm older, we still can't be together. And on top of that, he now hates me, for some unknown reason. But, turning my feelings off is easier said than done, so I caved to my desire to touch myself to thoughts of Asher. I imagined him sneaking into my room and slipping inside me. Only he wouldn't be sweet like Jackson was. It would hurt—because everything with Ash hurts—and I'd beg him not to stop. I couldn't even hate myself for it afterward because I was finally able drift off to sleep, blissfully sated.

This morning, however, is another story. The moment I opened my eyes, at six A.M. for some god-awful reason, a sense of dread blanketed my mood, like a dark cloud hanging over my head. I didn't know why, but I was pretty sure Asher had something to do with it.

Now, I'm standing in the kitchen in an old white T-shirt that reaches mid-thigh, making breakfast burritos for the hungry men who will be infiltrating my kitchen soon on the griddle of the restaurant-style range. I look at the clock on the microwave—seven thirty. I have a good hour before everyone wakes up and shows up, but the food can be reheated. And I can guarantee the drinking will start before ten A.M., so these assholes will need sustenance.

The silence is too much, so I grab my earbuds and hit shuffle on my playlist. An acoustic version of "Hoodie" by Hey Violet filters through my headphones. Jesus, I'm pathetic because everything always comes back to Asher. This song included.

I'm sprinkling shredded cheese onto the potatoes, swaying and singing, when I feel a hand brush across my neck before clamping down. I whip around, wielding the spatula in front of me like a weapon, only to see Asher standing there, looking highly unimpressed.

He has on a thin, black tank top with the sides cut out and gray board shorts. His hair is wet and slicked back, as if he just got out of the shower, and I can't help but wonder if he used my conditioner again. Now my heart is racing for another reason entirely.

"Jesus, Asher!" I whisper-yell. He tugs on the white cord, ripping the bud from my ear with a wicked smirk plastered to his face.

"I said your name. Multiple times." He shrugs, like that gives him an excuse to scare the life out of me.

"Where have you been?" I ask, without meaning to, turning back to switch the griddle off and scoop everything onto plates.

"Don't tell me you've missed me, Sugar Plum," he whispers, still crowding my space, and I feel his breath on the back of my neck.

"Don't call me that."

"Why no—" Asher starts, but stops, and I twist around to look at him expectantly. The playfulness is gone, and his expression is back to being stone-cold.

"What?" I ask with a nervous laugh. "Why are you looking at me like that?"

"Is that my shirt?" he asks, jerking his chin toward the tattered, blood-speckled tee. The one he left behind in my brother's room the night he left. The one I snatched after he crawled back out the window, and sniffed in the privacy of my room for weeks afterward, until his scent was gone just like him. The one I don't even think of as being his anymore.

"It's mine," I say firmly, chin thrust forward. My ears are burning with embarrassment and I feel my face heat, but I don't show it.

"Funny, I bled on a shirt just like that."

"Well, even if it was yours, I think the statute of limitations would be up by now."

He laughs, more of a single huff, really, before scrubbing a hand over his face. "Why'd you keep it, Briar?"

I have two choices. I can either play dumb or tell the truth. The truth is awkward and uncomfortable, but I decide to go with it. Maybe if I give him a little morsel of honesty, he'll open up about why he left the way he did, leaving all thoughts of college and Dash and me behind. Or maybe I'm just a glutton for disappointment.

"Because I was sad. Because you left me, and I had —no—*have* no idea why. Because the only friend I had after you disappeared was my own brother and I missed you so much that it physically hurt. And because this stupid shirt was the only thing that made me feel closer to you."

Asher doesn't speak, just stands there with his mouth pressed in a flat line. His eyebrows pull together as if he's trying to work something out in his head. He opens his mouth to say something, but before I can get my hopes up, he snaps it shut.

Asher steps toward me, and I suck in a breath. He hooks a finger under my chin, and I have to tilt my head up to make eye contact when he's this close. My hands that are braced on the oven handle behind me start to feel clammy, and I'm afraid to breathe, afraid to do *anything* to ruin this moment. His dark, mismatched eyes search my blues, for what, I don't know.

But it all comes crashing down when I hear the last voice I expect to hear. Here. In *my* house.

"Uh, hope I'm not interrupting anything," Whitley says, each word dripping with disdain.

Asher snaps out of his trance, and the mask of indifference is firmly back in place.

"What the hell are you doing in my house?" I didn't even hear her come in. I haven't so much as laid eyes on her since the party where she bragged about hooking up with Asher, and if I never see her again, it would be too soon.

"Aw, didn't Asher tell you? I'm his date for your brother's party. Thanks for keeping him entertained 'til I got here."

I look at him, my eyebrows clear up to my hairline,

unable to comprehend the fact that he invited *her*, here, of all people. Of all places. That's a new level of low, even for him.

"You're not my fucking *date*," Ash spits with more venom than he's ever directed at me.

Before anyone can say another word, the front door swings open and Adrian, two thirty-packs of beer under each arm, and a couple of other people I don't recognize make their way toward the kitchen.

Asher's jaw hardens and he shoots a look to my bare legs, and it's only then that I realize I'm still standing here...without pants.

"Breakfast burritos are ready," I supply, keeping myself hidden behind the countertop.

Adrian notices Whitley being here and looks at me with an eyebrow cocked in question. I shoot him a look that says *tell me about it*. No one really likes her. I'm not sure why she sticks around, or why they allow it.

"You're too good to me, baby," he says, clutching his chest and making his way toward the food. He fixes his plate and is already inhaling it in three seconds flat. If you want to win Adrian's heart, food is the fastest way to it. Hands down.

"Damn, girl," he says through a mouthful, as everyone else starts helping themselves, "shit is the bomb."

"Briar," Asher says, his voice cold and hard. Just like him.

"What?" I snap at him. I'm not ready to play nice yet.

"*Clothes*," he says in a threatening voice. "Now."

Adrian stands up from the barstool at the counter and peers over at me, giving me a thorough once-over. Asher plants him back down with a firm hand to the shoulder as I walk away, fighting the urge to cover myself.

"I'd straight-up suck a fart out of that ass," I hear Adrian say, followed by, "Ow, motherfucker!"

I'd laugh if I weren't fuming. I'm not even mad at Whitley. This is what she does. But Asher? He knows how she's always treated me. He knows how I feel about her. And still, she's here. Smugger than Simon Cowell.

I quickly pull on my white bikini and some cut-off jean shorts and head back to the kitchen. Dash is awake now, already eating, and stands when he sees me. Asher is sitting on the arm of the couch, and Whitley is perched between his spread legs.

"Thanks for breakfast, Bry," Dash says, hooking an arm around my neck and giving me a quick peck to the top of my head.

"Surprise," I say half-heartedly, my eyes still locked on the man version of the boy I used to love.

Asher stands abruptly, causing Whitley to stumble. "Going to take a piss." He walks by me, not looking even a little sorry.

"I'm going to go grab some towels. Be ready to leave in five?" I ask. Everyone mumbles their agreement.

Once I round the corner, I pause at the bathroom door to make sure no one else is around, and before I can talk myself out of it, I'm barging in. Asher's standing in front of the toilet, peeing, perpetually unfazed.

"This gonna be our thing? Meeting up in the bathroom? Not exactly the most sanitary place, but I guess it will do."

"Why'd you do it?" I seethe, too angry to be mesmerized by the glint of silver as he shakes himself once he finishes, before tucking himself back into his shorts.

"Do what?" he says with a sigh, as if he's exasperated by my antics.

"Why would you invite her? You knew exactly what you were doing."

"I'm not your fucking *boyfriend*, Briar." He wields words like a weapon, and they hit their intended target, like a punch straight to my gut.

Of course, he isn't my boyfriend. Even if we were together, words like *boyfriend* and *girlfriend* would seem too trivial a label for us. But it's about respect. And intent. He intended to hurt me, and that is what stings the most.

"I'm done, Ash. With whatever this is." I wave a hand between us.

"Like I said, *I'm not your boyfriend.* So save the breakup speech."

I drop my gaze, hating how I can want him and detest him simultaneously.

"Are you going to fuck her?"

A shrug. "Probably."

"You're disgusting."

"It's about time you realized it."

I leave the bathroom first, grab my stuff from my room, and shoot off a text to Nat telling her how much I hate her for not being able to come today, while the boys load up the trucks with beer and snacks.

I ride with my brother and Adrian, while Whitley hops in with Asher—shocker—and the other guys. The lake is a good forty-five minutes away, and somewhere along the way, I decide I'm going to have fun with my brother and our friends, regardless of Asher and Whitley's presence. Adrian cracks jokes and keeps the conversation flowing, and by the time we pull up to the lake, I'm feeling lighter. Happier.

Ignoring the pain from walking barefoot on the rocky beach, I go straight for the water. It's a scorcher at one hundred fourteen degrees today, so I don't waste any time.

An arm is slung over my shoulder, and I'm tugged into Adrian's warm, tan side. Arms still crossed, I look up and offer him a big smile. Asher was my crush, but Adrian was always like another brother to me. Albeit, a perverted brother, but a brother nonetheless.

"Hey."

"Why do you look like you're about to off yourself?"

"Shut up, I do not." I laugh, throwing an elbow into his side. "I'm just thinking."

"Thinking about...?" he hedges.

"Just stuff."

"Stuff like the fact that Whitley is here and hanging all over Kelley like he holds the key to all the blow in the entire state?"

I cringe, not only at that visual, but also because, apparently, I'm so transparent that even Adrian can see through me.

"He doesn't want her, sweetheart," he says, ducking his head close to mine.

Giving up the charade, I ask, "How do you know?"

Adrian looks backward, a cocky grin plastered to his face.

"Because if he wanted anything to do with her, he wouldn't be staring over here, looking like he's about to commit murder right after he pisses on you to mark his territory."

Trying to appear as casual as possible, I glance behind me to see Asher sitting on the tailgate of his truck, white knuckling his beer bottle. Clenched jaw. Spine ramrod straight. *Yeah, he's pissed.* Meanwhile, Whitley is oblivious, prancing around in her hot pink bikini that barely covers her crotch and half a nipple, making every effort to be noticed by Ash—and every other guy at the lake.

"Then, maybe he should do something about it," I say, suddenly feeling so fed up with this game we're playing.

"Give him a minute." He chuckles. "Kelley doesn't catch feelings for anyone. Not once in all the years that I've known him has he had a legitimate relationship. Figures the first girl he falls for ends up being his best friend's little sister."

The first girl he falls for...

I don't know if what Adrian is saying holds any truth—Asher is a very different person than he was before he left—but those words dull my anger, just a little. Sweet, vulnerable Asher doesn't know how to love anyone. Doesn't know how to let anyone love him. I could've loved him enough for the both of us if he let me.

"Let's go!" Dash yells, and I look over to see him standing on Adrian's dad's pontoon that they've already managed to unload into the water. "Who's taking the Jet Skis?" he asks, holding two keys attached to bracelets.

Slipping out from under Adrian's side, I run up and snatch one of the keys from him. I love these things, plus the more distance between Whitley and me, the better.

"You sure?" Dash asks, concern etched into his features.

"I'll be careful, Dad," I tease, giving a reassuring smile. Dash tosses me a life jacket, and I strap it on over my chest. I unbutton my shorts and let them fall to my ankles before tossing them onto the pontoon.

"All right, who else?"

Adrian starts toward us, but Asher hops off the tailgate, tosses his empty bottle into the bed of his truck, and then claims the other set of keys without a word. Adrian shoots me a knowing look.

Lovely.

"Stay close to Kelley. I'll see you out there."

Everyone piles onto the boat while Ash and I make our way toward the Jet Skis.

"You know how to drive one of these things?" Asher asks, shrugging on his own life jacket—looking put out that he's not above the law and has to wear one —as I swing a leg over and hop on.

"Yep."

"Of course, you do."

"What's that supposed to mean?"

"Not a damn thing. Ready?"

Instead of answering, I stick the key in and hit the *start* button. Asher gets behind me, and we both coast, unspeaking, until we pass the no-wake zone. As soon as we hit the buoys giving us the green light, Asher speeds off ahead of me.

Dick.

I squeeze the throttle on the handlebar and manage to catch up to him. His head swivels over to me, and I see a dark brow lift in amusement behind his black sunglasses. He ups his speed, daring me to keep up, and I don't plan to back down. My hair whips in every direction, and I'm laughing like a lunatic, but I don't care. It's not like he can hear me, anyway. I can resume my anger once I'm done having fun.

We're in the pontoon's wake, and I hear Dash and Adrian hollering at us. They're holding up something that I can't make out... *Is that a beer bong?* Yup. It's definitely a beer bong.

Asher stands on his Jet Ski, hands still on the handlebars, and cuts out of the wake, hitting several waves that send him flying through the air. But, he doesn't lose control for even a second. He's always loved the water, and it loves him right back. His dark gray board shorts cling to him like a second skin and hang low enough to expose the defined crease between two toned ass cheeks. That, combined with the vibration between my thighs, has me feeling more than a little squirmy.

Instead of staying with the boat, I veer off and follow Asher. He glances over his shoulder, and I swear I see a hint of a smirk on those gorgeous, pouty lips of his. If I thought we were going fast before, we're flying now. I check the speed. Thirty-eight miles per hour. *Okay, so maybe it's not that fast.* But it feels a lot faster on water.

Every time we hit a wave, he checks back on me,

and some stupid, naïve part of me equates that as caring about me—at least in some capacity. *Baby steps.*

After playing around in the water a little more, Ash leads the way back to Dash and everyone. We're parallel to the pontoon, but this time, I'm in front of him. I look back at Dash for a split second before I hear Asher yell.

"Briar!"

My head snaps to my right, and I see another Jet Ski coming straight for me. Fear takes hold and I'm frozen, unsure of what to do. If I hit the *off* button at this speed, I'll be ejected. I can't go left, because the pontoon is there. My only option is to pull out the key and take a sharp right.

I just narrowly avoid being hit, water splashes onto my face, and the two guys on the Jet Ski look back, oblivious to the fact that they almost took me out. I'm still trying to calm my racing heart when Asher's suddenly at my side.

"You okay?" he barks out, his eyebrows cinched together.

"Yeah, I—" Before I can finish my sentence, he takes off after them.

"Asher! Don't!"

But there's no stopping him. He's off like a rocket, chasing them across the lake. He has to be going at least sixty miles per hour to catch up to them. This is the old Asher. The hothead, always looking for a fight.

"Bry!" Dash yells out to me, panic lacing his voice.

"I'm good!" I shout back, climbing back on and giving a thumbs-up.

Asher passes them, and I'm confused for a second, wondering if he thought better of it, until he turns back around, heading straight for them.

Is he playing chicken?

They try to dodge him, but he mirrors their every move. I hold my breath, watching through my fingers and hoping to God he doesn't hurt himself or anyone else, when he cuts right, just before they're about to collide, and soaks the shit out of them. The guy tries to take a sharp turn to avoid getting hit, but they end up tipping over and going under.

Adrian and Dash howl with laughter, while Whitley rolls her eyes because the attention isn't on her. I think I let out something between a nervous giggle and a relieved sigh, but I can't tell because my pulse is still pounding in my ears.

I'm not sure exactly what's going on from here, but I can hear Asher's threatening, booming voice, and then he's throwing his arms up and pointing back at me. One guy swims to the shore, and one mounts the Jet Ski, idling. A few more words are exchanged before they go their separate ways.

Once he's back, he tells me to get my ass on the boat. I idle as close as I can get and Adrian extends a hand to pull me up. I ditch my life vest, then pull the key bracelet off, handing it to one of Dash's other friends. Asher dives off his Jet Ski and climbs onto the boat behind me.

"Key's on the handlebar," he says to anyone and everyone, but staring at only me, and one of the other guys jumps in to get it.

"It wasn't—" I start, but he cuts me right off.

"No, it wasn't your fault. Those fucks were drunker than shit."

"Oh. Okay."

I didn't expect that. I don't know why, I just assumed he'd find a way to turn it around on me.

"But, you weren't paying attention." *Annnnd there it is.* "If you hadn't thought fast..."

"Thank you, Asher," I say simply.

He gives a short, forced nod, but then Whitley is there next to him, tracing her talons up and down the dips and grooves of his abs. Asher tenses ever so slightly, but I catch it.

"That's a really cute suit, Briar," Whitley says, her saccharine sweet voice dripping with insincerity.

"Thanks," I deadpan.

"It's really brave for someone so...*curvy* to wear white. I wish I was as confident as you are."

I roll my eyes, letting her comment roll off my back before walking away. Is this what we're resorting to now? Backhanded, mean girl compliments? Seeing her touch his body with such ease, such intimacy, was far worse than any insult she could sling at me. I sit on the cushioned bench on the very back of the boat, resting a forearm on my folded knees.

Dash, deciding this is as good a place as any, throws the anchor over the side, next to another boat full of partiers. There are probably ten or so guys and girls who look to be a little older than us. Maybe mid-twenties. Dash grabs the beer bong and steps over onto their boat and introduces himself. Ever the attention whore.

"Having fun, pretty girl?" Adrian asks, plopping down beside me, flashing that megawatt smile. He's ridiculously attractive with his inky black hair, caramel-colored skin, and golden eyes. Why couldn't I crush on a guy like him? *Because that would be too easy.*

"I was before I almost died." I laugh.

"I don't think it was the near-death experience that put that look on your face," he teases. But he's also right.

"When did you get so insightful?" I grumble.

We both watch as Whitley sits on an uninterested Asher. At least, he appears to be uninterested, with the way he stares directly ahead as Whitley bounces around on his lap to some shitty Ke$ha song playing from the other boat.

Adrian tucks a wayward hair behind my ear, and I must give him the dirtiest side-eye known to man, because he laughs and leans in, explaining himself.

"Trust me. He just needs a little push."

I swallow hard and give a shaky nod. Good thing

Dash is too entertained by his new friends to notice
Adrian's show. Though, somehow, I suspect that he'd
get away with it, anyway. Adrian just has that way
about him. He can bullshit his way out of anything,
and everyone loves him. Even Ash, though you'd never
know it by seeing them together.

"Don't look at him," Adrian says in a hushed voice.
"Keep looking at me."

I look into his usually mirthful eyes, but right now,
they're full of heat, and I'm wondering if this is still an
act. He cups the side of my neck, pulling me closer.
His lips are just an inch from mine, and even though I
know it's all for show, my stomach twists with nerves.

"Damn, Briar. I'm starting to think you'd be worth
the beating I'd get from your brother *and* Kelley."

Huh?

"I'm gonna kiss you. Go with it."

His fingertips touch my cheek, and for some
reason, my first thought is how they're so much softer
than Asher's calloused hands. It's a testament to how
different their lives have been. How different they
still are.

I'm about to say no. These kinds of games always
lead to trouble. I chance a look at Asher out of the
corner of my eye, and all I can focus on is his death grip
on Whitley's thigh.

All of a sudden, Adrian's soft lips meet mine. I
gasp, and he takes the opportunity to slip his tongue in
to tangle with him. Before I can process the fact that

it's happening, his mouth is ripped away from mine. And then a moment later, a *splash.*

My eyes shoot open to see Asher in front of me— face full of anger and clenched fists full of rage—and I hear Adrian sputtering and chuckling from the water. Asher pushed him off the edge? *That fucker was right.*

"Keep your fucking hands to yourself."

Anyone in their right mind would be afraid, but Adrian literally laughs him off.

"I mean, we can share. It's not gay if your balls don't touch!" Adrian yells, sending a wink in my direction.

Turning his attention to me, Asher grabs me by my bicep and drags me toward the other side of the boat.

"You're coming with me. Say whatever the fuck you have to say to your brother."

"Why should I?"

"Don't fucking play with me right now, Briar," he says roughly, snatching up a life vest and smacking it to my chest. "You're going to pay for that little show."

ASHER

I'm going to kill Adrian's bitch ass. I know exactly what he was trying to do. But I also know that he wouldn't pass up the chance to hook up with Briar if it came down to it, either. And what the fuck was she thinking, letting him put his hands on her? His *lips* on her?

After making up some excuse about needing to get back home, Dash hugged his sister and thanked me for offering to help her. I'm a piece of shit, but ask me if I care right now.

She was wearing my shirt this morning. *Just* my shirt. She kept it. When I saw her standing there with her back to me, bare legs and messy hair, I wished things were different. I wished I wasn't a fucking lowlife scumbag and that she wasn't the girl who purposely fucked me over because her pride was wounded.

Nothing makes sense. I was about to ask her why she did it, once and for all, if only to keep from crushing my lips to hers, but then fucking Whitley walked in.

I didn't invite her. Fuck that. If there's a party, or anything even resembling one, Whitley will find out about it. My guess is that one of the other guys who still risks his life by putting his dick inside her tipped her off. I know she still tries to talk to Dash, but he shut that shit down a long time ago. And if Dash won't touch her, that automatically excludes Adrian, seeing as how they like to share.

I'll admit that I've fucked her in the past, but it was never a relationship. We were just two lonely, miserable people who used each other. I used her for coke, and she used me for sex. She knew the drill. It's not like

I could sleep with my best friend's fourteen-year-old sister, so I didn't really care.

I let Briar *think* that I invited her. Maybe it was payback for having to see her with Jackson. Maybe it was my way of getting her to hate me so I wouldn't be tempted to forget her transgressions and make her mine. Maybe I'm just an asshole.

I step onto the Jet Ski and hold out my hand to help Bry on behind me, but she doesn't take it.

"Where's yours?" she questions.

"My what?"

"Your life jacket. It's illegal to be on that thing without one," she says, arms crossed.

A devious smirk spreads across my face. "You're stalling, baby girl."

She takes a fortifying breath before taking my hand and cautiously stepping down. Once she's on, her thighs hug mine, and I can feel the heat of her pussy on my back.

This was a bad fucking idea.

I spot the key hanging off the handlebar, and I start it up, ignoring Whitley's shrill protests from the boat. The ride back to shore does little to calm my anger. If anything, I'm only getting more pissed off by the minute.

Briar's only five feet tall, but the girl is all legs. And right now, those thighs have me in a vise grip as she holds on to me for dear life. After hitting a rough wave that forces us even closer together, she finally wraps her timid arms around my stomach. I'm hard from her touch alone. I feel her tuck into me, her forehead hitting the top of my spine—probably to shield her face from the wind—and her long, blonde hair whips in my face.

We hit another wave, and instinctively, my left hand shoots out to grip her thigh. But I don't remove it. Not even when we're in the no-wake zone.

Once we reach the shore, I yank the key out while she takes off her vest, exposing those perky tits covered by thin scraps of white triangles. Fuck, she looks good. I bend down and lift her around the waist, and even though she squeals, her legs immediately lock around me.

"Put me down!"

"Shut up."

She tries to wriggle down my body, but all she does is make my dick harder, and the moment she feels it, she freezes. I laugh darkly at her wide eyes.

Once we're to my truck, I lay her down in the bed of it, on top of an old quilt I keep back here to prevent tools from scratching the paint.

"Tell me, Briar. What was your plan?" I ask, leaning over her.

She lies there, and with the setting sun making her hair appear more golden than blonde, those faint freckles across her nose, and cheeks rosy from the sun, she looks even more innocent than usual. She shakes her head. "What are you talking about?"

"Your plan. With Adrian?" *Don't play dumb, baby.*

"He wasn't being serious."

"Bullshit," I say, trailing my hand up her soft thigh. Higher, higher, higher. "Were you going to let him touch this?" I grip her between her legs through her bathing suit bottoms, and she gasps.

"Huh? Were you going to let him touch your pussy?"

"No," she breathes, as the flat of my fingers start to rub up and down.

"Because he would, you know. He'd fuck you in a heartbeat if given half the chance."

"You're such a hypocrite," she says, eyes closing in pleasure. "You can be all over Whitley, but I can't kiss anyone?"

"Fuck Whitley. I don't want her." *I want you.* I don't say it out loud, but the insinuation is clear.

She pushes into my hand, and I feel her wetness through the fabric of her bathing suit.

"Who are you wet for, baby girl? Is it for him? Or me?"

Briar doesn't answer, too focused on trying to close her legs around my hand to stop my movements. Her eyes dart around, making sure we don't have any company. The sun is going down, so there are people only feet away, packing up for the day.

"No one can see you," I say, covering her body with mine. "But even if they could...let them watch."

"We shouldn't be doing this," she says on a gasp,

but she parts her legs for me anyway, and I rub her clit with the heel of my palm at the same time that I pull her bathing suit top to the side with my teeth. I suck the soft flesh into my mouth, leaving my mark on her.

"You wanted to play big girl games, Briar. Now, I'm going to treat you like a big girl."

Briar's head drops back, exposing her slender throat. A lone freckle where her neck meets her shoulder catches my eye, and without thinking twice, I bite into her. Hard.

She shrieks in pain before I feel her entire body tense up, and her knees clamp shut, effectively trapping my hand between her legs. Once she starts to shudder and shake, I realize she wasn't screaming in pain. She was screaming from pleasure.

Baby girl likes it rough.

"Did you really just come?" I ask wryly.

She throws an arm over to shield her face and rolls away from me.

"Fuck you."

"Why, so you can come on my cock this time?"

"You're disgusting. Take me home."

"How long has it been, Bry? You must be going through quite the dry spell to get off so easily. Or is it just me that has that effect on you?"

I'm just saying things to get under her skin at this point. Getting a rise out of her is my newest addiction. It's better than cocaine. Briar sits up and jumps down from the tailgate, then stomps around to the front of the truck. She hops into the passenger seat and slams the door.

I decide to let her stew in her post-orgasmic bliss-slash-guilt while I set the Jet Ski up onto the trailer. It takes a while, and by the time I get back, the sun has completely set.

Briar sits in the front seat, chipping away at her white nail polish. She doesn't glance my way when I open the door. Not even when I start the truck. And not even when we pull up to her house.

"You wanna tell me why I'm the one with blue balls and you're giving the silent treatment?" It was a joke, but apparently the wrong thing to say, because when she looks up at me, her eyes are shining with unshed tears.

"Why do you do this to me?"

"What exactly am I *doing* to you? Besides making you come on my hand?"

"You know exactly what you're doing. You've been stringing me along since I was fourteen fucking years old."

"You don't know what you're talking about," I seethe. Does she think I do this on purpose? That I like feeling this way? I want to hate her. I *do* hate her. But I also just *want her*. This is her fault. If it weren't for her, none of the past three years would've happened.

"No, Asher, I think I do. You don't want me until someone else does. But we're just friends, right? At least, we were. Now, we're not even that."

"Because you're so innocent," I snap back. "Little Briar fucking Vale. Such a saint. Such a victim. That's what you want people to think, isn't it? But they don't know you like I do. I see you."

Briar huffs, avoiding eye contact while clumsily slapping around for the handle.

"I was trying to protect you," I say grudgingly. "Jackson isn't a good guy."

"You're miserable. And you won't be happy until everyone is just as miserable as you. I'm done."

"Why don't you ask him about his list then?" I toss back, ignoring the fact there is some truth to her words.

She gives me an appraising look, probably trying to gauge whether or not I'm telling the truth before she storms out of the truck and slams the door. Her pale hair whipping around in the dark behind her is the last thing I see before I drive off. I can't be here right now, so I go to the one place I've been avoiding since I got into town.

Home.

~

I stand in front of the house I grew up in with its flaking, once-white paint, and front yard full of dirt for the second time since coming back. The first time, I took exactly one step inside before bailing.

The olive-green Oldsmobile sits in the cracked driveway, and nothing seems to have changed since

I've been gone, except the boarded-up front window. The mailbox is knocked over, almost completely horizontal. I kick it when I walk past, inadvertently causing it to stand *almost* straight.

Don't say I never did anything for you, you piece of shit.

Once I'm at the front door, I smell the old familiar scent of mothballs that my dad insists keeps stray cats away. I raise a fist to knock before deciding to let myself in. Inside, it's dark, hot, and smells of stale cigarettes. Years of smoking in the house have resulted in nicotine-stained walls, but I can still see faint white patches where pictures used to hang.

And then I see him. John Kelley, in all his glory. Passed out in his black, cracked leather recliner, in front of an old television with a rabbit-ear antenna. A cigarette dangles from his fingertips with ash a mile long, and below it sits a collection of beer bottles.

"You got somethin' to say, boy, or are you just gonna stand there and keep killing me in your mind?"

Okay, so maybe he isn't asleep.

Wordlessly, I scan his face, noticing his yellow complexion and clammy skin. I didn't know how I'd feel standing in this house, facing this man who couldn't seem to put his bullshit aside for one goddamn minute to be a decent father. Even a decent *human* would've sufficed. But, the bitterness, resentment, and flat-out disgust are all still there.

"Well, no need," he says with a cough. "My liver will kill me before you get the balls."

"Am I supposed to feel sorry for you?" I ask, the picture of apathy as I casually sit on the filthy couch. It's the same one that was old, even when I was a baby, with its plaid design made up of different shades of tans and browns and wooden arms.

"No," he says thoughtfully. "No, I guess you wouldn't have any reason to, would you?"

"If you think that we're going to be buddy-buddy just because you're dying, think again."

"Then, why are you here?" he rasps, taking a drag of his cigarette.

I look him dead in the eyes. "To bury you."

He nods once, before looking back at the TV. "Fair enough."

Minutes pass, him not knowing what to say, and me not wanting to say anything at all. Finally, he breaks the silence.

"I never meant for you to meet David."

"Shut the fuck up."

Even hearing that name has my blood boiling, but he keeps speaking.

"I didn't want him to know you so much as existed. And, hell, for the first few years, he didn't."

I give a heavy sigh, aiming for bored. "Is this going to be a thing? You're dying, so now you're trying to absolve yourself of all your sins and guilt?" I roll my eyes and sit back, propping one foot on my knee, arms spread over the itchy fabric of the couch. "Save your breath, because I don't give a fuck about any of it."

"My father..." he trails off, looking away before continuing. "He was rough with us both. But David was different. He'd always been...*off*, even from a young age. I don't remember a time in my life when he was normal."

I feel my smirk falter. "I said stop."

"Then, once your mother died—"

"What happened to your window?" I say, nodding my chin in the direction of the boarded-up mess, changing the subject. I'm not talking about David, and I sure as hell am not talking about my mother.

"Ask your little girlfriend."

My eyebrows pull together in confusion.

"Who?"

Maybe he means Whitley. She's the one who told me he was hospitalized a few weeks ago and begged me to come home. Her mom is a registered nurse, and even though we don't exactly live in a small town, it's hard not to know who my dad is.

"The little blonde girl you used to run around with."

"Briar?" That doesn't make sense. How would she know what happened?

He nods and reaches for the beer bottle at his feet, liver be damned. "Threw a brick right through window. She stood there seething for about ten minutes first. I didn't think she'd do anything. She was just a little girl. So, I went about my business."

His *business*. Also known as drinking enough vodka to kill a horse while watching Skinemax. Most likely in his underwear.

"I about shit my pants when it happened. Got my drunk ass up just in time to see her flip me off."

"When?"

"Right after you left." He shrugs. "Before I got my DUI."

Well, well, well. Briar isn't such an angel, after all. But I already knew that, didn't I?

It doesn't change what she did, but it does have my lips tugging into a reluctant grin. No one has the balls to stand up to John Kelley. Not even me, for a long time, anyway.

I stand and scan the hellhole I used to call home one more time before deciding to leave. I used to fucking hate this place. It made me physically ill to be here, to be around my dad. To face the memory of my mom. Now, I'm just glad I got out, even if I had to go through hell.

"See you around, I guess."

"Does that mean you're sticking around?"

If I didn't know any better, I'd say his voice sounds hopeful.

"For now."

When I'm sitting in my truck, I scroll through my phone to the one number I haven't used in years and press *call*. After three rings, I start to think she's not going to answer, but on the fourth, she picks up—voice all velvety and thick with sleep.

"Hello?"

"You asked me why I do this to you. The truth is, I don't fucking know why. But until I figure it out, you're going to stay away from Jackson, you're going to stay away from Adrian, and you're going to stay away from fucking Billy Bob working over at the Circle K."

"And why should I do that?"

"Because this isn't finished, Briar. You and I were never just friends."

I hang up without waiting for a response, tempted to sneak into her room and really drive my point home, but I decide to leave it. For tonight, at least.

I end up heading back to their house after driving around for a while. A couple of days ago, I called the number listed on the building permit posted in a yard a few streets over on a whim. Asked the dude if he needed a roofer, and without even wanting to meet me, he told me the house would be ready for the roof by tomorrow and to show up ready to work.

Fuck, I love my job. I don't have to talk to anyone. I'm my own boss. I can work at my own pace, for the most part. I only take jobs when I feel like it, and if I don't hire anyone to help me, I can bust a roof out in a few days and make a good chunk of money. That also means I'm not tied down to any one place for too long. Plus, I've found that when you're hammering into shingles all day, you don't have time to get lost in your head. And my head is not a pretty place to be.

I'm not exactly rich. Not compared to the people of Cactus Heights. But it's sure as fuck more than I ever dreamed of making, and more than John ever made. We didn't have money growing up, so I'm used to living modestly. Dare was the one who convinced me that I needed to spend a little to live a little, and I finally caved and bought my truck. It's the first thing in my entire life that's ever been mine and only mine. *Besides Briar,* I think, but she never really was mine.

As I'm dozing off, I remember to set my alarm and notice a text from the little devil herself.

Briar: Same goes to you. No more Whitley, or no deal.

Me: Easy enough.

I know she fell back asleep, judging by the silence when I came in, so I don't wait for a response.

CHAPTER 5

BRIAR

Asher's words have played on a loop in my head for the past couple of days.

"You and I were never just friends."

Understatement of the century.

Our little agreement has me giddy, though I know better than to think it means anything other than Asher being territorial. Little does he know, I've already distanced myself from Jackson. It didn't feel right, and I didn't want to string him along. It hasn't stopped him from texting me, though. His behavior has become slightly erratic, accusing me of being a tease for not responding to him one second, and then apologizing in the next breath. I chalk it up to him not being able to handle rejection. Guys like him never can. *Pathetic.*

But, after Ash's cryptic comment about a list, I've

wondered if there was something more sinister going on. So, against my better judgment, when he asked if he could come over to talk, I said yes. My brother and Adrian are both here—sleeping off hangovers, but they're here—should anything go wrong. I doubt it will. I don't think Jackson is dangerous, but I guess you never know.

I step out of the pool to get dressed before Jackson comes over. I'm bending over, grabbing my towel off the patio chair when I see him come waltzing through the sliding glass door.

"You're early," I say, not even having to check the time to know he's at least forty-five minutes early. Not only that, but he let himself in. Jackson's eyes zero in on my chest, and I look down to see that my top has slid over a little, exposing the two purple spots Asher left as souvenirs. My face burns with embarrassment as I wrap the towel around me.

"I'm going to get dressed. Stay here," I instruct, and he nods, taking a seat on one of the cushioned lounge chairs. I run inside to throw on some skinny yoga pants and a plain white tee before meeting Jackson back outside. He's wearing crisp, dark jeans and a baby blue polo shirt, his usual attire, but something in his eyes is off. His easy smile is gone, and he appears to be on edge.

"How are you, Jackson?" Small talk is the worst, but I don't know what else to say. I want to ask him about the list, whatever it is, but I decide to ease into it.

"Same old, same old," he says, bouncing his knee. "I wish you'd talk to me, though."

I sigh, not wanting to go there right now.

"Jackson ..." I start, but the words fail me. He stares, waiting for an explanation that I can't give him. Nothing happened. At all. I just don't feel that way about him. I tried to make myself want him, but it turns out the heart is a stubborn, fussy bitch. And mine has only ever wanted Asher.

"I don't know what you want me to say," I admit.

"Just tell me the truth. I thought things were going well, and then it was like you just...lost interest." His eyebrows pull together, as if he's genuinely never been rejected before and can't begin to make sense of it.

"I just think we'd make better friends."

"It's because of him, isn't it?" he accuses, his eyes turning hard, and I know he's referring to Asher. I consider telling him the truth, but I can't risk other people finding out about us. And I don't trust Jackson.

"No," I say, taking a seat on the chair next to him. "But I do need to ask you something."

"Anything," he says casually, but his eyes scan me for clues. He knows I know something, but he doesn't know what. I'm starting to realize that there might be more lurking beneath that pretty-boy charade.

"Am I on a list?"

His knee ceases its bouncing, and his eyes widen. "What list?"

I can tell he's being deliberately obtuse, and that Asher and my brother were right to be concerned.

"Don't play dumb." I sigh. "Am I on a *list*?" I ask again. I stand, crossing my arms, and Jackson follows suit.

"It's not what you think," he says, taking a step toward me.

"No," I say, turning to walk back into my house. "That's all I needed to know." I feel sick. I don't know what the list entails, but I don't have to be a genius to know that it's not good. That it most likely has something to do with why he pursued me, and that he betrayed my trust. That's enough for me, without having the gritty details.

"Briar, stop," he demands, but I keep walking. When I open the sliding door, Dash is sitting at the breakfast bar, while Adrian fries some eggs. My brother's blond hair sticks up in every direction, and he looks half-asleep, but when he sees that I'm upset with Jackson on my heels, he snaps to attention. Adrian drops the spatula, and they both flank me in an instant.

"What's going on?" my brother barks.

"Nothing. He was just leaving."

Jackson swallows nervously, looking among the three of us, probably trying to gauge how close he is to catching a fist to the face. Ultimately, he decides to test his luck.

"There is a list, and that's why I was interested in you at the beginning," he admits, holding up his hands in surrender when both Adrian and my brother advance on him. "*But*, I never added your name. I swear to fucking God, Briar. Why do you think I kept pursuing you? If it was only about the stupid list, I would have bailed after..." he trails off, thinking better of finishing that sentence in front of my brother.

Dash's nostrils flare, and Adrian huffs out a humorless laugh, dragging a hand down his face.

"You have three seconds to leave before my foot meets your ass." This comes from Adrian.

"Briar," Jackson tries again, jaw clenched in frustration, but I shake my head in response. I don't know what to believe. I don't know if it changes how I feel, even if he is telling the truth.

Adrian arches a brow, and that's all it takes for Jackson to realize he isn't going to win this one. Then, he's out the door, leaving me with two pairs of expectant eyes focused on me.

"What?"

"Start talking."

Why are all the men in my life so damn pushy?

CHAPTER 6

ASHER

I finished the job I was doing over a week ago, so instead of working, I've been at my dad's house. He's getting worse—I can see it in his appearance, but his expression tells me that he knows it, too—and he refuses to go back to the hospital. He's basically just waiting to die at home, at this point.

Suit yourself.

I've mostly busied myself with cleaning this dump in silence, while my dad searches for the words to say. He watches me. I ignore him. He talks to me. I ignore him. There's nothing he could say to take back the past ten years of my life, but it doesn't stop him from trying.

"Where are you staying?" John asks from his place on his trusty old recliner. I fucking hate that chair. I'm surprised his skin hasn't grafted to it by now. I glance

up at him, debating on whether or not to respond, but
something in his hopeful expression has me caving.

"Dash's."

He nods, expecting that answer, but doesn't have
anything else to add.

I turn my attention back to the giant oak entertain-
ment center—probably about the same age as the
decrepit couch—that takes up almost the entire length
of the wall. The bottom is lined with cabinets sporting
broken handles, and inside is filled with newspapers,
my mom's collection of Disney movies on VHS, art
projects from when I was a kid, and old family
pictures. What's noticeably absent are photos of my
mom and me. I know they used to be in here. That old
bastard probably destroyed them.

I pick up a homemade Christmas ornament with a
tiny handprint and a picture of a child I don't even
recognize anymore—happy and toothless and carefree.
I turn it over. In jumbled, oversized letters, the back
reads "Asher Kelley, age 7, 2nd grade". A familiar
feeling washes over me like an old friend—a mixture of
anger and resentment—and I stuff it down into the
trash bag full of all the other useless shit.

"You're tossing that?" Dad asks, taking a swig of his
water bottle, and I almost laugh. The sight is so foreign.
I don't ever remember him drinking anything but beer
or liquor. The occasional cup of coffee, maybe. I want
to tell him it's too late for that, but I bite my tongue.

"Your mother loved that..." he trails off. Clearing

his throat, he adds, "*I* loved it." His voice is uncharacteristically gruff, and his eyes so sincere that it momentarily throws me off.

"Loved it so much that you threw it in with the rest of the crap you don't give a shit about?" I start grabbing junk by the handful and shoving it into the bag, not even sparing a glance at it. It's better this way.

"Son."

A turkey handprint from Thanksgiving. An article from the year I made regionals in swim. A birthday card.

"Son."

A Hot Wheels car. A photo of me with my first swim medal.

"Son!"

"What!" I snap, rising to my feet to grab another garbage bag.

"I'm sorry," he says simply, yet emphatically. "I'm sorry. I'm sorry. I'm *sorry*."

I shake my head, not wanting to hear this shit again. "I'm fucking here, aren't I?" What more does he want from me?

"I'm sorry," he says again. "Don't throw away the good things in your life on my account. I'll be gone soon, probably not soon enough for your liking, but you'll want these things one day. Trust me on that."

Tears well up in his eyes, and I look away. My dad has never had a problem expressing his feelings. Just the opposite, actually. He loved hard, and he fought harder. Whether he was crying happy tears at one of my swim meets or in an alcohol-induced fit of rage, he felt everything more than most people. Even when he beat the shit out of me, I knew that he loved me, as fucked up as that sounds. He'd always had trouble controlling his emotions, but after my mom, the calm to his storm, passed away, there was no one to help him reel it in. More than that, there was no *desire* to reel it in. I should've been enough. But I wasn't. And therein lies the problem.

If for some god-forsaken reason I ever become a father, I will live and fucking breathe for that kid. I will die before ever letting one single bad thing touch that kid. And I for damn sure wouldn't hurt my kid or send him off into the hands of a psychopath.

"I came for you, Ash," he admits in a quiet voice, shocking me. I don't show it, though. I stare blankly, waiting for him to continue.

"I know it doesn't matter now. But after I completed my court-ordered rehab, I went to David's house. I wasn't supposed to, not legally, but I didn't care. I knew you probably wouldn't want to stay with me, but I had a plan. I was going to help set you up with your own place. But you were already gone. Said you ran away, and he never bothered looking."

My fists clench at my sides. It's bullshit. All of it. My dad didn't have a dime to his name.

He continues, "I figured it didn't matter where you were, long as you weren't with him. You're strong.

Smart. Hell, you raised yourself after your mom died. I wasn't worried."

"I don't claim to know a damn thing about being normal, but I'm pretty sure normal people worry about their kids," I say sarcastically.

"That's not what I meant." He sighs, rubbing at his forehead with a shaky hand. "Of course, I worried. I wondered. But I had faith that you were safe."

I used to think my dad was the strongest man alive. I remember arguing with my friends, each of us bragging about the strength of our fathers, claiming they could lift cars and other ridiculously embellished tales. Now, he's sickly thin, except for his distended stomach. Weak. Frail. Pathetic. And fuck, if some part of me isn't starting to feel sorry for him.

"I was almost eighteen," I offer, staring at a cigarette burn in the carpet. "So, it was just a matter of laying low for a few months." I don't tell him how I stole money from my uncle and hopped the first bus out of there. I don't tell him how I met Dare on said bus, who could tell that I was running from something and offered me a job a few hours into the trip.

"Why didn't you come back after your birthday?"

Is he serious?

Tearing my eyes from the burnt spot, I look him in the eye.

"I didn't have anything to come back for."

"The Vale girl might not agree with that statement."

I bark out a humorless laugh.

"She's the reason I left."

He knows this better than anyone. But he inspects me, as if looking for a piece to the puzzle that he's missing.

"Look," I say, gripping the back of my neck and focusing on the popcorn ceiling. "I know you're trying to make amends before it's too late, but you can't force that shit on me. You're ready, but I'm not."

"I get it. I do," he says. "I just can't die with you thinking that I didn't—that I *don't*—love you," he stutters. "That you ever deserved one goddamn second of what I put you through. You lost both of your parents the night your mom died. My biggest regret is blaming you."

Inhaling deeply through my nose, I pace the living room.

"I don't need forgiveness. I just needed you to know."

"I gotta get out of here," I say, already walking toward the door. My dad gives a resigned sigh, and I pause, one hand on the door, looking back at him.

"I, uh, I'll see you tomorrow."

I thought about going back to Dash and Briar's, but I needed to clear my head. Instead, I found myself at a local hole-in-the wall bar. I had exactly three shots of cheap whiskey before a woman approached me. She was pretty, in that white trash, damaged sort of way. You could say she was the female version of me. And from the way her tongue flicked over her straw, I knew I could've had her in the bathroom. In my car. Right there on the bar, if I really wanted it. I looked her up and down, debating, but Briar's face was all I could see, and we made a deal, after all. I couldn't fucking pull the trigger, even if I wanted to. Even without the deal. Which, in turn, pissed me off even more. I slapped a twenty onto the counter and walked out without a word.

I've been driving around for the past two hours now, as "The Boy Who Blocked His Own Shot" by Brand New blares from my speakers. I light up a cigarette, relishing in the comfort and the slight buzz as the nicotine is absorbed in my bloodstream. I quit smoking in River's Edge—except for the occasional cigarette if I'm having a few beers—but I've been craving them more since I've been back.

I'm heading toward The Tracks, but at the last second, I cut across four lanes of traffic to take a different exit. The one that leads back to my old house. Something doesn't feel right. Or maybe it's just that I haven't eaten, and the whiskey is hitting me harder than usual, so I decide not to make the drive out there tonight.

When I pull up to the driveway, I know something is off immediately. There's a car that I don't recognize, and once I'm out of my truck, I hear yelling from inside the house. I run toward the sound to find the front door cracked open. Walking as quietly as I can, I nudge it open and step inside.

Whatever I thought I'd be walking into, this wasn't it. David, my uncle, has John against the wall with his hand around his throat.

"Not so tough now, are ya?" David spits. "Tell me where the boy is, for the last time."

"I told you," John wheezes, trying to loosen the hold on his neck. "He doesn't want nothin' to do with me. Haven't seen him in years."

"That's bullshit, and we both know it. Tell. Me."

"Fuck you," my dad says before spitting at him.

Before I can get to them, David's face contorts with rage, and his elbow cocks back before nailing John square in the face. He hits him one, two, three more times as I charge in their direction, both oblivious to my presence.

Coming up behind David, I sucker punch him to the side of the head, and he goes down like a ton of fucking bricks. I jump on him, raining blow after blow to his face, head, stomach, anywhere I can.

Three years and fifty pounds later, I can finally hold my own against him. I'm not the malnourished kid I once was.

"I gotta say, I didn't see this coming," David says. "It's touching, really." He laughs, and I hit him again, but he doesn't seem fazed. A sound from my left distracts me, and I look over to see my dad struggling to get to his feet. David jumps on the opportunity, striking my jaw with his fist. Flipping me onto my back and straddling me, he gets the upper hand. Out of the corner of my eye, I see John pull himself up, using the arm of the recliner as leverage. I take another hit to the eye, then the mouth, before I hear the unmistakable sound of a pistol cocking.

David freezes with his fist mid-air, and I give him a deranged smile through bloodstained teeth. I shove him backward with both of my palms, and then I stand above him.

"How does it feel?" I ask, my voice calm and steady. "How does it feel to be on the receiving end?" I give a swift kick to his ribs, and he clutches his side, the air leaving his lungs in a *whoosh*.

"I want my money," he wheezes.

I laugh, shaking my head. "How about a bullet instead?"

"Just give me the fucking money, and I'll leave," David says, not making any attempt to get up.

"If I wasn't sick, I'd beat you to a bloody pulp for touching my kid," John says, his gun still trained on David.

It's David's turn to chuckle. "That's fucking rich coming from you."

"How about this?" I interrupt before David gets himself shot. By the look in my dad's eyes, I know it's not out of the question. "You get the fuck out. Forget the money, and I'll forget the fact that I know all about your extracurricular activities." His mouth drops open in shock. "Yeah, you didn't think this through, did you?" I squat, not-too-gently stubbing two fingers against his forehead. "How many warrants do you have out for your arrest, anyway? You thought just because I didn't speak that I wasn't listening? I know details, David. Names. Locations. And if you come back here again, I'll sing like a goddamn canary."

My dad looks between us, thoroughly confused, but he doesn't let his guard down. He jerks the gun in the direction of the door, and David scrambles to his feet.

"This isn't over," he warns, and then he's gone.

"I guess there's a lot you haven't told me," my dad says, tiredly collapsing back into his recliner, like it's just another Tuesday night.

"Your brother likes to steal cars and sell them for parts. Among other things."

I even did it with him for a while. I was pissed off at the world, and the money was too tempting to pass up. Except I never saw a fucking dime. He kept me indebted to him by buying me nice cars, phones, shoes, whatever. It was nice not to have to worry about where my next meal came from for once, but I wanted my cut, and I told him that. He made excuses at first. It was always something. But still, I did his bidding. I was the youngest and the fastest. He could tell I was pulling away, and he started to lose it.

And then when I really wanted out, he got pissed that I wasn't doing his dirty work anymore. He and his lowlife friends took turns beating the shit out of me, not even stopping when I vomited from the pain. When they were finally done, I was unable to move, unable to open my eyes. I'm pretty sure he thought I was dead. He *left me* for dead.

I lay there, bleeding in the dirt, in a pile of my own puke, until the sun set and rose again. Once I could walk, I hobbled back to David's house when I knew he'd be gone and stole his chunk of cash. Booked a cheap hotel room for a few nights until I could move without being in pain and then took a cab to the bus station. When the lady asked for my destination, I told her I didn't care. I just needed the first bus out of there. I met Dare on the bus, and the rest is history.

But I don't say all that. No one knows those fucked-up details but me.

"Doesn't surprise me," my dad admits, bringing me back to our conversation.

I wipe the blood off my mouth with the back of my hand before I realize that it's pointless. My hands are just as bad as my face. I should've hurt him more. I should've made him pay. Instead, I let him fucking walk away.

"Why'd you come back?" John asks, looking like he's on the verge of falling asleep.

I shrug. "I don't know. Had a feeling."

He opens one eye and assesses me. "Well," he says after a long beat, "I'm glad you did."

My jaw aches—either from taking the hit or clenching it so hard the entire drive home, I'm not sure—as I haul ass down the dimly lit streets of the neighborhood. I glance at the dash, and the time isn't much more than a blur of neon blue, thanks to the swelling in my right eye. Two oh eight A.M.

I swing into the driveway with one, single thought. *Briar.* But I slam my bloody fist into my steering wheel when I notice that Adrian's car is here, too, which means Dash is still awake.

My body is moving faster than my brain can catch up, and then I'm sneaking around the side of the house and wedging Briar's window up with the heels of my palms. My head swims as I hoist myself up and through the window, but I ignore it. My boots hit the hardwood floor, and Briar gasps, sitting up in her bed.

"It's me," I say quickly.

"Ash? What happened?" Her voice is a whisper, and though the dark works to my advantage, I know she can sense that something is wrong.

This scene is all too familiar. Me wounded and belligerent. Her unwavering concern for me.

I stand there unmoving, unspeaking. I know what I want, but I don't want to ask for it. Don't know *how* to ask for it. But Briar knows, because she lifts her blanket in invitation.

Right now, I don't care about our pasts. I don't care about the bad decision she made back then, or the numerous bad ones I've made since. All I care about is crawling into her bed and leeching off her quiet and calm.

Wordlessly, I kick my boots off, then unbutton my jeans, dropping them to the floor along with my keys. Briar says nothing. She's completely still as she watches me. Her messy blonde hair is everywhere, and the moonlight shining through her window allows me to see the outline of her nipples beneath her thin, white tank top.

We lock eyes, and she sucks her bottom lip in a nervous gesture. I reach behind my neck, pulling my black T-shirt over my head, letting it fall to join the rest of my shit. Closing the distance between us, I slip in beside her.

Briar lies on her side, facing me, and her fingers reach out to touch my face. I intercept her, directing her hand away from my wounds, and instead, she curls her fingers into the short hair at the nape of my neck.

"Turn around, Bry," I rasp, lowering my head to hide my face. She massages the back of my head, and fuck, it's probably the most affectionate gesture I've ever received.

"Talk to me," she murmurs pleadingly. "You're drunk."

I squeeze my eyes shut and pry her hand from me, holding it away in a tight grip.

"Please."

Her voice is barely above a whisper, and then her nose grazes mine. I don't pull back, so she does it again, but this time, our lips brush, too. Briar hooks a bare leg over mine, her lips touching mine with every move, every breath, but we don't kiss.

I'm still holding on to her wrist between us, and she twists her arm to bring my hand to the curve of her hip. Her shirt has ridden up, and I feel the warmth of her skin against my calloused hands. *I shouldn't be able to touch anything this pure,* I think to myself. *I'll only taint it.*

Despite the fucked-up events of tonight, I'm hard as a rock. I want nothing more than to bend her over, shove inside, and forget all the bullshit. But she's not Whitley. She's not any of those girls. This is Briar, and she is fucking everything, even if she is a little liar.

"Turn around, Briar," I say, firmer this time, as I physically turn her over, then lock my arms around her waist. Her firm ass settles right on my cock, and I fight the urge to grind against her. If I were a little less exhausted and a lot less fucked up, things would go very differently.

Her fingers trace mine, and I know that she feels the gashes and tacky half-dried blood, but she doesn't speak. I wait for her breathing to even out before I dip my head forward, inhaling her scent and pressing my lips to the back of her neck. It isn't long before I start to drift off, too content to care about the consequences that tonight might bring.

BRIAR

I'm not sure what time it is when I wake up, but the sun has just barely started to peek over the mountains in the distance, so I know it must be before six.

I look down at the hand flattened against my stomach, halfway under my shirt. *He's really here. He's still here.* I almost expected him to be gone when I woke up, leaving me to wonder if it was all just a dream.

Carefully, I lift his hand to inspect the damage that I felt last night, and I notice streaks of dried blood on my stomach, on my shirt, my hip, and as I turn around to face his sleeping form, I see that it's on my white sheets, too.

Jesus, Asher. What did you do this time?

Underneath his nose is also caked with blood, and his right eye is bruised and swollen. I lightly kiss his knuckles before leaning forward to do the same to the corner of his eye, and then I feel his hands squeeze my ass, pulling me into him.

"Mmm," I moan, dragging my hands through his hair and dropping my head back as he peppers open-mouthed kisses all over my neck, shoulders, and chest.

He rolls me onto my back and settles between my spread legs, letting me feel his want for me.

Something about this time just feels...different. More intense. More *real*. We still haven't spoken. We let our bodies do the talking, and in this moment, we're the most honest we've ever been with each other. We show each other everything we're feeling with our gasps and tongues and teeth.

Asher shifts down slightly to take my nipple into his mouth and sucks it through the fabric of my shirt. *God, I love when he does that.* I arch into his hot mouth, and he brings both hands up to squeeze my breasts. Flattening his palms, he smooths them up my chest and over my shoulders to push the thin straps of my shirt down my arms.

With his forefinger, he pulls down the top of my tank, exposing one pink nipple. Looking up at me for the first time, he closes his mouth around the hardened tip and bites before licking and sucking away the sting. I feel myself growing slick at the mixture of pain and pleasure that Asher is so skilled at, and I shamelessly lock my legs around his waist, rubbing myself against him.

Ash reaches behind him, grasps one ankle, and unlocks my legs before moving down my body, kissing everything along the way. My heart hammers in my chest, and goose bumps assault my arms and stomach as he gets lower and lower.

This is something we've never done before, something *I've* never had done to me, but I'm too far gone to be nervous. I just want him. I want it all from him. Everything he has to give me, before he decides to take it all away, again.

Once he settles between my thighs, he pushes them open with a hand on each one, squeezing the soft flesh. Lowering his head, he rolls his face between my legs, then nibbles at my panty-covered clit.

Holy shit.

My hips rock against his face on their own accord, chasing that delicious friction. Asher hooks a finger inside my plain black underwear, pulling the crotch to the side, and exposes me to him completely.

He pauses, and I see his throat bob as he swallows. I think he's going to say something cocky, or maybe make me beg for it, but he just stares for a moment, looking conflicted, yet mesmerized. Angry, yet excited all at the same time.

I squirm under his attention, needing to feel more —to feel everything with him. Asher pushes my legs together before pulling my underwear down to my ankles. Smoothing his hands back up my closed legs, he spreads me, ever so slightly, with his thumbs. My entire body is trembling from my toes to my chin, but it's not out of fear. I'm literally shaking with need.

"My beautiful little liar," Ash breathes before closing the final distance and places a wet kiss on my clit. I suck in a breath at the feeling of his mouth on me. *God, I didn't know anything could be this good.* I try to spread my legs for better access, but Asher keeps them clamped shut with a hand on either thigh.

I look down at him, confusion painting my features, but then his tongue slides in between my lower lips. My back bows off the bed, and Asher's bruising grip on my legs keeps me anchored to the bed. To the earth.

"Quit squirming, baby," he mumbles between my thighs.

Baby. Not taunting. Not baby girl. Not little girl. *Baby.*

I tangle my fingers through his perfectly disheveled hair as he devours me, needing him closer. But we'll never be close enough. His tongue flattens against me, and with a few long strokes, I'm tensing up, ready to combust.

"Asher," I say, tilting his chin up to look at me. "I don't want to come like this." My voice is a whispered plea, and I know he understands.

Asher stares up at me and brushes his thumb across my bottom lip.

"Yeah?" he asks, pushing his thumb into my mouth, eyes full of heat. I suck on it, nodding my head, and he groans.

"How do you want to come then?"

"The only way I've ever wanted to. With you inside me."

Asher's jaw clenches, his nostrils flare, and I know that I'm finally going to get my way.

"You play dirty, baby girl," he says, moving up my body, bracing his palms on either side of my head. His lips hover above mine, and I wrap my arms around his neck, pulling him closer. I'm done talking. "Lucky for you, I do, too."

Asher takes my face in his hands before licking at the seam of my lips, and I open for him, letting his tongue in to dance with mine. His movements are unhurried and forceful. Intense, just like him. He kisses me like it's the main event instead of the opening act. I kiss him like he's my oxygen, and I'm afraid it's going to be taken away at any moment, leaving me deprived again.

Ash's hand trails down my neck, and his fingers dip under my tank top, squeezing and kneading. He circles my nipple, and I feel myself growing slicker. Everything he does is magic. I arch into his touch, and he takes the opportunity to pull my top over my head.

I'm laid completely bare before him, and he's still in his boxer briefs. I look at his tanned skin, the muscular dips and grooves of his stomach, the veins in his arms as he holds himself over me, his stormy eyes, and I can't believe this is real. This is happening. He's perfection, even bruised and bleeding. This beautifully damaged boy is about to give me the one part of him I've never had. And I'm about to give him what should've been his.

"Take me out," Asher says in a strangled voice.

I slide my hands underneath the elastic and lower

his boxers, smoothing my palms over his firm ass. His dick springs out, thick, and angry and *ready*. I can finally see his piercing clearly, and I realize that there is more than one. Two tiny, straight barbells underneath the head. For the first time, I wonder what that means for sex.

"It won't hurt you," Asher says, reading the thoughts that are written all over my face.

I give a shaky nod and reach between us to run the tip of my finger across the bars, and Asher shudders when I graze the thin skin. I bite my lip, tentatively wrapping my fingers around him.

"Harder," he demands and wraps his much bigger hand around mine, roughly guiding my movements. Together, we work his length, and I notice a bead of moisture appear at the tip. Without thinking, I swirl my thumb, spreading it over his head, and Asher jerks in my hand.

"Fuck," he swears, snatching my wrist and pinning it to the mattress next to my head. "If any part of you doesn't want this, you have two seconds to tell me to leave." His eyebrows pull together, and his eyes search mine for doubt that he won't find before roughly nudging my thighs apart with his knees. Then I feel him there, warm and unyielding, against my sensitive skin.

"Condom?" Asher asks, dipping just the tip inside me. I wiggle closer, trying to get more. "Briar," he snaps, forcing me to focus. "Condom."

"I'm on the pill," I say. "And I'm clean." I've only been with Jackson, and we used protection. I know Asher has had many partners, but some part of me still trusts him and believes he'd never truly put me at risk. He may do a lot of questionable things, but never that.

"Me, too," Ash says, still only giving me shallow thrusts that drive me crazy.

"I want to feel you," I whisper, wrapping my legs around him and pulling him into me. I lock eyes with pools of whiskey and jade, conflicted and guilt-ridden. "Please."

Asher's control finally, *finally*, breaks, and his hips snap forward, filling me in one move. The air leaves my lungs in a *whoosh*, and I close my eyes, unprepared for how it would feel to have Asher inside me, both physically and emotionally.

This. This is what I've been waiting for, and I could kill him for making us both suffer without this for so long. I tense and Asher pauses, buried to the hilt. He drops his forehead to mine while I adjust to the fullness. Slowly, *so slowly*, with more tenderness than I knew he was capable of, Asher starts to move. One of his hands comes up to cradle the back of my head, his elbow resting on the pillow, and the other one grips my thigh as he pumps into me. He was right about his piercing. I can feel *something*, but it doesn't hurt at all.

"Fuck, Bry," he groans. "I need to move, but I don't want to hurt you."

"Hurt me. Please." I love his tenderness, but I want his violence, his anger, his pain just as much.

Ash's jaw turns to stone, and his eyes fill with heat as he rises onto his knees and grips my middle, impaling me. I'm so full of him that it's painful, but I'll gladly take the pain because it means this is real.

"So fucking good. I knew you'd be perfect," Asher mumbles, looking down to where we're connected. His hands that are almost completely wrapped around my waist control the tempo, making my boobs bounce, and then he lowers his head to suck on my tightened nipple. His bruised, swollen lips against me only gets me hotter, and I feel myself clench around him.

"I'm not going to last if you keep doing that," he warns before pulling me upright to straddle his lap. My hands fly to the back of his neck while he guides my movements with his fingers digging into my hips. My clit rubs against the base of him in this position, and I start to ride him, shamelessly, desperately.

Ash mutters a curse and leans back on his palms. He sucks his lip in between his perfect, square teeth, watching me move on top of him. I rock my hips faster, about to shatter into a million tiny pieces, when I hear it.

A knock on the door, followed by a familiar voice.

"You awake in there, pretty girl?"

Fuck. Adrian.

My eyes shoot to the doorknob. *Locked, thank God.* Asher pushes me backward, and I yelp, causing him to cover my mouth with his hand. He settles in between my legs and immediately starts fucking me. *Really* fucking me.

"Ignore him. You're going to come on my cock," he whispers darkly.

My pleading eyes search his, and I shake my head.

"I can't anymore," I mumble from beneath his fingers. *Now that I know Adrian's listening.*

"You can and you will."

"Your brother and I are going to get breakfast. Wanna come?" Adrian questions from the other side of the door.

I look back to Asher, unsure of what to do.

"Answer him." He removes his hand from my lips, and my eyes widen, but Asher only moves faster.

"N-no," I say, a little more high-pitched and breathless than intended. "I'm really...tired."

Asher smirks and leans down to bite my nipple. I moan—loudly—and I hear a chuckle outside the room.

"Tired, huh? Okay, well, do you want us to bring you anything back?"

"God, yes," I breathe, as I climb higher and higher.

"Yes?" Adrian asks.

"I mean no!"

The asshole on top of me brings his hand down to rub his thumb in just the right spot, and that's it. I can't take it anymore.

"Well, which is it?" an amused Adrian questions.

I'm going to come. I can't hold back. I finally break

apart, practically convulsing. Asher crushes his mouth to mine to muffle my screams, kissing me deep and hard. Then he's pulling out, spilling on my thigh with a groan.

"Goddamn," he mutters into my ear. "You're beautiful when you come."

"Oh my God," I whisper, feeling myself flush with equal parts embarrassment and ecstasy. Ash collapses on top of me, face pressed into my sweaty neck, and a few moments later, we hear a vehicle starting.

"Do you think he knows?" I ask dumbly.

"He'd be a fucking idiot not to."

My heart hammers in my chest even harder now, and my panicked eyes meet his. Except now he looks...angry.

"My brother!" It hits me that if Adrian knows, my brother is going to in about five seconds.

"Don't trip, Bry. I'll handle it," he says, rolling off me.

The moment is gone.

The feeling is gone.

And why wouldn't it be? Because the boy I knew is gone, too.

"Okay," is all I say, feeling more vulnerable than ever as I pull the sheet up to cover my naked self. I'm done trying. Done hoping. I just slept with the ghost of the boy I used to love, and now I'm left feeling emptier than before.

"Okay," he repeats, swinging his legs over the bed

and pulling on his boxers. He hastily snatches up the rest of his clothes and storms away. Once he's to my bedroom door, he pauses.

"Fuck!" he shouts, and I jump as his fist hits the wall next to the doorframe, cracking the drywall. Tears spring to my eyes, and before my vision clears, he's gone.

And then I'm alone. With the evidence of our transgressions drying on my thigh and tears drying to my cheek.

Two weeks. Two weeks since I've laid eyes on Asher. I don't know if he's not staying here anymore, or if he's only coming around when I'm not here. It's safe to say we're avoiding each other. Or at least, I was for the first week. I stayed with Nat, not wanting to run into any of the boys who occupy my house at any given moment.

I'll admit it. I wallowed. Nat listened to the whole story, only interjecting to offer to kill him and throw out the occasional expletive, like any self-respecting best friend should. Then, she threw me the best pity party, full of Netflix and wine and pizza. The second day was full of manicures, pedicures, massages, followed by shopping at her mother's boutique. It stung knowing Asher regretted sleeping with me before our breathing even returned to normal, but buying pretty lingerie and being pampered helps even the most broken of hearts. Mine was just a little bruised.

Now, though, I'm not sad. I'm angry. No, I'm fucking pissed. I've done nothing wrong. So, I decided to go home. It's *my* home, after all. When I saw Dash later that night, he asked what I was doing staying with Nat for so long, and I blamed it on her, saying that she was going through something. He gave me a look that screamed *bullshit*, but he didn't push. And surprisingly, he didn't allude to knowing about Ash and me.

Now, I sit on the couch in the living room with my laptop on my crossed legs, attempting to decide on where I want to go to college and what I want to study. I startle when Adrian comes waltzing through my front door. He's wearing a plain, loose, white tank top, dark jeans, and black, designer sunglasses. Even when he's in casual attire, he looks like a million bucks.

Adrian smiles, his deep dimples on display, and plops down next to me on the couch like he owns the place.

"Hey, pretty girl," he says, taking off his sunglasses and giving me an expectant look.

"What?" I ask defensively.

"Your secret is safe with me," he says with a wink.

"Don't you have a job?" I say, avoiding that statement altogether.

"Don't change the subject."

"Ughhhh," I huff dramatically and close my laptop.

"What do you think you know?" I cut my eyes at him, giving him my best death glare.

"I know that I thought I caught you in the middle of your, you know, *me time,*" he says the words with air quotes, wagging his brows. "Until we walked outside and saw Kelley's truck. Weird, though, since we didn't see him come in."

I roll my eyes, dropping my head to the back of the couch.

"Don't worry. I told Dash that he was asleep in the media room and that he wouldn't wake up to come with us."

What? My eyebrows shoot up in surprise. I wasn't expecting that.

"Why would you cover for me?" I ask, genuinely confused. They're best friends. More like brothers.

"It's not for you. I was hungry and didn't want to get held up." He shrugs. "Besides, that asshole Kelley is just as much my friend as Dash is, whether he wants to admit it or not."

I think back to the day on the lake and how Adrian wanted to help me get Asher's attention.

"Why are you pushing this?" I ask him, suddenly wary of his motives.

"Dude deserves some good in his life. Besides, we'll never get rid of Whitley if she thinks she has a chance with one of us."

One of us?

"Oh my God, did you hook up with her, too?!" I slap his chest.

"You don't even want to know." He grins, squeezing my knee. "Trust me on this one."

"Gross."

"Downright *filthy*."

If the rumors are true, this means she's hooked up with all three of the boys in my life. Ash, *my brother*— yeah, found that out last summer—and now Adrian. My nails cut into my palms as I clench my fists. Why won't she just *go away*?

"Calm down, little killer." Adrian laughs, reaching over to uncurl my fingers, and then leans back, propping his feet up on the edge of the coffee table. He pulls on my hand, and I lie back with my head on his shoulder, kicking my own feet up. "You don't have anything to worry about with her."

I'm not so sure, I think, but instead, I say, "I'm not worried. Thoroughly disgusted," I add, "but not worried. Where's my brother, by the way?"

"Should be pulling up any minute. He had to drop his truck off at the shop, so he called Kelley to pick him up."

Fuck. My first instinct is to dread seeing him, but some pathetic part of me still feels a thrill run through me at the thought of it.

"We're gonna hit up the club later tonight," Adrian explains.

"The *club*?" I snort. Imagining Asher at a club is

straight-up laughable. I can just see him there, hating life, arms crossed in the corner. But my amused smile melts away when I imagine what would inevitably happen next. Gorgeous girls. Short skirts. High heels. Wanting one night with the bad boy with sad eyes.

"Yes, *the club*," he says, mimicking me in a high-pitched, Valley Girl voice. "I need some pussy tonight, and I'm sick of the same old places and faces. I need fresh meat."

"What you need, sir, is a damn filter. And condoms. *Lots* of condoms." I roll my eyes and cross one ankle over the other.

"And what *you* need is my d—" Before he's able to finish what's sure to be an inappropriate remark, the door opens and Dash and Asher walk in.

Holy. Shit.

He's wearing black jeans—not skinny jeans, but more form-fitting than I've ever seen on him—with holes in the knees, a dark green V-neck that hugs his biceps, and his trusty black combat boots. His signature unruly hair is styled and pushed back off his forehead. He's going out looking like *that*—meanwhile, I'm not old enough to get in even if I was invited.

That pang of anxiety about him going out morphs into pure, ugly jealousy. The kind that turns your stomach to lead and makes your ears hot. The thought of Asher hooking up with *anyone, ever* turns my stomach, but hooking up with someone three seconds after we slept together? That thought makes it hard to breathe, especially since he clearly wasn't happy with what I had to offer.

Dash and Adrian jump into making plans for the night, but I don't hear a word they say. I'm still stuck in my head when I finally look Asher in the eye, only to realize he's staring at Adrian and me with narrowed eyes, looking more than a little suspicious. Lifting my head off Adrian's shoulder, I stand, and he reflexively extends his hand to help me step over his outstretched legs while still in conversation with Dash.

"Briar," Dash says my name, just as I'm about to turn down the hall toward my room. I pause, looking over my shoulder. "You okay?"

"Yep. I was a little disappointed over a boy." I turn and aim a pointed look at Ash. "But he turned out to be kind of a douche, anyway." Asher's jaw ticks once, then he looks away.

"Jackson? The fuck did he do?" my brother says, instantly riled up.

"Not Jackson," I'm quick to assure. He's texted me here and there, but I haven't responded. "It doesn't matter anymore. I'm over it."

Lie, lie, lie.

Not wanting to stick around for their inevitable pre-gaming, I stalk off to my room and text Nat.

Me: I need you.

Nat: Is this you finally coming out of the closet?

Me: Not today. When are you getting here?

Nat: Pulling up in 2.5.

Me: Tell me you brought alcohol.

Nat: Among other things…

Me: Low-key suspicious of your "other things," but I love you anyway. Come straight to my room when you get here.

Five minutes later, Nat arrives, arms full of bags, looking frazzled.

"Damn, your brother looks good tonight," she says, unloading different bottles and jars of things onto my long, white dresser. "I almost got pregnant just from walking past him."

"I don't think that's how it works." I laugh, picking up a jar of maraschino cherries. "What's all this?"

"I jacked a bottle of vodka from my mom, then I decided to get fancy and googled different cocktails…" She digs her phone out of her shorts pocket and taps a few times before turning the screen for me to see. "I present to you…the Cherry Blossom."

"God, yes. You are my favorite. Let's take this party to the pool."

I dig through my drawer full of bathing suits and pull out one in a peachy color for me, and toss a mint one in Nat's direction. Some girls collect shoes or purses or jewelry. Arizona girls collect swimming suits for every occasion.

After getting changed, we grab the vodka, grenadine, cherries, and pink lemonade before heading to the kitchen to get cups and ice. As I'm filling our glasses, Dash and Adrian appear.

"We're leaving," Dash says, eying our little setup. "Lock the door behind us and *do not* get drunk if you're going to be swimming alone." He points a stern finger in my direction and then Nat's, making sure we're both clear.

"Yes, *Dad*," I say, barely containing my eye roll. The hypocrite's favorite pastime is drinking and swimming.

"Hey, Natalia," Adrian says, looking her up and down. "Do you have any Mexican in you?"

"No. I'm fucking Italian," she scoffs.

"Do you want some?" He wiggles his brows, and I bust out laughing. Nat rolls her eyes, but she's unable to smother her grin.

I look back to Adrian, expecting to see his perpetually amused smile, but instead, he looks uncomfortable and maybe even a little pissed off. And he's staring directly over my shoulder.

I hear Asher's boots slapping against the tile floor, but what I don't expect to hear is a pair of decidedly feminine footsteps click-clacking behind his. I turn, moving in slow motion like something out of a horror movie. Except this is real life and so much worse. Whitley is, once again, in my fucking house. Dark hair, sleek and parted down the middle, flat ironed to perfection. Pale breasts pushed up to her chin. My smile melts away.

"You have got to be fucking shitting me, right?" This comes from Nat. "If I'm ever too dense to realize that I'm not wanted somewhere, please tell me." She looks Whitley up and down before adding, "Better yet, just shoot me."

I'm afraid to say a word, to even make a move, in fear of everyone seeing right through me. Dash, luckily, is thrown off enough by Nat's reaction that he doesn't pay me any attention. Adrian angles himself in front of me in a defensive stance, under the guise of making himself a drink. Whitley looks victorious, and Asher looks...the same. His face is completely devoid of any emotion. He doesn't even have the decency to look ashamed or contrite, and that right there is what hurts the most.

I'm stuck, fighting to keep my emotions in check. I want to tell Dash that I don't want her here, but that would lead to unwanted questions. But, this is my house, and I shouldn't have to be blindsided on my own turf.

"Welp, you assholes have fun tonight!" Nat says in a cheery voice, no doubt sensing me flounder. She grabs our drinks, handing me one before trying to usher me out back.

"We will!" Whitley pipes up, leaning forward to pluck a rogue piece of ice that fell to the counter and sucks on it in an embarrassingly transparent attempt at being seductive. "Too bad you guys can't tag along, but you know, it's twenty-one and up and all. Grown-ups only." She fake pouts, careful not to say anything that can be seen as outright offensive in front of my brother, and I stop in my tracks.

Fuck it.

I pivot back around on my bare toes. "That's okay. I wouldn't want to get in the way of your *fun*," I say with a pointed look and gesture to the white residue coating her left nostril. "Clean it up, coke whore." Whitley's hand flies to hide her nose, her shocked expression quickly morphing into one of contempt.

"I don't want to see her in our house again," I say, focusing my attention on Dash.

I try to catch Ash's eye to gauge his reaction. If he's surprised or disappointed, it doesn't show. I don't know what would be worse. Doing drugs with Whitley in my bathroom, or doing *her* in my bathroom.

"Agreed," Dash says, crossing his arms. "What the fuck are you thinking, bringing that shit around my baby sister?"

Or, you know, at all.

"Annnnd, that's our cue to leave," Nat drawls out, and this time, I listen. Adrian gives me an awkward head pat as I walk past, like he wants to comfort me but doesn't quite know how, and Dash casts me a suspicious look—seeing through my shitty façade—that says *we'll talk about this later.* I give him a short, reluctant

nod before walking out to the pool without sparing a
backward glance.

"Fuck him," I announce for what is probably the
eighteenth time in the past two hours.

"I concur. Fuck him with something hard and
sandpaper-y," Nat agrees, blowing out a cloud of smoke
from the blunt between her fingertips. Turns out, this
is the "other things" she mentioned earlier. Nat is
pretty much the female Snoop in that sense. It's not
usually my thing. Not that I have anything against it, I
just always end up eating everything in a ten-mile
radius, then passing out—in that order. Tonight seemed
like a good night for it, though.

"Without lube," I add, and we both erupt into a fit
of laughter. The pool deck is cool against my skin, but
the pool that I'm swishing my feet through feels more
like bath water. I look up at the stars as our giggles fade
into the night, feeling content to stay in this spot until
morning. Until forever. We lie in comfortable silence
for a few minutes, side by side, before I break the quiet.

"I think something bad happened to Asher...and I
think it's my fault," I whisper, voicing my fear aloud for
the first time.

"What?" Nat coughs, turning on her side to face
me. I stay on my back, eyes on the stars. "Why would
you even think that?"

"I don't know," I say, dragging my fingers through my hair. "He keeps insinuating that I've betrayed him somehow, and there's only one thing I can think of." I've never told anyone this before. Not Natalia. Not Dash. And *definitely not* Asher.

"Okaaay," she says warily.

"I was so upset when he left, Nat. You have no idea. I felt abandoned and hurt and *so stupid* for ever thinking he could return my feelings. After he left, I rode my bike over to his house. I guess I couldn't believe that he was really gone. But then, I saw his dad in the window, stumbling through the living room, and it all shifted. I just wanted to hurt him. I wanted to hurt him for hurting Asher.

"I hated him in that moment. Every bad thing that ever happened to Ash was because of him, or at least that's what I thought back then. So, I picked up a rock and threw it right through his window."

"You what?!" Nat sputters out a laugh.

"I totally did." Despite my mood, I feel my lips tugging into a grin at the memory. "And it felt good for a whole two seconds."

"What happened then? And why did you say that's what you thought *back then*?"

I exhale loudly, feeling particularly ashamed about this part.

"Instead of running, I just stared him down through his open window like a creep. I wanted him to know that I wasn't afraid of him. But, he ended up telling me that I needed to fix his window or else he'd tell my parents what I'd done."

"You *didn't*." Nat cackles. "Only you, Briar Vale, would bust someone's window and then put it back together."

"Shut up." I roll my eyes. "I didn't want them finding out. You know how my mom is about keeping up appearances, and my dad and Dash were constantly at each other's throats then." Nat nods, because she knows better than anyone. "I did the shittiest job in the history of ever. I had no idea what I was doing. I thought I'd show up and he'd at least give me some kind of direction, but nope." The word pops from my lips. "He just sat in that recliner, waiting for me to figure it out."

"Anyway, it took a while, and in that time, he told me stories that made me see things...differently. Things that I'm not even sure Ash knows. I still hated him for how he treated Ash, but for the first time, I realized that nothing was black and white. People are flawed, and sometimes, good intentions aren't enough."

"I realized fairly quickly that he wasn't doing well. So, I checked on him a couple of times a month, brought him food, made sure he had clean laundry, and he'd tell me stories about Asher as a kid. It made me feel closer to Ash."

Dash told me about John having liver cancer, and I wondered if that's what had been wrong with him. If I would have said something, insisted he go to the doctor, maybe, would he still be dying right now?

"But how does that make what happened your fault?"

"I don't know."

And I don't. I don't even know what happened, but it's the only thing I have to go on that makes even a little sense.

Suddenly, there's a splash at the opposite end of the pool, and we both scream and sit up, not having heard anyone come out here. I squint my eyes, trying to make out the details in the dim patio lighting. All I can see is a mop of dark hair, and broad, powerful shoulders gliding through the water. *Asher.*

Sure enough, it's Asher that comes up, stopping directly before us. His shirt is molded to his chest, showing off the muscles in his arms and stomach, and his hair hangs in his eyes. Water drips down the bridge of his nose, onto those full lips. He stares directly at me, not breaking eye contact when he reaches for the towel bunched up next to me and rubs it across his face and hair before tossing it back to the deck.

Ash reaches over, plucking the blunt from Nat's hand, and takes a big hit.

"You can leave now," he says, eyes still focused on me.

Nat looks to me, silently questioning whether I want her to go or not. I give her a nod, and she stands, pointing a finger in Ash's direction. "Break her heart again, and I'll break your dick." She knows better than to wait for a response, so she walks off.

Ash takes another couple of hits before flicking it behind him to land in the pool.

"How did you get here?" His truck has a very loud, distinct sound that I've memorized over the past few weeks. I didn't hear a thing...until he dove into my pool, anyway.

"Cab. Rode with your brother and Adrian. They weren't ready to come home yet. I was."

"Oh." I don't know what to make of that. I wonder what Whitley thought about that, but I don't care enough to ask.

"Funny," he says, in a way that lets me know what he's about to say isn't going to be funny at all, "you made such a big deal about Whitley doing blow— meanwhile, you're out here getting high."

"Please. Weed isn't a drug. Not really."

"The point is, you're not only a liar, but now you can add hypocrite to the list. That's a far cry from the perfect little Briar that I used to know." Asher stalks toward me, and I put my foot out to keep him from getting too close. His words cause something to snap, and I'm suddenly so sick of his vague put-downs.

"What the hell did I do to you, Asher?! Just spit it out already or shut up about it!" He comes closer, my foot pressing against his chest.

"Maybe I want *you* to spit it out. To take responsibility for something for once in your privileged little life," he grits out.

"I'm done playing these games." My voice is quiet. Resigned. "We'll keep going around and around on this merry-go-round forever if one of us doesn't get off. I'm getting off, Ash." I push off his chest and twist my body to stand up, but before I can do so, his hand grips my ankle and he yanks. Hard. My ass slides across the smooth stone deck, and then I'm in the water, wrapped around him.

"You're getting off, all right," he says menacingly, locking his arms around me to keep me in place. "But not in the way you think."

I struggle against him, unlatching my legs and trying to slide down his body. My center rubs against his abs, and then I feel something harder prodding at me.

"You don't make any sense," I say, feeling more confused than ever. "You've made it abundantly clear that you despise me."

"I don't have to like you to fuck you, baby girl."

"You fucked me and *left me*," I remind him. My voice cracks, and I hope he doesn't catch it. "You ignored me for weeks, then you bring *her* to *my* house."

No longer struggling to get away, my legs float lifelessly on either side of him, and his hands start kneading my ass, making me rub against him again.

"I heard what you said about John," he says, calling his father by his first name like always, and my body goes rigid, eyes go wide. I have no idea how he's going to react to hearing that I not only saw his dad after he left, but inadvertently ended up with some sort of unlikely friendship. Although, friendship might be too strong a word for the relationship I had with John. It was complicated and unconventional, but we had both lost Asher, even if his actions were the catalyst.

"Seems you're keeping more secrets than I thought." He rubs my sides up and down before tugging the strings on my bottoms, causing them to fall off.

"That's it, I swear," I say on a gasp.

"You're a liar, Briar." He licks a tear that I didn't know was there as his hand curves around my butt cheek and two fingers circle my entrance before hooking inside me. My head drops to the soaked shirt plastered to his shoulder, and I grind against his fingers. "But I want you, anyway."

Before I can respond, he frees himself from his pants, and I'm sliding down his formidable length. A moan slips free as my arms wrap around his neck, holding his head to my chest, and my legs lock around his waist. I'm so full of Asher, physically, emotionally, mentally. This is pathetic. No matter how many times he burns me, I go back for more. I need him like a bad habit—one that I don't want to kick. He cradles me—one hand wrapped around my waist, the other forearm spans the length of my spine, and his fingers curl around my shoulder—holding me close as he pumps into me. Using his teeth, he pulls the thin triangle of my top to reveal my nipple that hardens in response to the night air. Asher sucks it into his mouth, reaching to untie the strings around my back and neck.

My movements become a little more frantic—a little jerkier—as I grind against him, using my weight-lessness in the water to my advantage.

"Fuck," Ash groans after pulling away from my chest. Gripping me by the waist, he abruptly lifts me to sit on the edge of the pool again.

"What?" I ask breathlessly. He can't stop now.

"Spread your knees and put your heels on the edge." It's an order, and I'm all too eager to comply, scooting close to the edge and leaning back on my palms. Ash peels his T-shirt off and flings it. Before I hear the wet plop of it landing, his hot mouth meets my slick center. I jerk forward, and he grips my ankles, chuckling darkly, holding me in place.

His tongue takes another long swipe, and my head falls back at the sensation. I'm completely naked, on display for anyone who might decide to walk out here as Asher eats me wildly, savagely. He laps at me, from top to bottom and everywhere in between. Releasing one of my ankles, he uses his free hand to fist his length. Asher pulls back to look at me as he strokes himself, the glistening head of his cock barely visible above the surface, but I can still make out the glint of his piercings.

"Sexiest fucking thing I've ever seen," he mutters

before diving back in. The sight of him working himself, getting off to tasting me, has me gripping his head, holding him in place.

"Make me come, Asher," I beg in a voice that I don't even recognize.

"Gladly."

His fist around his cock moves faster, and then he's shoving two fingers inside me as he pulls my clit between his teeth and sucks.

I explode, unable to keep quiet and uncaring of the repercussions, as Asher groans, his own release spilling into the pool.

CHAPTER 7

ASHER

B riar slumps back to the deck, completely boneless, as I hoist myself up and over the edge. I struggle to pull my soaked jeans off, opting to leave my boxers on for now. Through it all, she doesn't make any move to get up.

Briar's outstretched arms lie limp at her sides, her bare tits heave, and goose bumps prickle her skin. Her eyes are closed, wet lashes hitting the tops of her cheeks, and her plump lips are parted. My dick jerks, already wanting round two.

Fuck, I need to get it together. This girl is fucking with my head. I don't know how to feel about her little story about my dad. My initial reaction was to go find a wall to smash my fist through. Not only did she have me sent away and stripped me out of my chance at college, but then she spent time with the person she was so concerned about? John conveniently left that part out. Briar wants to see the good in everyone. That's just who she is. *Was.* Fuck, I don't know anymore. Who knows what lies John filled her pretty little head with, and she probably fell for it, hook, line, and sinker. Not even that could keep me from wanting her, though.

I don't know why I let Dash and Adrian talk me into going to the East Side tonight. Clubs aren't my scene, and the whole time all I could picture was Briar's face when she saw Whitley and me walking out of the bathroom together. Then, I got mad at myself for giving a shit how she felt. Nothing happened—*of fucking course, nothing happened because I wouldn't even touch Whitley with someone else's dick*—but even if I wanted to explain, Dash might wonder why I'm defending myself to his little sister.

The second Whitley showed up, sniffling, bouncing from foot to foot, and talking a mile a minute, I knew she was coked-up. I know because I used to do it with her. So, when she decided to go powder her nose—literally—I followed her and tore her a new asshole for doing that shit here. I honestly don't know why any of us put up with her anymore. She used to be cool, once upon a time, and like the horny, asshole teenagers that we were, we took advantage of the fact that she threw herself at us. But then, she got into drugs, and while I'm guilty of partaking, it was never a problem for me. Whitley definitely has a problem, and I think we all just feel stuck with her, and tolerate her, like a drunk uncle during the holidays.

Whatever the fuck Briar and I are doing is point-less. There are too many obstacles standing in the way for this to end well. Allowing Briar to believe that I invited her, yet again, or that we hooked up, was my way of ending shit between us. Yet, here I am, scooping her listless body into my arms and carrying her through the house and back to her room right after finding out that her betrayal goes even deeper than I thought. Because I can't fucking quit her.

I went back to River's Edge for two weeks to do just that. I took on another job and caught up with Dare and our other friends. I just needed some distance, to recalibrate without Briar inadvertently seducing me at every turn. But the time away has done nothing to dull the attraction. Three years didn't do it, so it was stupid to think two weeks would suffice.

"What are you doing?" she asks, covering herself with one arm. The other curls around the back of my neck.

"Taking you to bed," I say, kicking her bedroom door open.

"Are you staying with me?"

I falter, not expecting the question, before looking down at her big blue eyes.

"Do you want me to?"

Briar nods wordlessly, and I lay her down before taking off my boxers. She arches a brow.

"I'm not sleeping in wet clothes," I explain, and she bites her lip, looking directly at my cock.

"Don't look at me like that," I warn.

"Or what?"

"Or else I'll fuck you again, and this time, I won't hold back."

"You've been holding out on me?" she asks, a playful lilt to her voice. I groan and climb into bed next to her.

"Don't tempt me. Go to sleep."

"Yes, sir," she mumbles, nuzzling her way under my arm and resting her head on my chest.

"Comfy?" I ask, sarcasm lacing my tone.

"Mhm."

We're both silent, her naked body against mine, as I trace her soft skin from her ribs to the curve in her hip. I'm drifting off when I hear her whisper, "I've missed you."

You can't miss something you never had, but I don't correct her, because I feel it, too. Being with Briar like this feels like what I've been missing my entire life.

It's a shame it won't last.

≈

I wake up, my mouth drier than Gandhi's flip-flop, to curious, delicate fingers, tentatively skimming the sensitive underside of my cock. Briar traces my frenum piercings, and I groan at the sensation, my hips jerking forward of their own volition. Her eyes snap up to mine.

I got these piercings on a drunken dare before I was even old enough. Adrian's doing, of course. Instead of simply accepting the challenge, I had to show off by getting two. I figured I could remove them, but it turns out they make sex a lot more fun. And right now, as Briar plays with me like I'm her new favorite toy, I'm definitely not regretting it.

"Good morning," she says, part seductress, part innocent, before she licks the length of my dick. I shudder when her tongue brushes over my barbells, bringing my hands to rest behind my head.

"I'd say so." My hips flex. Briar flicks underneath the tip with her tongue a couple of times before closing her mouth around me.

"Wrap your hand around it," I say. She does as instructed, her tiny fist working my shaft while her mouth works my head.

"Yeah. Fuck yeah, like that. Squeeze harder."

She does.

"Look at me. Let me see those pretty blues while your perfect lips are wrapped around my cock."

I'm already close to coming, but when her eyes

meet mine, I'm ready to flip her over and bury myself inside her. I start to do just that, but then I hear a voice that stops us both dead in our tracks.

"Hello? Where are my children, and *what* has happened to my house?"

"Oh my God," Briar whispers, panic infused in her voice. "What is my mom doing here? You have to go!"

"No shit," I say, already feeling around on the floor next to the bed for my boxers. Fuck. We left our clothes by the pool. And a blunt. And alcohol and my semen, but who's counting? Briar grabs a white dress out of her drawer that looks like something the old Briar would wear and carelessly pulls it over her head before smoothing out her just-fucked hair.

"Shit, shit, shit," she whispers, pulling her under-wear up her legs. "I'll see you later."

Knowing we don't have time for pleasantries, I give her a nod before I crawl through the window and jump down, ready to hit the back entrance for my keys and clothes. Before I can take a single step, Briar jerks me back by my shoulder, catching me off guard. She smashes her lips to mine, her hands gripping my hair, and kisses the shit out of me. She sucks on my tongue, and when I nip at her bottom lip, she moans into my mouth. She pulls back slightly, lips puffy, cheeks flushed, and eyes wild, ending the kiss just as abruptly as it began.

"Come see me tonight?" she asks, nervously sucking on her lip. Only our foreheads touch, and my hands are braced on either side of the window frame. Those four insignificant words trip me up. I've never had anyone waiting for me, wanting to see me, not for anything other than a quick fuck, at least. I take that back. I've never *wanted* anyone waiting on me. I've had the occasional stage-five clinger, and with anyone else, it always felt like the walls were closing in on me. But, when Briar does it, I feel like maybe I have a place in this world.

My initial thought is to say no. I tell myself that I shouldn't let her get attached. But who the fuck am I kidding? We're beyond attached. She's in my head, my fucking veins, and in whatever's left of my heart, whether either one of us likes it or not.

"I'll be here."

CHAPTER 8

BRIAR

The moment Asher walks away, my mom barges into my room. I whip around, trying to look casual as I lean an elbow on the windowsill.

"What happened to your hair?" she gasps, pinching the strands between two fingers to inspect it.

"Nice to see you, too, Mom," I say, leaning in for an obligatory hug. "What are you doing here?"

"I'm sorry. Am I no longer allowed in my own home?" she asks, dramatic as ever.

"You know what I mean," I say, barely containing my eye roll. Mom sighs, smoothing my hair out of my face.

"You'd know if you ever picked up your phone.

Your father is speaking at the Smiles 4 Kids gala tonight."

My dad may not be up for the father of the year award any time soon, but he still manages to impress me from time to time. I remember hearing about this fundraiser, but I'd forgotten all about it. It's to raise money for kids, mostly in other countries, whose families can't afford corrective surgery.

"Oh! Where is he?"

"He had some work to do on the other side of town. We're only here until morning, so we're going to stay at the event's hotel to stay close to the airport," she says, pulling an envelope out of her purse. "Here are your tickets. It starts at eight. Make sure your brother is... decent." Decent. In other words, *sober*. Dash just graduated from college and is about to start law school, but you'd think he was a burnout who dropped out of high school and does nothing but party by the way my parents talk about him.

"Does Dashiell know?"

"I'm sure you can talk him into it," Mom says, avoiding a straight answer. Which means that's a negative. "It'll mean a lot to your father."

"Fine," I relent. I feel guilty for ignoring her calls, and she's only in town for one night, so I'll play along.

"Perfect. By the way, whose truck is that outside?" She says the word *truck* like one would say *dog shit* as she points her manicured finger in the direction of the driveway.

"Oh, uh, one of Dash's friends." Not technically a lie. "I'm pretty sure they're still asleep."

"Well, you tell him I want this house back to the way I had it."

"Will do. What's new with you guys? How is California?"

"Oh, you know. Busy," she says vaguely. "We'll talk later. I have a hair appointment to get to." She kisses my cheek, and I stand to walk her out.

"Oh, and Briar, I almost forgot to tell you. You have a date for tonight."

Uh, what?

"I'm sorry?"

"You're seeing that Jackson boy, aren't you? His mother is also attending, and she said he'd love to escort you."

"Mom. No." I shake my head. No way am I going with Jackson. "I am not dating him. In fact, I'm going out of my way to *not date him*."

"Oh, don't be so dramatic. You can't say no, now."

"I didn't say yes to begin with!" I protest, my voice rising in volume.

"Briar Victoria Vale. Two hours is all I'm asking. Two hours out of your life to play nice for your parents that you haven't seen in weeks. Is that too much to ask?"

If there's one thing Nora Vale is good at, it's guilt-tripping. And passive-aggressiveness. And don't forget manipulating.

"There better be cake," I say, defeated, plopping back down to my bed.

"I'll make sure there's a chocolate one just for you." She's joking, but I know it's her way of playing nice. "Now, go get showered. You smell like bad choices, and that hair is going to take nothing short of a miracle to tame."

"Goodbye, Mother." I laugh.

Unfuckingbelievable. I have managed to stay away from Jackson this whole time, and now I'm forced to go on a date with him. This should be tons of fun.

Hair curled: check. Lips in Scarlett Empress by Nars: check. Winged liner: double check. I turn to my bed, admiring the dress I got from Natalia's mom's boutique. It's burgundy with spaghetti straps. The top is skintight lace with a deep scalloped neckline. The bottom flares out, hitting mid-thigh. It's gorgeous, but the back is my absolute favorite part. The thin straps form an "X" across my shoulder blades, leaving the rest of my back completely bare. I pair it with black pumps, black bracelets, and a simple black choker. It's feminine, yet edgy, and perfect for me.

I walk into my closet to find a matching clutch, and all I can think about is how I wish I was going to this thing with Asher instead of Jackson. But that would never happen. Even if Asher were the suit and tie kind of guy, my parents would probably have a coronary if I showed up on his arm. I would, though. If Asher called me up right now and told me that he wanted to be official and tell our families, I would in a heartbeat. Fuck what anyone else thinks. The only person I'd worry about is Dash. I don't want to hurt him. But I think, in time, he'd come around. He'd want us both to be happy. Would it be so bad to find happiness together?

Deciding on my black studded Michael Kors wristlet, I walk back into my room.

"Why so blue, baby girl?"

My head snaps up to find Asher sitting on the end of my bed.

"Jesus!" I whisper-yell, rushing over to close my bedroom door. "I need to put a bell around your neck. You're like a goddamn ninja."

Asher smirks and pulls me to stand between his spread legs. His hands grip my waist, his thumbs rubbing my stomach. My heart pounds in my chest, and I feel myself already growing slick. My eyes close, and I lean into his touch. His hands flatten against my stomach, then move down to grip the hem of my dress.

"Show me what you have on underneath." His voice is thick and gruff, and I nod in acquiesce. Bunching up the skirt, he exposes the black lace.

"Turn around."

I comply, and he mutters a curse. I'm wearing a high-waisted thong that laces up in the back, showing a lot of skin and little to imagine.

"Fuck, this ass," he says, bringing his hands up to squeeze my cheeks in his palms. He spins me back around to sit on his knees, my legs straddling his. "I missed you today," he says grudgingly, like he's mad at me for it, as his thumb starts to circle my clit through my panties.

"God, I missed you, too," I say on a gasp, wrapping my arms around his neck as he continues his ministrations.

"I know you're not all dressed up for me," he says, his lips ghosting across the shell of my ear, his voice low and deadly. "Where are you going?"

I freeze, like a bucket of ice water has been dumped over my head. How do I tell him that I have to break our plans to go on a date with someone else? Someone that he already can't stand.

"Briar," he warns when I don't respond. His thumb still rubs me.

"I have to go to this fundraiser gala for my parents tonight."

"And?" he questions, knowing I'm not spilling everything.

"And I have to go with Jackson."

"Say that again." Venom laces his tone. "I must have heard you wrong. I thought you just said that you were going on a date with the guy that your brother and I have repeatedly warned you to stay away from."

His thumb moves faster, pressing harder, and I can't focus, let alone form coherent sentences.

"It's not like that," I manage to get out.

"Tell me what it's like then, Briar." His other hand comes up to fist my hair at the back of my head, forcing me to look at him while he continues his interrogation as he gets me off.

I moan, my hips jerking forward on their own accord. "My mom..." I start, but I'm lost in the sensations running through me. My body feels like a live wire, threatening to explode at the next touch.

"Your mom?" Asher prompts, sliding his fingers underneath the lace.

"She set it up. It's not a real date."

"So say no."

"It's not that easy," I say, as a finger slips inside me. It's slow and teasing, enough to make me crazy, but not enough to get me off. "I have to. I'm sorry."

Losing patience, I grip his wrist, moving his hand at the speed I need.

"Does that feel good, baby?" he whispers, adding another finger, pumping harder.

"God, yes. That's what I need, Ash."

"Good," he says simply, abruptly pulling back and leaving me feeling empty. My mouth drops open, and he lifts me by the waist, plopping me down beside him.

"What are you doing?" I ask incredulously. He can't leave me like this.

Picking up the tickets from my nightstand, he scans the information and then drops them down on my shaking legs. "You're going to be late. Might want to get going."

"You're an asshole," I say, standing to straighten my dress and smooth my hair.

"So you keep telling me," Ash deadpans.

Grabbing my wristlet, I decide to do the opposite of what he's hoping for. Asher wants to get a reaction out of me. He wants a fight. But I'm not going to give it to him. I'm going to walk right out of this room, shaking my ass a little more for his benefit, without another word. And that's exactly what I do.

"Dash!" I yell once I'm in the kitchen, plucking my keys off the hook. "Let's go! We're late!" We're not late yet, not technically. But Friday night traffic is going to make it difficult.

"I'm not ready yet," he calls back over the music blasting from his room. "I'll meet you there."

Great. Just *awesome*. There goes my buffer. I was counting on Dash's presence to scare him off, even if a little. Though, on the other hand, I must admit I'm somewhat relieved. I don't think I could face my brother right now after what just happened with Asher in my room. I don't know how I'm going to focus on anything other than his fingers inside me. *Jesus, take the wheel*.

∾

I'm delightfully bored. I say "delightful," because it's better to be bored than to be with stuck in awkward conversation with Jackson. For the past thirty minutes, I've done nothing but shake hands, kiss cheeks, and hug necks. My face hurts from smiling politely, and my feet are already killing me. But, I'll take it. Because I haven't seen Jackson once. Maybe he decided not to show.

A server walks by, and I pluck a glass of champagne off his tray. Even though I'm clearly underage, he doesn't so much as bat an eye. No one cares at these types of events, my parents included. Everyone here is rich enough to buy their way out of any trouble they may find themselves in, anyway. My parents are busy schmoozing and mingling, so I decide to go to the bathroom just to have something to do.

My heels click-clack across the hard floor, and I stare straight ahead, hoping to avoid eye contact with another one of my dad's clients or my mom's friends. Standing in front of the bathroom mirror, I scan my appearance. Besides the lingering flush in my cheeks, you'd never know that a little over an hour ago, I was grinding on Asher's lap, begging him to take me higher.

After fluffing my hair and reapplying my lipstick, I've run out of things to do, so I decide to head back out. As soon as I open the door, a hand darts out to clutch my elbow in an almost painful grip.

"Jackson, what the hell?" I tug my arm back, and the champagne splashes onto his shoes.

"I thought I saw you go in there," he says, still staring at the liquid on his dress shoes. "I didn't mean to scare you." He shakes his foot off and flashes me an easy smile. I don't apologize.

"So, I hear you're my date," he says, when I don't respond.

"We're here as *friends*," I stress. Even that much is a stretch after our last conversation.

"Friends?" He laughs. "Do you *fuck* all your friends?" he spits angrily.

"Okay, we're done here." His ego is wounded, and I get that. But I won't be spoken to like that. I stand and spin around to walk away, only to run into a solid, six-foot wall of Asher. He steadies me by my shoulders, and I gasp when I realize he's wearing a suit.

I'll always prefer casual Ash over anything, but seeing him in a suit literally takes my breath away. His usually disheveled hair is slicked back in a pompadour style, and those beautiful, multicolored eyes shoot lasers in Jackson's direction. I bring my hands to his face, forcing him to look at me, before dropping my hands and looking around, frantically, making sure no one saw us.

"Asher, don't," I whisper.

Ignoring me, he moves around me, standing chest to chest with Jackson.

"If you so much as fucking look in her direction again, I will put you in a fucking coma."

His words aren't loud, but quiet, intense Asher is far more dangerous. Jackson's eyes dart to me briefly, but if he's expecting me to stick up for him after that, he's sorely mistaken. Shaking his head in disbelief, doing his best to hide his fear, he stomps away like a scolded child.

"What are you doing here?" I ask, turning my attention back to the bad boy turned GQ model in front of me.

"I knew that piece of shit was bad news." His fists at his sides clench and release, clench, and release again.

"Relax." I discreetly grab one of his hands, uncurling his fingers and rubbing his palm with my thumb. His hard eyes soften at my touch, and being the one person who can get through to him when he's like this cracks the last piece of my hesitant heart wide open. It's his. It's always been his. I just wish he'd realize it.

"What the fuck was that about?"

At the sound of Dash's voice, we drop each other's hands like they're on fire.

Dash jerks his chin in the direction Jackson ran off. "Do we need to take care of this guy?"

"What are you, the mafia?" I joke, shooting a pleading look at Asher. I know he wants nothing more than to make Jackson hurt right now. I can see it in his eyes. But, I don't want them involved in this. I don't even want my brother knowing that I slept with him.

Asher hesitates for a beat, indecision warring on his face. "He was just talking shit," he explains, purposely downplaying the situation, and I let out a relieved breath.

As if I needed more chaos, I spot my mom heading right toward us, zeroed in on Dash. Maybe she won't recognize Asher, being three years older and in a suit of all things.

"Dash, darling, how nice of you to—oh. *Asher*. What are you doing here?"

Okay, so I guess she recognized him.

"Dash here asked me to be his plus one," he says, that mask of cool indifference firmly back in place. "I couldn't say no to that pretty face. You know how it goes."

"Mhm," is all my mom says with a forced smile, turning her attention to me. "Where's Jackson?" She scans the crowd.

"Probably to change his pants," Asher mumbles under his breath, and I elbow his side.

"I don't know. He was just here. I'm sure he'll be back." I shrug.

"Well, make sure you find him. Dinner will be served soon, then I'm certain he'll want to dance."

"I'm not—"

"Oh! And Lara wants a picture of you two," she says, cutting me off, referring to Jackson's mother. I swear I hear a growl come from Asher. And then she's off, making her way to her next victim before I have a chance to object.

There are so many things I wish I could say to Ash right now, but I can't, because Dash is right here. My brother takes his seat, and Asher follows suit, picking up the place card with *Dashiell Vale +1* in gold script.

"Guess this is me," he says, arching an eyebrow, daring me to argue.

I roll my eyes, lowering myself to my seat, which happens to be sandwiched between Asher and Jackson's empty chair.

"When he comes back, play nice," I warn them both. "You don't have to like him, but we can't cause a scene here."

Dash takes a swig of his Jack on the rocks that I can smell from here and throws up a hand gesture.

"The fuck is that?" Ash asks, and I laugh.

"Scout's honor."

"Dude, that's the Vulcan salute from *Star Trek.*"

Dash shrugs. "Same difference."

"Idiot," I say, but I can't keep from smiling. It feels good to be together like this again, just the three of us.

Until I see Jackson, heading back our way.

CHAPTER 9

ASHER

This fucking kid can't be serious. He ran off with his tail between his legs, but he seems to have picked up some new-found courage during his little bathroom break, judging by the cocky fucking grin he's sporting that's going to get his teeth knocked out here in a minute. He sits down next to Briar, and she looks at me with wide eyes, knowing that my patience is hanging by a thread.

Dash leans forward, resting his elbows on the table. "Keep your mouth shut, and we won't have any problems," he says in a low voice as to not draw any attention.

Jackson smirks, bringing his ankle up to rest on his knee. "You know what I think? I think you can talk all the shit you want, but you won't make a scene. Not here."

"He won't, but I will. Don't fucking test me, pretty boy. I have nothing to lose with these kinds of people."

"Because you're not one of us. You can put on a suit and tie, but you're still trash."

I feel a delicate hand rub my thigh, and though I know her attempt is to calm me down, she's doing the opposite. She's making my dick hard, and all I want is to fuck her, right here and now, to prove that she belongs to me. Only me.

"At least he's not a snobby, elitist douchebag with a tiny dick," Briar shoots back, shocking all of us. Dash spits out his drink, and Jackson is completely speechless, eyes as wide as saucers and face burning with what I assume is a mix of anger and embarrassment. I'd laugh if she hadn't confirmed—for the second time tonight—that she fucked him. The thought of him touching her, of being inside her, I can't fucking handle it. I know I'm no good for her, but he doesn't deserve her, either. Not by a long shot.

I clutch her wrist and bring it back to her lap before curling my hand around her thigh in a squeezing grip. I feel her stiffen, but I don't look at her.

"I'm going to pretend I didn't just hear that," Dash says, shaking the liquor off his hand. I glance at Briar to find her cheeks bright red—either from embarrassment at her outburst. Or maybe the fact that my hand is making its way underneath her dress with her brother on one side of us and her wannabe boyfriend on the other has something to do with it. I trail my calloused fingers up her silky-soft thighs, and she presses them together. I hook my leg under hers, thankful for the floor-length tablecloths, and pull, forcing her legs to widen. Briar makes a small sound of surprise, but no one else hears it.

I wonder if she's still wet from earlier. It took every ounce of my self-control not to unzip myself and thrust inside her when she was straddling my lap, riding my fingers. I wasn't going to come tonight, but the more I thought about her being alone with Jackson, the more I knew I couldn't stay away.

I went into Dash's room and questioned where he was going. I played dumb, making him think it was his idea to invite me.

"What are you up to tonight?" he'd asked. "My mom is forcing me to go to this fundraiser to keep up appearances."

"You want me to go with you?"

He paused in the middle of adjusting his tie, thrown off by my offer. "You'd go? I've never gotten you to agree to this kind of shit before."

I shrugged, feigning nonchalance, and feeling like a dick for it. "Will there be free booze?"

He smiled and handed me one of his suits that was a little tighter than I'd have liked, but it would do. And here we are.

Dash gets up and announces that he's getting another

drink, and I take the opportunity to slip my finger inside her panties. Fuck, those underwear. All strappy black and lacy framing her perfect little bubble butt. I take a sip of the water in front of me with my right hand while sliding my fingers through her slick heat with the other hand. She's wet, *so wet*, and smooth. Someone takes the stage and begins their speech, but all I can focus on is the way Briar clenches around my fingers when I shove them inside her pussy, the way her breathing becomes ragged, her eyelids growing heavier, her tits heaving, and nipples hardening against the thin fabric of her dress. *Fuck this.*

I lean in close and whisper, "Go to the third floor. Wait for me by the elevator. Now."

She nods her head yes rapidly, and the fact that she doesn't even hesitate sates my inner beast. "Okay," she whispers back, and she lets a quiet moan out when I slide my fingers from her pussy. Jackson looks over, a combination of shock and jealousy written all over his face, and I'm one thousand percent sure he knows what's going on under this table. I raise a brow that says *can I help you?*

Briar rights her dress under the table before getting up onto shaky legs, making her way to the elevator. I give it a good five minutes, daring Jackson to say a fucking word, while also keeping an eye on Dash. A pretty little thing at the bar has distracted him, so I doubt he'll be back any time soon. I'm a piece of shit for this—for being so sneaky with my best friend's little sister—but I've fought acting on my feelings since she was fourteen years old. This thing between Briar and me is like a runaway train. It can't be stopped, and it'll take us both straight to hell.

"Enjoy your night," I say to Jackson, sucking the taste of Briar off my finger before wiping my hands with the linen napkin. I ball it up, drop it on his plate, and walk away. Heading into the elevator, I stab at the number three with my finger, having zero patience left. I need to be inside her. Now. The doors ping and then open. She's waiting, biting back a nervous smile, hands twisting behind her back.

"Hi," she says.

"Hi."

Eating up the distance between us, I take her face in my hands, kissing her hard. She moans into my mouth, her tongue sliding against mine. Both of us are too far gone to care about getting caught now. We've been teasing each other all night, and it's coming to a head right here and now. Her hands grip my suit jacket as I swallow her cries of pleasure. This kiss is frantic and messy and desperate. I pull back, both of us panting.

"You let him fuck you?"

"Ash—"

"Tell. Me."

She nods reluctantly.

"When." It's not a question. It's a demand. I need

to know if she fucked him after this thing between us started.

"Months ago. Before you came back."

"Why?" Why *him*?

"Why?" She gives a bitter laugh. "Because you left me. Because Whitley came in bragging about hooking up with you. Because he was *there* and I was mad. That's why. Was I supposed to keep waiting for you?"

"No." Fuck. "But it doesn't mean I'm not going to be pissed about it," I say petulantly. Something she said isn't adding up. "I thought you said this just happened a few months ago."

"It did," she says, confusion painted on her face. "Just the one time, at his party before school even ended."

"I haven't fucked Whitley in years." We both stand there, soaking this information in. Whitley is a fucking liar, for one. And Briar gave up her virginity based on that lie.

Briar shakes her pretty, blonde head, walking to the balcony that overlooks the fundraiser. She rests her elbow on the bannister.

"I hate her, Ash." Her voice is a whisper.

"I know, baby," I say, coming up behind her, palming the outsides of her thighs. "Fuck her. Fuck all these people."

"Ash," she breathes my name as my left hand curves around her hip and dips underneath the thin scrap of lace. Her dress is bunched up above her ass, which is pressed right up against my crotch.

"What would they say if they saw you like this? With me?" I rub her clit and bite the shell of her ear. "They don't know you, Briar. They think you're a good girl, but they don't know that you like sneaking around with me. That you like the idea of being fucked up here, right out in the open. Right underneath their noses."

Her sharp intake of breath tells me that I'm right. And thank fuck, because I don't know if I could wait another minute.

"We can't."

"We are." I unzip my slacks enough to pull my cock out and tug her panties to the side. "Stop me."

"I can't," she says, low and keening, pushing back against my bare, engorged dick.

"Because you need this just as bad as I do. You like the idea of getting caught almost as much as you like getting away with it."

I push inside her slick pussy, giving us both what we want. *What we need.* Her head falls forward, but I grip the front of her neck, forcing her chin up.

"No," she gasps as I start to fuck her harder.

"No? Are you sure?"

"Yes."

"Say it. Say what you want."

"I want to be up here with you. *Fucking you.* So fuck me." The dirty words coming from that pretty mouth spur me on, and I pull one of her straps down, then pinch her nipple. She sucks in a breath, and I feel her clench around me.

"That's right. You don't belong with them. You never have. You may have been born into this life, but you're not like them, Briar. You and I are the same. And that's why you've been mine since you were fucking eleven, even if we didn't know it yet."

"Yes, God, yes. Don't leave me again. Don't ever leave."

"Careful what you wish for." I pump into her, my cock growing even harder. She plants her hands on the rail in front of us, bracing herself, meeting me thrust for thrust. I turn her face to the side, holding her there as I suck and bite and lick her shoulder, her neck, her cheek, and everywhere in between. I bring my other hand to rub at her clit while I pound into her. I can hear how wet she is, and our skin slaps together. Her hushed moans turn louder, and neither one of us cares if anyone knows in this moment. Because this is our truth, up here in the shadows.

I pull out abruptly to slide her underwear down, ignoring her protesting whine. I tug them down her toned thighs, and they fall to the floor around her slender ankles. Scooping them and clenching them in my fist, I waste no time burying myself back inside of her velvet heat. I squeeze her hips in a bruising grip, still holding on to the scrap of lace, and I don't hold back. I fuck her like I hate her, because part of me still does. I don't fully understand the depths of my feelings for Briar, but make no mistake, I'd kill for this girl.

"You're so fucking beautiful like this." We're sweating and panting, completely animalistic. "Look at them, Briar. Look at them when you come on my cock. Anyone could look up at any moment." I place my arms on top of hers, my hands covering hers that grip the rail, and I nip at her spine. "They'd act appalled, but they'd go home and jerk themselves off to this image. I promise you that."

Briar cries out, contracting around my dick, but she bites down on my arm to muffle her screams. I fuck her through her climax, trying to hold back from coming inside her. Finally, she slumps forward, spent, and I pull out, shooting my load inside her wadded-up panties.

We take a minute to catch our breath, unspeaking, before I straighten the skirt of her dress and zip myself up. She turns to face me, flushed cheeks and sleepy eyes. Her hair is damp, and little curls spring near her hairline.

"What are we doing, Ash?" Briar asks, as reality crashes down around us. We're getting sloppy. Just begging to get caught. I don't know what this is, either, but I know I'm not stopping. So, I give her the only answer I can.

"Whatever the fuck we want."

CHAPTER 10

BRIAR

I can still feel him between my legs, his fingers on my hips, his teeth in my shoulder. I clamp my legs shut in the passenger seat of my car, looking over at Asher. His left hand squeezes the wheel, hard eyes staring straight ahead. His suit jacket was thrown in the back seat, leaving him in a white dress shirt with rolled sleeves. He glances over and eyes my crossed legs pressed together, knowing I don't have any underwear on. Giving me a cocky grin, he slides his right hand in between my thighs, gripping the inside of one.

After we caught our breath and the weight of what we did settled around us, we both decided that we needed to go somewhere to be alone. We're getting careless. Practically begging to be caught. He didn't say where he was taking me, just snatched the keys out of my hand and started driving us out of the city limits. As we get further west, I realize I know exactly where he's taking me.

"We're going to The Tracks?" I ask, equal parts unsure and amused. "That's an interesting choice."

He shrugs. "It's quiet. No chance of being interrupted."

Yeah, I think, *unless fifty high schoolers decide to have the same idea.* But, The Tracks has always been his safe place.

We pull up to the old building. It's pitch-black and eerily quiet, the only sound the crickets chirping and the hum of the cars on the freeway in the distance. Asher takes my hand and wordlessly leads me through the gate, the hole in the fence, and finally into the building. Dapper and demure meet damaged and dilapidated as we walk inside, still in our gala attire. I wonder if this place ever held events like the one we attended tonight. If two star-crossed lovers ever resorted to stolen moments in the middle of a crowded building like we did, I wonder how their story turned out.

We wander around, aimlessly, neither one of us speaking, but both having so much to say. I decide to finally bite the bullet and break the silence.

"Where did you go?" I ask, cutting to the chase. He knows I'm referring to the past three years and gives me a long look before deciding to answer.

"It's a long story," he starts. "But the important part

is that I ended up in a small town in Northern California called River's Edge."

"And?" I prod, needing more of an explanation than that.

"And, I met a guy named Dare who has his own roofing company. He took me in, taught me the trade, and then when he started the process of opening up his own tattoo shop, I sort of took over."

"Oh."

I'm not sure what else to say. He always wanted to leave, and I understood why. It's the timing that never made sense to me. I guess I had it in my mind that there was some big secret that stole him away from me. Like jail or boarding school. But the fact that he just... started over elsewhere? That stings, though it shouldn't.

"What about you?"

"What do you mean?" I ask, confused.

"What did you do while I was gone?"

I shrug. "School, mostly. Acted as a referee between Dash and Dad whenever they were together. The usual."

"Still want to be a nurse?"

I look over at him in shock. I mentioned that in passing once, when I was maybe fourteen.

"I do..." I say, trailing off.

"But?"

"But, my dad wouldn't ever go for it. He's still pissed at Dash for not going to Harvard." What he doesn't know is that I have a pile of acceptance letters that have lapsed in my dresser drawer. I didn't make a decision, and now it's too late for any of them.

"Fuck your dad," Ash says darkly and with more anger than is warranted for this conversation. "What do *you* want?"

"Honestly? I have no clue. None." The problem is that I want to do everything and nothing all at once. I can't commit, and regardless of what I do, I'm letting someone down.

"Then, be undeclared. Or take a year to figure out what you want to do. Life is too short to live for someone else."

I nod, knowing he's right, but he doesn't understand, not really. It's not easy saying no to my parents.

"Let's play a game," I suggest, changing the subject. Asher looks at me warily.

"Okay..." he drawls out. "What do you have in mind?" He rakes his fingertips up the sides of my thighs and back under my dress, meeting my bare skin. I already want him again.

"Not that kind of game. A question game. I ask you a question, and you give me a straightforward answer, *no bullshit*," I stress. "Then you get to ask me a question. Deal?"

"Deal," he agrees, and we both head in the direction of the grandstand, through what used to be the food court. The place is so quiet that I could probably hear a pin drop from the other side of the building.

"So, you weren't hooking up with Whitley while you were gone?"

Asher stops short and turns to face me, his expression dead serious. "Not even once. I never saw her while I was gone."

I nod, waiting for his question.

"Does any part of you still want Jackson?" He doesn't waste any time asking. I think he more than knows the answer to this question, but I give him the reassurance he needs.

"Not even a little bit," I say with the same sincerity in which he answered me. "He was nice. You were gone." I shrug, as if that's all there was to it. There wasn't much more than that, to be honest.

"Are you going to leave again?" I ask, voicing my biggest fear.

"Probably," he answers honestly. His head is down, hands in his pockets, as he angles his body toward the dark sky through hollow windows while I die a little inside.

"Why did you help my dad?"

I suck in a breath. I knew this one was coming. "I'm sorry," I start, but he puts a hand up and stops me.

"That's not a straightforward answer, Bry."

"Okay." He's right. "Um, because I felt bad for him. I felt that he truly regretted how he treated you. And I knew that he was still your father. I wanted to take care of him for *you*. It made me feel closer to you, too."

Asher doesn't speak. He stares out at the silhou-
ettes of palm trees against the night sky, and I can see
the tension in his jaw. I decide to hit him with a not-so-
loaded question.

"Did you miss me?"

"Every fucking day. Even when I despised you."

"Why did you—" I start to ask, but he tsks and
wiggles a finger at me.

"It's my turn." *Oh. Right.*

"Did you miss *me*?"

"So much it hurt."

His eyes snap toward mine.

"What are we?" I ask, even though my heart is in
my stomach waiting for his response.

"I don't know," he says, coming closer. He moves
my hair off my right shoulder, bringing his mouth close
to my neck. "What do you want to be?" His breath
dances across my exposed skin, and I shudder with
anticipation.

"Everything."

"We can't," he rasps, curling a hand around my
thigh and lifting. I wrap both legs around his waist, and
he backs me up against the pillar behind me. "I can't
give you that. Not yet."

"But, I don't want to stop this," I argue.

"I *can't* stop this," he agrees, reaching to unbutton
his pants. I use the heels of my shoes to push them
down, and then I feel him there. Warm and hard
and ready.

"So, we keep doing this, but—"

"But we don't tell anyone," he finishes.

"What are you waiting for then, Kelley? Fuck me."

His eyes fill with heat, and he thrusts forward, showing me exactly how much fun secrets can be.

"Can't say I didn't see this coming," a raspy, familiar voice grumbles, startling me out of my slumber. It's dark, and it takes me a second to remember where I am. Asher brought me to his dad's house last night, because neither of us wanted to deal with people or the hassle of sneaking around. I wasn't sold at first, but I figured any time Asher spends around his father is a plus.

Ash is wrapped around me. His nose is in my hair, his arm banded around my waist. I reach behind me to shake him awake. He barely budges.

"Leave me alone," he growls in his sleep-sexy voice, squeezing me tighter to him. It rumbles in my ear, leaving goose bumps across my neck and down my arms. "This is the best sleep I've had in years."

I melt at his words, all vulnerable and unfiltered due to his sleepy state, and my face heats because John's lifted eyebrow and amused expression tell me that he has heard every word. Asher is an adult, and he doesn't strike me as someone who ever followed the rules, even as a kid. But, I'm still seventeen, and I've just been caught in a boy's bedroom. I should feel the need to apologize or make excuses, but somehow, I know the normal rules don't apply. At least not here.

"I'll leave you two to it," John says, before slowly making his way back down the hall. Asher finally opens his eyes when he realizes we aren't alone, but he doesn't offer up any explanation. Once his dad is gone, I cover my face with both hands.

"Well, that wasn't weird at all," I deadpan.

"You're fine," Ash says, his voice still thick with sleep. "He doesn't care about this kind of thing. Trust me."

I know Asher's a bit of a man whore, but the insinuation that he brings a lot of girls home still stings. And my face must show it.

"What?" he asks, confused. I turn away from him, but he turns me onto my back by my shoulder and props himself on one arm to hover over me. His mussed-up hair that hangs in his right eye, his square jaw full of day-old stubble, his muscular arm braced on the pillow next to my face. How could anyone *not* want him? He's perfection personified. The bad boy with a good heart. I know it's there, even if he tries his best to hide it.

"Briar..." he coaxes, smoothing my hair off my face.

"I'm being stupid," I answer honestly. Because I *am* being stupid. What happened with Asher and other girls before me is irrelevant. Even if we were technically together—which we aren't—it still wouldn't matter. I'm not going to be one of those girls who obsesses over every single person he's ever come in contact with.

"Tell me."

"I was just wondering how many girls have been in this bed."

He smirks and opens his mouth, but I cover it with my palm.

"I don't want to know!" I say quickly. Ignorance is definitely bliss in this scenario. Asher chuckles into my hand and then bites the skin of my palm. I jerk it back, and he pins it to the pillow next to my head, lowering himself onto me.

"I've never brought one single person into this room. Male or female."

"Even Whitley?"

"Even Whitley," he agrees.

How is that possible?

"Come on, Briar. You know how my dad was. I wasn't bringing anyone over here. *I* didn't even want to be here. You're the only one."

I love feeling like I'm different than everyone else to Asher, as juvenile as that sounds. Maybe even special. He doesn't say it in flowery words or extravagant public declarations of love, but that makes it mean even more to me. Ash is like an onion with many layers. With each one, I find something more to him.

"Oh," I say dumbly.

"Oh?" he repeats, cocking a brow. "That's all you

have to say?"

"I've never had another guy in my room, either."

"Good."

And then he lowers his head, pressing those full lips to mine, before trailing them down my neck, collarbone, the curve of my breast. I arch under his touch, never needing anything more than the slightest touch to burn for him. He reaches for the hem of the old P.E. shirt from high school that he let me borrow and sprinkles open-mouthed kisses up my stomach. Just before he exposes me completely, I hear John erupt in a coughing fit from the other room, reminding me of our surroundings.

"Ash," I say, already breathless. "We can't. Your dad."

He growls, biting the underside of my boob before rolling away.

"Guess I'll go make sure he didn't hack up a lung," Asher grumbles, and I laugh, righting my shirt.

"Don't be an ass. I'll be out in a minute."

Asher reaches over to turn on the lamp on his nightstand before standing and pulling on some thin, mesh basketball shorts. I bite my bottom lip as I take in his lean swimmer's torso. The sharp V, the two freckles right at the waistband of his shorts that I want to trace with my tongue. I wish we had a place that was ours— just ours—so we could be alone and I could have my fill of him for hours, days, weeks. I don't think I'll ever get tired of being with him like this. I've never felt this desperate, *can't eat, can't sleep, need you, bleed for you* type of addiction before.

"You're doing it again," he groans, balling his fists at his sides.

"Doing what?" I ask, batting my eyes innocently. He shakes his head, exasperated, and walks out the door, leaving me to drool at the sight of his shirtless, muscular back.

I take a second to look at the room around me—the glimpse into teenage Asher's mind that I never got to see. Most everything has been packed into boxes that line the wall, but a few things remain. A couple of posters—Brand New, Underoath, and Thrice. The usual suspects. His window is covered by a black sheet, the same shade as his bedding. A skateboard with a Volcom sticker peeks out of the closet, with one of the trucks missing. I always thought he planned to leave, and it only felt sudden to me, but seeing his room appearing so lived-in has me wondering if it wasn't planned.

I stand, ignoring the ache between my legs, and reach for my dress that was flung over the box in the early hours of the morning when Asher and I made up for lost time, yet again. I pull the dress over my head, and I can't help but notice the medals and trophies collecting dust inside. I pick one up and turn the cool, heavy metal in my hand. I wonder why he doesn't swim anymore. Swimming was his *thing*. The one thing he seemed to actually enjoy.

I make my way over to his black dresser and hope to God he has some boxers or shorts or something, considering he never gave me my underwear back. I try the top left drawer. Empty, except for a few socks. I try the top right—*jackpot!* I sift through the drawer, looking for the smallest pair, when I see something stashed underneath. It's a folded piece of paper. I shouldn't open it. Asher's already so private, and I don't want to do anything to betray his trust. Even if it's nothing more than a grocery list, he wouldn't want me looking through his things.

But, curiosity gets the best of me, so I pick it up. It's heavier and thicker than notebook paper, like the kind that people use to sketch on. I carefully unfold it and gasp when I see what's inside. It's a black and white skull with vibrant, colorful succulents and roses around it, covering one half of the face. They kind of look like the ones in my mom's garden. It's dark and sad and beautiful all at once. *Did Asher draw this?*

"What are you doing?"

His voice is cold and curt, and I jump, dropping the picture to the floor. His arms are crossed, stance guarded, eyes suspicious.

"I was looking for some shorts," I stammer, plucking out the first pair I get my hands on and sliding them up my legs. He eyes the paper on the floor, but doesn't say anything. Stalking over, he bends over and picks it up, inspecting the art.

"It's beautiful," I say honestly. "Did you draw it?"

"No."

"What does it mean?"

"It's just a tattoo idea. Dare sketched it up for me when I went back."

I nod, unsure of what to say, rocking on my heels. Ash crumples the paper up and tosses it back into the drawer.

"Come on," he says. "I'm making us breakfast."

"You can cook?" I ask, amused, thankful for the subject change.

"I've been cooking for myself since before you grew tits."

"Touché," I say, rolling my eyes. I guess he would've had to learn how to cook at a young age. Between his mom dying and his dad being too busy self-destructing, it was mandatory.

I sit at the old oak table while Asher does his thing in the kitchen. John is firmly planted in his favorite recliner, watching the NFL draft on TV. I haven't seen him since Asher's been back, and I'm in this weird place where I feel guilty for not coming by, but also guilty for ever coming in the first place.

"How's he doing?" I ask quietly, as Ash flips the eggs in the frying pan like a pro.

"Hanging in there, I guess." He shrugs.

"Are *you* okay?" I know Asher doesn't have much of a relationship with John, and I know he plays it off like he couldn't care less, but deep down, he does care. He has to. He's twenty-one years old and about to be parent-less. That would be hard on anyone. Something dark passes over his features, but then it's gone, leaving me to wonder if I imagined it.

"Why wouldn't I be?"

"Just making sure."

Ash loads up three plates with eggs—sunny side up —bacon, and toast. I walk one of them over to John so he can eat in his chair. Asher sets our plates at the table in the kitchen. Risking his wrath, I snatch his plate from under his nose and grab my own before bringing them to the coffee table in the living room. Next to John. Ash isn't happy about it, but he follows suit, glaring all the way.

"So, you two have become fast friends, I see," Ash says, his accusation clear, but if he's looking for a reaction from John, he's not getting one. *Like father, like son*, I think. Both of the Kelley men are so adept at keeping their emotions concealed. They aren't easily ruffled, at least on the exterior.

"Yep," John mumbles around a mouthful of food. "Got our BFF necklaces and everything. You jealous?"

Ash lets out an unamused huff.

"The house looks good," I note. It's much cleaner than it used to be, and it's mostly packed up. I can't help but feel a little sad thinking about it. I can't imagine preparing for my own death. Seeing my entire life reduced to a few boxes. Trying to make amends before it's too late. My heart hurts for both of them.

"Mostly Asher's doing," John says. "He's been

sorting through everything, cleaning, packing, you name it."

I'm slightly thrown by the almost-compliment, until he tacks on, "Anything to avoid actually talking to his old man, right?" He laughs it off, self-deprecating as always, but I sense the pain behind his words. I know Asher is conflicted. You wouldn't be able to tell by looking at him, but I know him. His words are his weapons, but when it comes to his father, he doesn't always bite back, and that speaks volumes. I want him to give John another chance, but that doesn't mean he should ever, for one second, feel guilty about not being able to forgive him.

"Two months of sobriety doesn't erase the past six years," I say, shocking even myself. It just slips out. "I didn't mean to say that," I confess, eyes wide. "But it doesn't make it any less true."

"She's right," John says after a beat of silence. "I'm glad you have someone in your corner." Then he goes back to eating as if nothing ever happened.

Ash squeezes my knee, and I let out a relieved breath. That little gesture says more than words ever will.

"Do you want to go somewhere with me?" Ash asks, catching me off guard.

"Now?"

"Right now. I want to show you something."

I beam at him.

"Let's go."

CHAPTER 11

ASHER

I glance down at Briar's sleeping form. She's so tiny that she's curled right up on the bench of my truck with her head on my lap, living up to her namesake. When I asked her if she wanted to go somewhere, she wasn't prepared for a twelve-hour drive. I've done it so many times that it's nothing to me. Once we left my dad's house, we stopped at Briar's to pack a bag and change our clothes, then we were off.

After spending time with her at my dad's, without fear of anyone seeing us, I decided I needed more of that feeling. We wouldn't have to sneak around, I wouldn't have to share her with other people, and most of all, I'd get to fuck her whenever I wanted.

I shoot Dare a text, informing him that we're close.

The air has turned crisp, the roads windy, and the pine trees outnumber the people.

"Wake up, Sleeping Beauty," I say, tucking her hair behind her ear. She lets out a sleepy moan, and the sound goes straight to my cock.

"Where are we?" she asks, rubbing her eyes.

"Almost there. I didn't want you to miss this," I say, gesturing to the scenery that's vastly different from Arizona. Everything is green, and there's nothing but mountains and pine trees, as far as the eye can see.

"It's beautiful," she says. "I can see why you stayed so long."

"It's a lot better than the alternative."

"Arizona isn't *that* bad." She laughs.

"Not Arizona," I surprise myself by admitting.

"Then what do you mean? Where else did you go?"

"With my uncle in Southern California, at first."

"You have an uncle?" she asks, her nose crinkling in confusion.

"I didn't really know him until recently."

"Then why would you stay with him?"

I blow out a breath and decide to tell her everything. I know her well enough to know she'll get it out of me sooner or later. From the drugs and the cars to the stealing and the fights, I tell her all of it, including the day my uncle left me for dead, and how Dare came into the picture, bailing me out in more ways than one.

"Jesus," she says quietly, eyes glistening with unshed tears. "I had no idea."

"Well." I shrug. "Now you do."

We sit in silence as she takes in the trees and the lake along with the information I just dumped on her. The thing I love about Briar is that she didn't even bat an eye when I told her about stealing the cars or snorting the coke. She doesn't judge me. She's probably the only one who never has.

Finally, I pull onto Dare's street. His house is secluded, far away from town, and the roads are so narrow that you have to pull over for oncoming cars to be able to fit. I thought I was anti-social, but Dare makes me look like the freaking prom queen in comparison.

"We're here," I say, cutting the engine. Briar's wide eyes take in the luxury cabin before us.

"*This* is where you lived?"

"Yup."

"Why the hell did you ever leave?" she asks, incredulous. The cabin itself isn't very glamorous, but it's right on the water, and people pay millions for that. Literally.

"I had something prettier waiting for me in Cactus Heights," I tease.

"That's sweet, Ash, but your dad really isn't that cute."

I snort, hopping out of my truck before walking

around to the other side to help her down, too. Instead of stepping down, she launches herself at me, wrapping her arms around my neck. I squeeze her ass as she brings her lips to mine, her tongue seeking entrance.

"Are you guys going to come in, or are you just going to fuck in my driveway all night?" Dare asks from his open door. Briar jumps at the sound of his voice and sheepishly slides down my body.

"Briar, this is Dare. Dare, Briar," I say as we make our way inside. Bry surprises me by hugging his middle. And Dare looks even more shocked, arms held out to his side, not knowing what to do.

"Is she always this friendly?" he asks, cocking a brow and pointing a finger at her arms wrapped around his tattooed torso.

"Thank you for helping him," she says, and once he understands, he returns her hug, even if it is one-handed. I don't think I'll ever get used to the way she cares about me. It never fails to surprise me.

"*Kelleyyy!*" someone slurs from far away.

"Cordell or Camden?" I ask.

"I have no fucking clue." Dare laughs. "But it's one of them. They're all out back."

Remember how I said Dare was anti-social? Our friends, who happen to be brothers, don't seem to realize it. Or more accurately, they just don't care. They're the complete opposite of Dare, and myself for that matter.

Briar takes in everything from the high ceilings to the old wooden floors, and everything in between as Dare leads us through the house and into the backyard.

"I can't believe we're only in the next state over. It feels like we're in another world."

"You should see it during the winter. It's like living in an actual snow globe."

"I'd love to live somewhere like this. You know, with actual seasons."

I nod, because that's my favorite part about being here, too.

We make our way toward the rowdy voices in the backyard, finding Camden and Cordell in the hot tub with three chicks. They're randoms. Tourists. I'd bet my life on it.

"Well, if it isn't the fucking King of the Mountain," I say to Camden. He and Cordell both snowboard, like everyone else who lives here, but Camden went pro, and he's achieved somewhat celebrity status around here.

"What's up, motherfucker? Who's that fine ass looking female?"

"You're not going to be very good at snowboarding with two broken legs," I warn, and he holds his palms up, laughing. "This is Briar."

"Oh, shit, you found someone to deal with your brooding ass?"

"Seems that way," I grumble, but fuck, it feels good

to be with her like this. I link my fingers with hers, just because we can, and she smiles up at me.

"This is Serena and Sasha," Camden says, referring to the two blondes next to him. "They're from Canada. And this is beautiful creature is Mila. I'm not really sure where the fuck she came from, to be honest." The girls giggle, thinking he's joking, but I can tell by his expression that he genuinely has no clue.

"You guys coming in?" Cordell asks. "There's beer in the cooler."

Usually, that would be a hard pass. But the Jacuzzi is big, and they're only taking up one side. Plus, any excuse to see Briar in a bikini has my vote. I look at her to see what she thinks, and she shrugs, as if to say *might as well*.

I lead her up to my room, tossing our bags onto my bed.

"I really love it here," she says, taking in the plain walls and minimal furniture. Just a bed, a dresser, and a TV.

"It's not much, but living in this environment, you don't need much else."

"I can see that," she says, plucking her bathing suit out of her bag. This time, it's plain black.

"Well?" she asks, lifting a brow.

"Well, what?"

"Aren't you going to turn around?"

"Fuck no."

Briar giggles, and surprises me by dropping her shorts and underwear. Next is her tank top and her bra. She's standing in front of me, completely naked, and I gulp at the sight. Tiny waist, curvy hips, flat stomach. Her light blonde hair falls over her perfect little tits.

I take a step toward her, but she holds up a palm.

"Nuh-uh," she says, already reading my intentions. "That can wait. Your friends are waiting."

"Fuck my friends. You're naked."

"I told you to turn around," she teases, pulling her bottoms up her toned legs. "Later."

"Fine."

We both finish getting dressed and join everyone in the hot tub. They all love Briar, and I'm not surprised. The girl could make friends with a brick wall. Even Dare seems to like her, which is saying a lot. He only tolerates most people.

Eventually, they move the party to the fire pit a few feet away. Briar's on my lap, and I squeeze her thigh, letting her know I want to hang back. Once we're alone, she turns to straddle my lap.

"Thanks for bringing me here."

I nip at her lip and grip her ass, pulling her into me. I'm hard as a fucking rock, and I know she feels it when she flexes her hips toward me on a gasp.

"Can you be quiet?" I ask, tossing a look over my shoulder to make sure no one else is watching.

"Asher..."

"Yes or no?" I ask, pulling my cock out of my swim shorts, and it bobs between us.

Briar reaches down to pull her bikini bottoms to the side before sinking down onto me.

"I can try."

"That's my girl."

CHAPTER 12

BRIAR

I t's been a few weeks since Asher brought me to River's Edge. Something shifted that day, or maybe the night of the gala, but things have been different. *Good* different. After we finished in the hot tub, he brought me up to his room and we showered together before calling it a night. We had to leave the next morning, before people started wondering where we were, and I was surprisingly sad to go. And if I wasn't mistaken, I could've sworn that Asher looked a little disappointed to leave Dare's, too.

Dare. That man. He's equal parts intimidating and beautiful. Jet-black hair peeking out from under his beanie and striking blue eyes. Both of his arms were covered with vibrant, intricate art, and his eyebrows were cinched together in a perpetual scowl. He was the broodier version of Asher, and that's saying a lot.

Asher was quiet on the way home, but so was I. I think we were both contemplating what our futures held. The deeper we fell, the harder it was to hide. So, tonight, when I got a text from Ash earlier, saying he wanted to talk, it was just vague enough to worry me. I can't help but think he already has one foot out the door. That our secret is already taking its toll.

My dirty black Vans struggle to keep up with Natalia's nude pumps as she quite literally drags me toward the music blaring from the two-story house that's only a few minutes' walk from the university. Of course, Adrian's spoiled ass wouldn't even entertain the idea of staying at the dorms. Unless they were co-ed. He's going on his fourth year of college, and I'm convinced he's only here for the parties and fresh meat. It took a fair amount of time convincing me to come, so there's a good chance that we're the only sober ones. And judging by the two chicks that are trying to lift their friend, who is doing a fantastic impression of a limp noodle off the lawn, I'd say that's a safe assumption.

I wasn't going to come tonight. Wasn't in the mood after receiving that text, but Nat insisted she needed a wingman. Apparently, she and Adrian have some kind of bet going on, so, she went full-on predatory female tonight. With her incredibly tight, incredibly short, black bandage dress from her mom's boutique, you'd think she was hitting up the Las Vegas strip instead of a college party. Her dark red, messy hair is tussled in that perfectly imperfect kind of way. Adrian doesn't stand a chance. Me, on the other hand? I'm wearing black jean shorts, a black tank, and a flannel. Her pursed lips told me that she wasn't happy with what I chose to wear, but she knew better than to argue once I agreed to come if she wanted a wingman.

We step over the drunk girls, who are now all three sprawled out on the ground, and walk in the front door. "Do Re Mi" by Blackbear assaults my ears as we shuffle through the sweaty, drunk bodies and the cloud of smoke from some dude's bong rip. Natalia is on a mission, pulling me by my elbow straight toward the kitchen, ignoring the looks and whistles. Once we're in the kitchen, I'm immediately aware of Asher's presence. I haven't even spotted him yet, but I know he's close. And like a magnet, my eyes find him through the glass patio door, sitting on the beer pong table, smoking a cigarette with my brother. He nods as someone talks, but I know he's not paying attention, not really. I'm focused on those thick, calloused fingers and the way the cigarette sits between them. The way he draws it up to those full lips and his eyebrows tug together before taking a drag. I hate smokers—I hate that *Ash* is a smoker—but there is something undeniably sexy about watching the act. I'm just glad he only does it when he's drinking these days.

"Here." My attention snaps back to Nat when she

shoves a blue plastic cup of God knows what into my line of vision.

"What is it?" I ask, raising a brow.

"Whatever that is," she says, gesturing toward some mysterious red juice in a bowl. She takes a tentative sip. "Vodka. I think."

I take the cup, but I don't drink it. I'm not in the mood tonight.

"So, where is he?" I look around for Adrian, but I don't see him.

"Oh, he's here," Nat says, looking like she's preparing for battle with the way she scans the room for her victim, eyes narrowed to slits. "*Somewhere.*"

Just then, Adrian walks around the corner, and his jaw drops when his eyes land on Nat. She ditches her drink and saunters toward him with a victorious smile. He checks her out from head to toe, biting his bottom lip as she gets closer. Once she's within reach, he holds out his hand, but she bypasses him instead, wrapping her arms around some random guy's neck. The guy is clearly caught off guard, but he doesn't dare complain. She leads him into the living room where the music is, and his hands land on her hips, squeezing. She's putting on a show, rolling her body seductively, and the poor guy doesn't even know it's not for him. Adrian's eyes burn a hole into the back of his head, and I can't help but laugh. When I grow up, I want to be just like Natalia. Balls of steel.

I stand near the counter, not really wanting to

venture outside, but also not having any desire to mingle with randoms. I recognize a lot of these people—some of them friends with my brother, and others that graduated when I was a freshman—but I don't know any of them well enough to call them friends.

"Hey, little Vale, right?" a guy who's vaguely familiar says, invading my personal space. He has light brown hair and kind eyes. Very red, high on marijuana eyes, but kind nonetheless.

"Heyyyy," I say, letting the word linger between us, unsure of his name.

"Tanner," he supplies.

"Right." I snap my fingers. "You graduated with my brother. How are you?"

"I'm good, I'm good. Just graduated from MIT and came back for a visit."

A stoner engineer. Impressive. Before I can respond, the sliding glass door opens, and Asher is suddenly at my side.

"Can we talk?"

"What, now?" *Surely he wouldn't break it off in a public place. Right?*

His nostrils flare, cutting a glare at what's-his-face, probably not liking the fact that I'm making him talk in front of him.

"Yeah, now."

I lift a brow.

"Please," he grudgingly tacks on.

I give an apologetic wave to stoner engineer guy and reluctantly follow Asher.

"I really don't think this is the place," I say, pausing before the stairs. "My brother is here. All his friends are here. And this," I say, gesturing between us, "does not look good."

"I don't give a fuck what it looks like, and I don't give a fuck who knows anymore."

There it is. That little spark of hope that Asher is so good at giving me, just enough to keep me on his string. I hate that it's there. I hate that some part of me believes it's different this time. And I hate that it has me accepting his proffered hand and following him upstairs.

He tries a door, but it's locked. The next one is the bathroom. But the third time is a charm. Or so we think. The room is dark except for a light from the closet off to the right, but I can just barely make out two figures on the bed. I laugh when I hear moaning and go to close the door, until I hear something that stops us both in our tracks.

"Fuck me, Jackson. Fuck me like you want to fuck her."

Whitley? I'd know that voice anywhere. Like nails on a chalkboard. And Jackson? I don't even think they know each other.

"You get off on this, don't you?" The voice that I know to be Jackson's asks as his bare butt moves between her spread legs, and I can't look away. Why are we still watching this? "You like knowing you can have what she does? That it?"

"Yes," Whitley whines.

"Briar," he growls. "Fuck yeah, Briar." My eyes widen, and I feel like I'm going to vomit all over my shoes.

"Don't fucking call me that," Whitley grits out.

"Why not? It's what you want, right?"

"No!" Whitley smacks him in the face, and to my shock, he slaps her right back. Whitley moans, clearly enjoying their depravity as Jackson pins her hands to the bed. I sneak a glance at Ash to gauge his reaction, but he doesn't look at all surprised. Disgusted, maybe, but not surprised. It makes me wonder what kind of sex they had together.

I've seen enough of their fucked-up little games. Tugging on Asher's hand, I start to lead him away from the doorway. He's stiff. Unmoving. And the hard angles of his jaw are sharp enough to cut glass right now.

"You wanna do something Briar never did for me?" Jackson asks, and Whitley moans her response. Asher's head cocks to the side—like a predator zeroing in on his prey—hands squeezed into fists, and I know I need to get him out of here in about one second, or all hell is going to break loose.

"Suck me off."

I hear some rustling around, and I try again to pull Ash away, to no avail. He's rooted to this spot.

"She won't suck my dick, but she'll get finger fucked in public like a whore. Do you want to be *my* whore, Whitley?"

Whitley gives a breathy *yes*.

Ash lunges forward, and I bring both hands up to clasp his face between them. To force his focus on me. I shake my head, silently begging him to walk away. This isn't worth it. *They* aren't worth it. Who cares what two shitbags say or do together?

"I've seen the bite marks he leaves on her. Maybe that's what she's into. Maybe she just needs a little more *convincing* next time," Jackson says darkly.

Everything happens in slow motion. I see the minute his eyes turn black. I see the second there's no going back.

Ash rips his face from my hands.

Kicks the door open.

Whitley screams.

Jackson springs away from her.

There aren't any words exchanged. Asher charges at him in the dark, and I hear the sickening sound of fist meeting flesh and bone. I slap at the wall in search of the light switch. I finally find it, bathing the room in brightness, and see Asher straddling a very bloody Jackson.

I bolt toward them, trying to pull Ash off Jackson without leaving him vulnerable to getting hit.

"Stop!"

"Briar, get the fuck out of here!" Ash yells, not

taking his eyes off Jackson, one hand gripping his polo shirt by the collar. Jackson's jeans are around his ankles now, exposing his boxers. He tries pulling them up, but he can't reach with Asher crushing his abdomen with his weight. Jackson throws a fist, grazing Ash's cheekbone, but he doesn't even flinch.

Whitley takes her time adjusting her skirt, then stands back by the window, arms crossed. Asher lifts Jackson by fisting his collar with both hands and throws him into the desk, sending a computer and a lamp flying.

"I told you what would happen the next time you so much as looked at her," Ash says menacingly before cracking his forehead against Jackson's. He pulls back, and Jackson's head lulls to the side against the wall for a beat, dazed, before he regains control. "You're lucky you're even alive, motherfucker."

Ash cocks back and lands punch after punch. Whitley still stands there, looking mildly entertained, if anything. This isn't going to end well. If I don't break this up soon, Asher is going to end up in jail, and Jackson in hell. Because he's going to kill him.

Coming to a decision I know I'll regret even before I act on it, I run out into the hallway, stopping at the top of the stairs. I have no other choice.

"Dashiell!" I scream, cupping my mouth with my hands. "Adrian! Someone get my brother!" The music is still loud, but my screams are louder. I run back to the room, hoping someone heard me. I can't get through to Ash right now, and I don't have the physical strength to stop him.

They're rolling around on the floor, and it's all Jackson can do to block his face from the blows.

In a last-ditch effort to get through to him, I wrap my arms around Asher's waist as he pummels Jackson. He pauses, hesitating, fist poised for another hit. I press my lips to his spine, resting my forehead in between his shoulder blades.

"Please, baby. *Stop*," I beg him.

"What the fuck?" Pools of blue that match mine meet my guilty ones as Dash barges in, taking in the scene before him.

Asher whips his head around, panting and heaving with exertion. His black hair has fallen into his eyes, and he flips it out of the way with a jerk of his chin. Dash shakes his head in disbelief, and Adrian stands with his arms folded across his chest, eyebrows pinched together, with his usually playful demeanor nowhere to be found.

"Dash—" I start, backing away, but before his name leaves my lips, Jackson takes advantage of the distraction and clocks Asher. Not expecting the hit, his head flies back, and he stumbles, almost taking me out. I lunge for Jackson, suddenly no longer concerned with his safety. I slap and claw at his face for all of two seconds before he shoves me away and all three guys are on him, pinning him back against the wall.

"What the fuck!" my brother yells. He has Jackson's right shoulder, Adrian his left, and Asher? Asher has his throat. "Somebody better start fucking talking. Now."

A feminine giggle reminds me of Whitley's presence, and we all turn to see what could possibly be funny. She stands there, black thigh-high socks askew, laughing and shaking her head. Next to her is a glass mirror with little white lines cut into rows, a rolled up hundred-dollar bill, and a credit card on top of the nightstand.

"You're so fucked up, Whit," Adrian says. "This is low, even for you."

Her face falls, her eyes narrow, and I already know what's coming. She's about to drop a bomb that's going to leave my world in ashes without giving one, single fuck.

"*I'm* fucked up?" she screeches, pointing a finger in our direction. "You four want to act like you're all so close. So *loyal*. Untouchable to outsiders. But you're the fucked-up ones. You're keeping more secrets from each other than you know what to do with."

I lock eyes with Asher, both of us mentally bracing ourselves for what we know is coming. I want to tell my brother about us. I want to tell the world about us. But not like this. It shouldn't come from Whitley.

Adrian huffs out a laugh, letting go of Jackson, and starts toward the door. "I'm out."

"Let's start with you, then, Adrian," Whitley says.

He pauses and turns around, throwing his arms out in a
hit me with your best shot gesture.

"I bet no one here knows that you can't get it up. At
least not without your best friend there. Why is that?
Could it be that pussy just doesn't do it for you?"

What is she talking about?

"No, it's just yours that tends to kill my boner," he
strikes back, but I can tell her jab hit its intended target
from the way that he grinds his jaw and clenches
his fists.

"He's not gay. That's enough, Whitley," Dash says
in a low, threatening tone. She turns her attention to
him, lifting one perfectly arched brow. Dash releases
his hold on Jackson, but Asher keeps him pinned by his
throat.

"Why? Because you don't want your precious little
sister to know how messed up you really are? How you
like to share girls with Adrian. How you both fucked
me *together*, night after night, even in high school."

Her eyes glow with victory, dying for my reaction. I
bite the inside of my cheek to keep my jaw from hitting
the floor. I knew Adrian was into some freaky shit, but
there are just some things you don't need to know
about your brother. Dash won't so much as meet my
eyes, and I hate Whitley right now. I hate her for all
of this.

"And what about you?" I snap. "You have literally
slept with everyone in this room besides me. Did
Daddy not love you enough? Or is this because of

Asher? He doesn't *want you*, Whitley. Why can't you accept it? Sleeping with all his friends isn't going to make him jealous."

I know I'm being harsh. I hear the words being spewed from my mouth like verbal diarrhea, but I can't stop myself. Whitley is toxic, and she's hurting every single person I love with her brand of poison. I've put up with her for years. But this? This is too far.

Whitley's mouth snaps shut, and her face reddens.

"You," she says, pointing a finger at me, "are one to talk, Little Miss Make Out Slut. You'll shove your tongue down anyone's throat, but when it comes to fucking, no one gets you off like your brother's best friend."

And there it is. My pulse races, and I hear my heartbeat in my ears that are now on fire. All eyes are on me. No one speaks. Dash begs me with his eyes to deny it, but I won't lie to him. Jackson laughs, despite Asher's fingers closed around his neck, but Ash doesn't show any emotion whatsoever. His face is completely blank, but I know what he's doing. He's bracing himself for the fallout. Slipping that mask back into place.

"I mean, sure, you screwed Jackson in an attempt to get over Asher. But even that was a one-off. Not that I blame you, though," she whispers conspiratorially, holding her finger and thumb an inch apart in the universal sign for tiny penis, with her bottom lip jutted out in a fake pout.

"What the hell, Whit?!" Jackson yells, while my brother says, "You fucked my *sister*?"

"Since we're all sharing secrets," Jackson shoots back, "do you want to know the real reason Asher had to leave?"

"Jackson, no." Whitley shakes her head, looking genuinely nervous for the first time. My heart sinks, stomach full of dread. Even Asher seems confused. What could Jackson possibly know about Asher leaving?

"Whitley saw you guys that night," he starts, and Asher's grip on his throat tightens. "In Dash's room. She saw you in the window."

"What the fuck is he talking about?" my brother, who is rapidly losing patience, asks.

"She knew right then she'd lost him, so she snapped a picture before Dash caught up and sent it to Daddy Vale. He's the one who had him sent away. All because she was *jealous*."

What? How?

My dad has made his feelings for Asher clear, but he would never do something like that. And if he did, he would've mentioned knowing, right? Asher drops his hand abruptly, bringing both hands behind his head as he paces back and forth, letting this new information sink in. She did this. I underestimated her. I thought she was just a typical high school mean girl: Gothic edition. I never thought she'd be capable of something like this. I shouldn't be surprised, yet I still am.

"She was fourteen!" Dash shouts, and from the sheer outrage in his voice, I know this is going to be bad. "You were with my sister when she was *fourteen*?"

"No, it wasn't like tha—" I try, but Dash lunges at Asher, only to be held back by Adrian.

"You fucking piece of shit," my brother says between clenched teeth. "I let you into my house. I trusted you with her. Instead, you fucking preyed on her! She's a child!"

Asher wipes his bloody nose with the back of his hand and sniffs.

"I didn't fucking touch her, man."

"So, she's lying?" Jackson stabs a finger in Whitley's direction. "You two haven't been seeing each other behind my back?"

"Not back then, we weren't. I fought it when she was younger. I fucking fought it as hard as I could."

"I'll kill you."

"I love her."

My mouth drops open. *Love.* Asher loves me. And he's admitting it in a room full of people. The words are right, *so right*, but the timing is so wrong.

Dash rushes Asher, and they both go down. Jackson takes the opportunity to slip out of the room like the coward he is, and both Adrian and I try to break them up. Asher is doing his best to block my brother's hits without actually doing any harm, but after a few good punches, I can tell his graciousness is wearing off, and he's close to fighting back. In all the years that Dash and Asher have been friends, they've never come to blows.

"Knock it the fuck off!" Adrian shouts, separating them with a palm to each of their chests. I step in front of Asher just as Dash throws another punch. Ash shoves me out of the way and I stumble toward Whitley, but I catch myself. I turn my attention back to Dash and Asher, still trying to find my footing when I feel something abruptly pull me backward by my hair. I throw my arms out and try to twist around to brace myself for the fall, but something sharp hits my temple and then...nothing.

Black.

Just black.

CHAPTER 13

ASHER

I'm going to fuck Dash up. That's my only thought as I push Briar out of the way right before his fist makes contact with her face. I get it. I fucked up. But he's putting Briar in danger because he can't see past his anger.

I hear Whitley scream, and from the corner of my eye, I see Briar go down. She hits the side of her head on the table next to Whitley, sending the tray of coke flying. *Fuck. Fuck, fuck, fuck.*

"Briar!" I scream her name, but she doesn't move. Whitley stands there, gaping, and brings her hands to her mouth. I drop to my knees. I want to shake her, to lift her head and force her to look at me, but I know I shouldn't move her. Blood pools under her head, and I look to Dash, who's white as a fucking ghost.

"Call 911!"

Adrian breaks out of frozen fear, frantically feeling around for the phone in his pocket.

"Briar, baby, wake up. Why the fuck isn't she waking up?!"

This isn't happening. This isn't happening. Memories flash through my head of seeing my mom just like this, and I shake my head, violently, to rid myself of the images assaulting my mind. This is Briar, and this is different.

Everything is muffled, but I recognize Adrian's voice relaying the address to the police. The party below us still goes on, completely oblivious to what's taking place above their heads. Carefully, I try to move Briar onto her side. I think I remember reading that you're supposed to do that somewhere, and I can't sit here and do nothing.

"Get the fuck away from her," Dash says, breaking out of his shock. "You've done enough!" He steps forward and kneels next to her. His shaky hands reach out to touch her, but he stops himself. "You fucking pushed her. You did this!"

No.

No.

"Walk the fuck away, Ash."

But I can't. I won't. Even if that means the end of my friendship with Dash. I pick Briar. I'll choose Briar every fucking day if I have to.

She's still not waking up. Shouldn't she have

woken up by now? I want to argue with him. Tell him that I was trying to protect her from *him*, not hurt her. But, as I see her crimson blood spreading across the hardwood floor, I know that there has never been a clearer sign in my life. I'm no good for her.

"Whitley!" Adrian snaps, and she jumps, her eyes darting up to his. "Get everyone out of here. The party is over." She nods, panicked. "Now!" Adrian shouts, and she finally runs out of the room.

"Dash, keep her head and shoulders elevated, but don't move her neck." Dash closes his eyes and blows out his breath. "Okay. Okay, I got it."

"Kelley, go get a clean towel or a washcloth or something. We need to stop the bleeding."

I don't want to walk away from her. I feel like if I do... I can't even go down that road. She's going to be fine. She just bumped her head. Ignoring the fear that grips my throat, stealing all my air, and the blood on my boots, I bolt into action.

"How do you know all this? She's going to be okay, right?" I hear Dash ask Adrian as I'm walking out the door.

"When your mom is a doctor, you pick up a few things over the years."

I don't hear Dash's response. I run down the hall toward the bathroom we almost went into before. Fuck, how was that only twenty minutes ago? How did everything get this bad in so little time? I barge in on a couple—some guy getting head as he sits on the toilet and a redhead between his knees—and yell at them to get the fuck out. They both jump up, and he trips over his pants as they run away.

"Fuck!" I can't find a towel. Darting back into the hall, I see a door that's narrower than the others and hope to fuck it's a linen closet. I grab two thick, white towels and one washcloth and rush back to the room.

"She hasn't woken up?" I ask, sliding the towels underneath her head. The longer she's unconscious, the more I'm filled with a feeling of pure dread. Wisps of her blonde hair are stuck to the blood on her temple and cheek. Dash balled up his T-shirt, stopping the flow of blood, and he removes it to let me hold the washcloth there.

"Where the fuck is the ambulance?" Dash's panic-stricken voice echoes my thoughts. It feels like it's been hours, but in reality, it's probably only been about two minutes since she fell.

"I'm going to make sure everyone's out of the way and wait for them," Adrian says, leaving us alone with Briar.

"I can't..." I start, but my voice cracks. I clear my throat and try again. "I can't lose her. She's the only fucking good thing in my world."

"Stop. The only reason you're still here is because my sister needs me right now."

I want to tell him to try it. Just fucking try to make me leave. But now isn't the time. So, we wait in tense silence for what seems like days, until the paramedics or EMTs or whoever the fuck they are pile into the room. There's about six of them, two of them carrying a stretcher.

Natalia comes barreling in on their heels, all the color gone from her face.

"Oh my God!" she shrieks.

"How long has she been unconscious?" one of the paramedics asks.

"I don't know, fuck, maybe ten minutes?" Dash answers.

"What's her name?"

"Briar Vale."

"Briar, can you hear me?" another one asks, squatting down and checking her pulse. When she doesn't respond, he presses his knuckles hard against the center of her chest.

"The fuck are you doing?" I bark, just barely stopping myself from smacking his hand away. I think I see her stir, but I can't be sure.

"I'm testing her level of consciousness. Has she had anything to drink?"

"No, I don't think so," I reply, but, fuck, I'm not sure. "She hit her head on the corner of the table." I gesture to the nightstand and realize that no one even thought to clean up the drugs and paraphernalia. It's the last thing I'm worried about—it's not my shit—but the disapproving look the medic shoots me tells me he thinks he's got us all figured out.

"She wasn't drinking," Natalia chimes in, twisting

her hands together. "I gave her a cup of that punch, but she set it on the table without taking a sip."

"And she doesn't fucking do drugs," I add pointedly.

"Okay, let's get her to the hospital."

Briar's loaded up onto the stretcher and carried downstairs. My stomach rolls, and for a second, I think I'm going to throw up. I can't help but draw parallels to the way I lost my mom. The unresponsiveness, the blood. My phone rings, but I don't even look at it before hitting the *fuck you* button.

She's fine. She has to be.

Once outside, they ask who's riding with her to the hospital, and both Dash and I step forward.

"Only one," the medic snaps, looking between the two of us impatiently. "And figure it out soon or neither one of you is going." He turns his attention to lifting Briar into the ambulance, and even though I want nothing more than to fight for my place next to her, I know I need to let this one go.

"The only way you're riding in the ambulance with her is if you're in a goddamn body bag," Dash says in a low, threatening voice.

Shaking my head, I walk off wordlessly toward my truck. Except I'm blocked in by two other cars.

Fuck!

I'm seriously debating on hot-wiring a car—it's what I fucking do best, after all—when Natalia rolls up and motions for me to jump in.

"Need a ride?"

Tears are streaming down her face, but she tries to play it off with a shaky, unconvincing smile. Most of the time, Natalia is a pain in my ass. She's loud and opinionated, and I wish she came with a mute button. I tolerate her at best. But right now, we are the same. Two people who are trying to keep their shit together while the most important person in their lives is sitting in an ambulance.

I climb into her flashy little sports car that costs more than most people's homes. Her hand trembles as she reaches for the gear stick, and she stalls out. She smacks the steering wheel, and a frustrated growl leaves her mouth. I can tell she's losing it. Really fucking losing it. We don't have time to waste, so I place her hand on the shifter and cover it with my own. Her eyes shoot up to mine.

"Get it together. Briar needs us."

"Okay. Okay," she says, sounding like she's trying to convince herself.

"Breathe."

She does, inhaling and exhaling deeply.

"Now, let's fucking go."

She turns the key and pushes in the clutch, and this time, she doesn't stall. She accelerates, weaving in and out of traffic to catch up to the blue and red flashing lights, and stays on their tail all the way to the hospital. She follows it all the way up to the emergency entrance and lets me jump out before going to park the car.

I run toward the ambulance as they unload the stretcher that carries my fucking heart. The first thing I notice is that Dash is talking to her, reassuring her that everything is okay.

She's awake. She's fucking awake.

"Briar!" I yell as I get closer, and her panicked eyes follow the sound.

"Asher? What happened? Asher, please." She sounds desperate and confused, and I tell myself not to panic that she doesn't remember. That it's common with head injuries. *Right?*

"You're okay. It's going to be okay. I promise."

They wheel her into the hospital. The bright fluorescent lights and bustling of the busy ER are a stark contrast from the quiet night sky.

"You both need to wait out here," one of the paramedics says over his shoulder. "Someone will be out to update you soon."

"Asher, please don't leave me," Briar says, right before they go through the double doors that we aren't allowed to pass.

"I'll be here, baby. I'm not going anywhere," I shout after her.

And it's true. Nothing and *no one* could make me leave her. I pace the waiting room, hands crossed behind my head, while Dash opts to take a seat. I try to distract myself by counting the square tiles on the ceiling and making out shapes in the water stain that seeped through.

After a while, I notice him staring at me, his eyes following my every move with his arms crossed, expression contemplative.

"What?" I snap, annoyed.

"She asked for you."

Briar?

"When?"

"She asked for you right when she came to, and then she told you not to leave her. Not me. Any time she fell and scraped her knee or any time she forgot her lunch, she'd call me. Not my parents. *Me*. But she asked for you."

I don't know what to say to that. I don't know where he's going with it, either. So, I don't respond. After another minute or two, he breaks the silence again.

"She loves you," he says grudgingly.

I pause my pacing, and even though the words aren't coming from her, my heart starts to pound harder at the thought. I know he doesn't mean like a brother or a friend, or he wouldn't be upset at the idea.

"Yeah, well, I fucked that up."

Why couldn't I have just walked away? My actions caused this.

I take a seat two chairs away from him, with my elbows on my knees and my head in my hands. My phone rings again, and I silence it. Not a second later,

Natalia comes barging through the doors like a bat out of hell. She's still in her party dress, but her shoes dangle from her fingers.

"Where is she? Is she okay? Have you heard anything? They need better fucking parking. It took me ten minutes to find a spot. That's not really conducive to an *emergency situation*," she yells.

Annnnd, the motor mouth is back.

"Calm down, turbo. She's awake, but we aren't allowed to go back yet," I say, dropping my head back down.

"She's awake," she repeats, equal parts shock and relief lacing her Dash tone. "Thank fuck." Natalia tosses her shoes underneath the chair between Dash and me before collapsing into it like a sack of potatoes.

My phone goes off again from my pocket, and this time I'm ready to kill whoever is calling me. I check the screen—it's a private number.

"What?" I bark into the phone.

"Hi, yes, may I speak with Asher Kelley?" a man's deep voice asks.

"This is a bad fucking time. Whatever you're selling I'm not interested." I almost hang up, but his next words stop me.

"It's about your father. John Kelley? This is Doctor DuCane from Banner North. I need you to come to the hospital." His voice is firm, but somehow soft, and deep down, I already know what's coming.

"I, uh, I'm actually here already," I say, plugging

one ear with my finger and angling my body away from Dash and Natalia. "Is he okay?"

"Oh," he says, sounding surprised. "Where are you? I'd like to come speak with you personally."

The burning dread that had lessened to warm coals is back with a vengeance with each passing second.

"I'm in the emergency waiting room. Is he dead?" I ask bluntly, cutting to the chase. "Just fucking tell me."

I feel two sets of concerned eyes on me, but I ignore them both. I don't need anyone's pity, and I don't need this fucking doctor to come hold my hand.

"I'm on my way to you now," is all he says. I hang up the phone, flipping it around in my hands without looking up.

"Everything all right, man?" Dash asks tentatively.

I don't respond.

"Asher?" This time it's Natalia's worried voice.

"I'm fine." My harsh tone is enough to shut down any further questions. We sit in tense silence for I don't know how long before a man in a white coat calls my name.

"Asher Kelley?" His eyes scan the room. There aren't many people in here, which is unheard of for a weekend. A couple of moms and their sick kids, an elderly couple, and us. I stand, stuffing my hands into my front pockets.

"Is this your family?" he asks.

"No," I say at the same time Dash says, "Yes."

The doctor looks confused, but doesn't press.

"Can you both come with me?"

Dash hesitates, looking back at Natalia, and she assures him that she'll call him if there is any news on Briar. He nods, and we follow Dr. Bad News to a private room.

The room has a couple of chairs, a coffee table with magazines, a TV, and some miscellaneous games for kids, but is otherwise empty.

"Can you tell me what you know of your father's condition?" he starts.

"He has liver failure." I scratch at the stubble on my jaw. "That's about all I know."

"Yes. His condition has been worsening over the past couple of weeks. Were you aware?"

I clench my jaw. He didn't tell me that. He didn't even *hint* at it.

"No," I say through gritted teeth.

"His nurse found him when she went in for her shift."

"His nurse?" I ask, my eyebrows drawing together in confusion. Maybe he has the wrong guy. "My father didn't have a nurse."

"He finally agreed to hospice care about a week ago. He didn't tell you that, either?"

"No, I guess not."

He steps forward, his hand coming down to my shoulder. I stare at it. He continues, "We did everything we could. Unfortunately, his cirrhosis was too advanced."

He keeps speaking, but I don't hear the words. *"We did everything we could."* Everyone knows what that means.

At some point, Dash starts answering for me, though I still can't make out any of their conversation. My mom is dead. My dad is dead. Briar is lying, hurt, somewhere in this hospital. And the common denominator is me.

"Would you like to see him?" The doctor's voice breaks through my thoughts. I shake my head. What's the point, right? He's dead.

"Let me know if you change your mind, but it needs to be relatively soon," he says gently, holding out a card. Dash takes it. "My cell is on the back. Let me know if there's anything I can do. Again, I'm very sorry for your loss."

Another shoulder pat, then he's gone.

"Asher…" Dash says, letting my name hang between us. The words sound foreign from his mouth. He doesn't call me Asher. He calls me Kelley. I don't think he's called me by my first name once in the six years we've been friends. And for some reason, it enrages me. It makes everything more real. He wouldn't be calling me that if shit weren't fucked up.

I knew this was coming. It's the whole reason I came back. So, why does it seem like the rug has been pulled out from beneath me?

Dash's phone buzzes, and he reads the message on his screen.

"The nurse said Briar's okay. She just has a mild concussion, and we can see her in a few minutes."

I'm relieved, so fucking relieved, but I feel heavy. Like a dark cloud is over my head, tainting everything and everyone I come in contact with.

Dash walks toward the door and pauses, looking back at me when he realizes I'm not making a move to leave. "You coming?"

"I just need a minute."

He dips his chin in acknowledgment and pats the doorframe. He hesitates—searching for the right words —but there aren't any, so he walks out, leaving me to the maelstrom of emotions going through me.

My mom died because of me. My dad essentially died because he couldn't handle life without her, which again, comes back on me. He died alone. That one's my fault, too. And Briar. If I hadn't insisted on going upstairs. If I had walked away from Jackson, instead of letting my rage control me, she wouldn't be here. I shouldn't have come back. And if I stick around much longer, I'm sure it will be too late for her, too.

Dash and Natalia are waiting on me. Briar's fucking waiting on me. My father is waiting on me. I don't want to face any of them, and stronger than anything I've ever experienced is the urge to bolt. I can't fucking be here. I feel like I can't breathe. My pulse hammers in my ears, and the room spins around me. Bending over and bracing my hands on my knees, I squeeze my eyes shut and try to suck in air, to no avail. I can't get enough into my lungs.

I need out. Out of this room. Out of this hospital. Out of this town. Then, maybe I'll be able to breathe again.

CHAPTER 14

BRIAR

My head is pounding. That was my first thought when I woke up in an ambulance, followed closely by *how did I get here?* Dash explained what happened, and slowly, the events of the last hour started coming back in pieces. Fighting. Lots of fighting. Lots of revelations. More fighting. Whitley pulling me backward by my hair. Then, darkness.

Once we got into the room, the nurse took my vitals and helped me change into a hospital gown before the doctor came in to examine me. Now, besides having a splitting headache, I feel fine. I want to get out of here so I can talk to Asher—privately—about everything that went down. I can't wrap my mind around everything that came out tonight.

The door slowly creaks open, allowing a sliver of light into the room, followed by a light knock.

"Bry?" my brother asks.

"Come in."

Dash and Nat step in with uncharacteristically long faces.

"Whoa, who died?" I joke, trying to lighten the mood, but they don't laugh. They share a look that sends my heart free-falling to my feet.

"Are you okay?" Nat asks, changing the subject. She comes to sit on the bottom of the bed next to me and brushes my hair out of my face to assess the damage.

"I'm good," I say, looking between them. "Did something happen?" Natalia looks up to Dash for permission, and that right there tells me that it's bad. Since when does she defer to him? Or anyone, for that matter? Dash shakes his head.

"Tell me," I demand. "Is it Asher? Is he okay?"

Dash's nostrils flare, and I don't even care to have the good sense to be sensitive to the fact that he just found out that his little sister and his best friend have been sneaking around behind his back.

"He's fine, but his dad died tonight."

My hand flies to my mouth, and I feel my eyes welling with tears. I swing my legs over the edge of the bed, needing to find him.

"Where is he?" I ask, hopping down. "I need to be with him."

"Hell no, sis," Nat says, pushing me back toward the bed. "I get it. I do. But you need to make sure you're okay before you go saving someone else."

"She's right. Besides, he said he'll be here. He just needed a minute to wrap his brain around everything."

I reluctantly agree, sitting back and pulling the cover over my freezing legs—why are hospitals always so cold, anyway? But somehow, I know Asher isn't coming. I can feel it in my bones.

The doctor walks back in, stopping to wash his hands at the sink. "So, I have good news and bad news. Which do you want to hear first?" he says by way of greeting.

"Good," I answer, because I'm not sure how much more bad I can handle in one night.

"Well, the good news is that you'll be fine. Slight concussion. No need for a CT scan or anything like that since you weren't unconscious very long and you're not having any prolonged amnesia. It's been about two hours since you got here, so we probably would've noticed by now if things were going to take a turn for the worse."

I nod, relieved.

"And the bad news?" Dash asks, arms folded across his chest.

"The bad news is that you have a nasty gash there," he says, pointing two fingers in the direction of my head, "and you're going to need a couple of stitches."

"That's it? When can I go home?"

"Well, seeing as how it's..." he turns his wrist over to check his watch, "three in the morning, I'd rather have you stay here for a few more hours just as a precaution. I'll let you go before shift change at around eight. Sound good?"

No, it doesn't sound good at all, I want to say. Ash needs me. But I don't. I let him stitch me up, try to convince Nat and Dash to go get some sleep, and watch *Supernatural* reruns for the next six hours, all while calling Ash over and over until my phone finally dies.

It's eight forty-six by the time the doctor comes in with my discharge papers. I've been dressed and ready to go since seven.

"All right, Miss Briar," he starts, flipping through the paperwork. "You have a mild concussion. You might have a headache for a few days, so try to take it easy. Unless you're planning to play any contact sports, you should be good to go back to life as you know it.

"Here are the do's and don'ts and what to watch for. If you experience any of these things," he instructs, circling a section with his pen, "come straight back to the hospital. Any questions?"

"Nope," I say, signing his copy. He gives me one more warning about taking it easy, and then we're free to leave.

"I need to find Asher. Do you know what room his dad is in?" I don't waste any time asking. Both Dash and Nat shake their heads. Ignoring their protests, I run in the direction of the nurses' station with both of them trailing behind me. I smack my hands down on the desk, feeling out of breath and a little dizzy, but I can't focus on anything other than finding Ash right now.

"Hi, can you tell me what room John Kelley is in?"

The tired nurse doesn't even look up from her computer.

"Are you family?"

"No. It's my boyfriend's father," I lie, ignoring the disapproving look on Dash's face at the word *boyfriend*. I don't know what we are, but "my sometimes fuck buddy, and sometimes enemy" isn't going to get me the information I need.

"I'm sorry," she says, finally looking up at me beneath thick-rimmed glasses. "I can't release patient information unless you're family."

"Okay, then that's *my* father," I say through clenched teeth as Dash pulls me away by the elbow, apologizing on my behalf.

"Briar, you need to calm down. He wouldn't be in his room. He'd be in the morgue by now. You've had no sleep and a fucking concussion. Let's go home. Maybe he's there," Dash says, and Nat nods in agreement.

I know he's just trying to get me back home, but I agree because he could be right. If I know Asher at all, he's not sitting at John's bedside. He's either running or trying to numb any of the feelings that threaten to penetrate his wall of indifference. And everything he owns is currently at my house, so it's a good a place to start as any.

Ignoring the throbbing in my temple, we make our way toward the exit and pile into Nat's little car. I take the back seat, thankful for the chance to be alone with my thoughts. I close my eyes and rest my head against the black leather. So many different thoughts war for my attention. My dad sending Asher away and never saying a word. Whitley's part in all of this. God, all these years, I thought she was just an annoyance. I had no idea that she was at the root of everything. What must Asher have thought of me? This entire time, he thought I betrayed him. That explains why he was so cold to me at first, but why would he ever get close to me again? And John. Gone, just like that. It's hard to believe we just visited him, and he was up, walking around, eating food, and carrying on a conversation. It's funny how everything can change in an instant. And by funny, I mean fucked up.

Any hope that I had dies the moment we pull up to the house and Asher's truck is nowhere to be found. My pulse quickens as I punch in the code and walk inside. I can smell the faint trace of his cologne, and I can't figure out whether it's real or just my desperate mind willing it to be.

I go straight for the media room. His bag is gone. I check the hall closet that he sometimes used—nothing but sheets and blankets—and right here and now, I know he's gone for good. Only this time, it's so much worse. He let me fall in love with him. And he let me have just a taste of what it felt like to be loved by him, too. Then he took it away, leaving that hole inside of me even hollower than before.

I don't know what it is—the weight of everything hitting me at once, or maybe just the lack of sleep—but I break down. Tears flood my face before I even feel them coming.

"He's gone," I cry, turning around, and Natalia's in front of me in an instant, bringing my head to her chest and shushing me like a child as she runs her hand down the back of my head in a soothing gesture. "Why did I let it happen again? Why do I do this to myself?" I knew I was playing with fire. I was bound to get burned. But rebellious hearts know no consequences. Bad habits are easy to make and impossible to break, and Asher was the worst addiction of them all. I let him crawl inside my body, and he burned me from the inside out, leaving nothing but ashes in his absence.

"Bry," Dash says in a hushed tone, and then I feel his hand on my shoulder. I turn to face him, and he pulls me in under his arm. I hug his waist to keep from slumping to the floor. I'm just so tired. Tired of lying, tired of sneaking around, of being hurt, of trying to please everyone.

"Why would Dad send him away?" I ask through the lump in my throat. "None of this makes sense."

Dash kisses the top of my head and squeezes my shoulder.

"I don't fucking know, but I'm going to find out."

He says it with such conviction that I don't doubt him for a second. And even though Asher is gone and nothing in my world seems good, I take comfort in the fact that I have my brother on my side. Someone who loves Asher as much as I do.

"Listen to me," Dash says with more authority than I'm used to hearing in his voice. "I know you're upset, and I know that everything is fucked up. But, I need you to get some rest. I'll make you something to eat, and then you need to sleep."

I don't argue, because I know he's right. Only I don't know how I'm supposed to sleep when my whole world was just turned upside down. Natalia follows me to my room, and I pull out my favorite bloodstained T-shirt before climbing into bed and curling up in a ball on my side. Nat settles in behind me. We lie in silence for a while, waiting for Dash, as she plays with my hair—my occasional sniffle or hiccup the only sounds. I must be a pathetic sight right now, crying into Asher's T-shirt as my best friend tries to console me, but I'm too pathetic to even care in this moment. My head hurts from crying—or the fall, or maybe both— and my stomach growls, reminding me that I haven't eaten since yesterday afternoon.

I close my eyes, pretending that Ash is still here. He'd sneak into my room and wrap his arms around me, telling me that everything would be okay. That no one else matters but us. If I try hard enough, I can feel his breath on my neck and his stubble against my cheek. Eventually, exhaustion beats heartbreak, and I feel myself drifting off to sleep with Asher's ghost.

CHAPTER 15

ASHER

ONE WEEK LATER...

"The fuck!" I groan, my voice hoarse as hell as I'm woken up by freezing water being sprayed on me. *Where the fuck am I, and why is it so bright?* I shield my eyes from the sun with my forearm and survey my surroundings. I'm in someone's front yard, facedown in the grass. Not just anyone's lawn—Dare's—and he's standing over me with the hose pointed in my direction.

"Morning, Sunshine," he deadpans. I have a solid thirty seconds of being blissfully unaware before I remember why I'm here and the events that led up to it. I ran, literally *ran*, the four miles from the hospital to Adrian's place. Hopped in my truck, drove to Briar and Dash's to grab my shit, and then hit the highway, heading straight for River's Edge. I showed up at Dare's door twelve hours later, then told him about the last couple of months, while I drank myself into oblivion. *How did everything get so fucked up?*

"You had your pity party. Time to man up and deal with it."

"Fuck off, Dare. I don't need your big brother shit right now."

"I don't really give a shit what you think you need. I know from experience that you're about to spiral, and then you're going to spend the rest of your life regretting it. Trust me on this one."

That might be the most Dare has ever divulged about himself in one sentence. I know something happened, and I've always gotten the feeling that it was a tragedy, but I've never asked him. Dare likes to talk even less than I do.

I stand up, brushing off the pieces of grass stuck to my bare stomach and follow Dare inside. The house is just like I remembered it. A cabin style home with vaulted ceilings sitting right on the lake. It's still pretty bare. A couple of couches in front of a huge stone fireplace. A couple of rooms with beds upstairs—one of them mine—and not a lot else. Not even a TV, which has made for a very boring week. Dare's been tattooing at the new shop he opened, and I've been doing a lot of drinking myself into oblivion and sleeping. Rinse, repeat.

"It's been a week," Dare says, handing me a cup of coffee, his not-so-subtle way of sobering me up. "You need to bury your dad, man."

The mug is scorching, but I ignore the burn as I clench it so tight that I expect it to shatter in my hands. I've been in contact with the funeral home. John made most of the arrangements on his own. He's to be buried right next to my mom. He was an organ donor, which is pretty goddamn ironic if you ask me, so the process takes a little longer than it would otherwise. And now, they're just waiting on me. But I can't go back. I won't.

Briar. Just thinking her name feels like a fist around my heart. I left her in a fucking hospital bed. She was only there because of me in the first place.

"Asher, please don't leave me."

Her voice haunts me, and I squeeze my eyes shut. I promised her I wouldn't leave her, and even though it's for her own good, I can't stop picturing how it must have felt when she realized I wasn't there, and again when it was clear that I wasn't coming back. I told her this would happen. This, right here, is what I was trying to avoid. But, what I feel for Briar transcends logic, rules, and societal norms. She's so deeply ingrained in me, that I'm not even me without her. My best side was her worst creation.

None of that matters, though. I'm not the one for her. I don't belong in that town with those people. Briar is inherently *good*, while I'm rotten, and it only takes one bad apple to spoil the whole bunch.

CHAPTER 16

BRIAR

DAY EIGHT

My parents are coming. It took them an entire week to check the voicemail that the doctor left on my mom's cell phone, informing them that their daughter was hospitalized. To their credit, they hopped on the next flight out, as soon as they heard. The utter despair I've been feeling for the past week shifts into anger, and my blood boils thinking about my dad's part in all this. My father isn't the softest man in the world, not by a long shot, but I didn't think he was capable of something like this. Especially not when it hurts his own children. But, clearly, I was mistaken.

I stretch out my legs from the fetal position I've spent the majority of the past week in and yawn. I've done nothing but sleep and watch *Tombstone* from my bed. I can't even use the media room anymore because it hurts too much. He managed to ruin my favorite place.

"Fucker," I mutter under my breath.

I've called the funeral home, but they didn't have any information on services planned for John. He wasn't a bad man. He was a man who sometimes did bad things. A man who couldn't deal with all the hurt inside him, so he pushed his son and everyone else away while he quite literally drank himself to death. My worst fear is Asher suffering the same fate. I thought I could be that person for him. I thought I could make him happy. Because even through all the dysfunction, the sneaking around, and the lies, he made me happy. He made me whole. I promised myself I wouldn't let him complete me. I didn't want to fall in love. Falling in like, and then losing him, was hard enough.

I hear the shrill, neurotic voice of my mother coming through the front door, her heels clacking against the hardwood floors. My father is silent, but I know he's with her. I blow out a deep breath, rolling onto my back, bracing myself for them to come barging through my door. Swinging my legs over the side, I sit up on the edge of the bed.

"Briar!" Mom shrieks, running into my room. She

bends at the waist, taking my face in her hands, checking to see if I'm still whole. And I am, on the outside, save for some stiches and some gnarly bruises. But the inside is another story. I don't speak. I don't move. I'm limp as I stare straight at my father while she checks me over. He's foreboding in his sharp suit and crossed arms. He looks ruffled. Concerned. But it's all an act. His tall frame takes up the entire doorway, but he doesn't intimidate me one bit. Not right now. A loaded gun wouldn't scare me at this point.

"Sweetheart," Mom says, tipping my chin up to force me to look at her. "What's going on?"

"Ask him," I say, jerking my chin out of her bony fingers.

My dad doesn't even have the decency to look guilty. He arches a brow, jaw clenched, and straightens his tie.

"What is she talking about?" Mom asks, looking genuinely confused. Maybe she wasn't in on it. Maybe he didn't even tell her.

"That's a good question, Nora. Because I don't have a goddamn clue."

"Oh, so you didn't have Asher sent away?"

"Asher?" Mom questions. "What does that boy have to do with anything?"

I roll my eyes at her referring to him as *that boy* when she's known him for years.

"Of course, I did," he shocks me by saying, not an ounce of apology in his tone. "I get an anonymous email, at work, no less, containing a photo of my four-teen-year-old daughter lip-locked with the trash of the town."

"*Excuse me?!*" Mom interrupts.

I'm fuming. My face and ears get hot, and my nails dig into my palms, leaving bloody, little half-moon indents.

"He was nearly an adult, preying on my *child*. A drug addict. He was corrupting both you and Dash. I could've had his ass thrown in jail. Probably should've. I was pretty generous, if you ask me."

"You're kidding, right?" I stand, walking closer to him. He appears slightly taken aback. Like I'm overre-acting, and he hasn't a clue why.

"You have no idea what you set in motion. What your actions caused. He thought I betrayed him this whole time. That I sent him away and used you to do it."

"No, dear daughter, that was all him. He's respon-sible for his own actions."

"You almost got him killed!" I scream, unable to stay calm any longer. "You sent him to someone even worse than his father, and he almost didn't make it out alive."

My mom's eyes dart back and forth between the two of us, like she's watching a tennis match, as she struggles to put the pieces of the puzzle together.

"How could you just play with someone's life like that? You think you're God? You're a coward hiding behind money and power. And you're not the man I thought you were."

I've finally broken through that cool exterior. He takes a calming breath, nostrils flaring, as he steps closer, pointing a finger in my face.

"Not God. But I am your father. And I will do what I think is best for my children, regardless of how it rates on your moral meter. He's bad news, Briar. A *predator*. And I wasn't going to wait around until you figured it out for yourself."

"That's where you're wrong," I say, batting the angry tears away from my face. God, I'm so sick of *crying*. "Because you'll never be half the man he already is. He's kind and *good* and loyal and resilient. He's overcome more in his twenty-one years than you could even dream of."

He scoffs, rolling his eyes toward the ceiling, and his reaction pushes me to hammer in the final nail in my coffin. What's the worst he could do? The damage has already been done.

"I love him."

My dad's face reddens, and I think his teeth might crack under the pressure of his steeled jaw. Without saying a word, he turns on his heels, slamming the door behind him. He slams it so hard that the framed picture of Dash, Ash, and me falls from the shelf next and shatters onto my desk below it. My mom scurries over to clean it up, sweeping the shards into her hand.

"Mom. Stop."

She doesn't.

"Mom."

She bends down, picking pieces out of the carpet.

"Mom! I don't care about the fucking glass right now!"

That finally gets her attention. Her head snaps up, eyes wide.

"Of course, you don't. You've never cared about making messes. *Someone* has to care about the mess!"

I get the feeling that she's not talking about the state of my room. She looks like she's holding back tears, and I wonder if something else is going on. Her tone softens when she sees my shocked expression. She drops the glass into the trash can next to my desk and brushes off her hands.

"I'm sorry," she says softly. "I was so worried about you when I got the message. And then I felt like the worst parent on the planet. What kind of a mother doesn't know her own child is in the hospital?"

"It's okay," I'm quick to assure her. "I had Dash." But the truth is, it's not okay. And I don't know why my first instinct is always to placate her.

"I envy you, Briar Victoria. Your brother has the title of being a rebel, but you... You've always marched to the beat of your own drum, even when it drove me insane." She laughs bitterly.

She couldn't shock me more if she decided to slap me in the face.

"Doing the right thing comes naturally to you," she adds. "That's why I wasn't worried about you staying behind when we moved. Knowing the right thing is easy. *Doing* it is the hard part. You've never had that problem. So, if you think that Asher is worth your heart, then I have to trust that. I know better than anyone what happens when you don't follow your heart."

This is the first time my mom has ever, in my life, said something like this. She's always been so closed-off, and though I've never once doubted her love for me, I never felt like she understood me. She's prim and proper, and everything is black or white in her eyes. I'm messy, and I see the world in shades of gray. But seeing her this raw and unfiltered humanizes her. I feel like I've seen the first glimpse of Eleanor Vale the person, not the mother.

Closing the distance between us, I wrap my arms around her neck, hugging her tightly. She's stock-still for a moment before she hugs me back just as tight and kisses the uninjured side of my head.

"So, where is he?" she asks, pulling back, wiping the wetness from under her perfectly lined eyes.

"Asher?" I ask.

"I'm assuming he's the one who's been staying here? It was his truck that was in the driveway that day, wasn't it?"

I nod, feeling guilty for the first time about keeping it from her.

"And to say that he's why you disappeared from the fundraiser would be a safe assumption?"

I clear my throat and look away and sit down on the bed, suddenly feeling embarrassed. Like she knows exactly what happened up on that balcony.

"I figured as much," she admits, raising a brow. "You were always close. A little *too* close. And very protective of each other."

I almost laugh, because it's true. Asher has always been that way. But I'm just as protective of him. I've always felt the need to come to his defense and shield him from the condescending comments and judgment from the people of Cactus Heights, even when I know he'd rather I kept my mouth shut. He always thought he wasn't good enough, but the opposite is true.

"That's because he's worth protecting. I knew it even then." I feel those stupid tears stinging my eyes again, and I pick at the nonexistent lint on my duvet.

"I feel like I'm missing something," Mom confesses, her forehead wrinkling in confusion. "Why are you upset?"

"John Kelley died the night I was in the hospital."

"Oh my God," she says, sitting down beside me on the bed.

"Ash didn't take it well." I don't know why I'm telling her any of this. It doesn't feel natural, like I need to keep my secrets and feelings guarded. I keep waiting for her disapproving look or her condescending tone. But at the same time, I so desperately want to have this kind of relationship with her. She made an effort, so now it's my turn. "This time it's over for good, and I'm scared to death about what that means."

"I doubt that very much."

"What makes you say that?"

"He thought you sent him away, right? And he still came back to you."

"He didn't," I argue. "He came back for his dad."

"That's not what I said. He may have come back *for* his dad, but he came back *to* you."

It doesn't matter, anyway. It's a moot point. If he cared, he wouldn't have left me in that hospital room after I begged him to stay. Even if he did decide to come back, it's too little too late. I could forgive him, but I couldn't ever forget.

CHAPTER 17

ASHER

I stare at the old message on my screen, like I've been doing for the past hour, ignoring the texts from Dash and Adrian and everyone else. Briar was texting me "Glycerine" lyrics the other day before any of this happened. Lyrics about not letting the days go by. Lyrics that I could admit are fitting, if I wasn't so stubborn.

I can still remember the night I played it for her. She closed her eyes, her long lashes resting on the tops of her still-round cheeks. Her black combat boots—that I was ninety-nine percent sure she begged her mom to buy her because I wore the same kind—were covered in dirt and dust and dangled off the hood of my car as she listened. She fell in love with that song, and I watched it happen. It was one of the first times I had ever felt like I had anything to offer Briar. I didn't have money. I didn't have anything, but I gave her a song and she liked it.

I think about responding. I type and delete, type and delete, before deciding against it. *This is how it needs to be.* I smooth my hair back with both hands before dropping my head to the back of the couch. *She didn't do it.* This entire week has been a daze. I haven't had time to process anything that went down except for Briar getting hurt and my dad dying. Fucking Whitley. I should've known she would stoop to that level. That girl is made up of equal parts jealousy and daddy issues.

All this time, I thought Briar was lying. And she had no idea why I hated her—no idea that her own father was in on it. *Fuck, there's no going back now.* I've put her through too much. The sound of her pleading with me not to leave haunts me every fucking day. Every hour. Every minute. I couldn't set aside my feelings for once and just fucking *be there* for her.

Sound familiar? A voice in my head taunts me. The realization hits me like a goddamn freight train. I've turned into my father.

"Hey, fucker," Dare barks, snapping me out of my self-loathing. "I need your help on the roof tonight. There's a storm coming, and I have about three days to finish it. That is, unless you've got someplace else to be..." he trails off, in a not-so-subtle hint to deal with my life back in Cactus Heights.

"Jesus Christ, you nag worse than a chick."

"Well, fuck. Someone has to. So, either get your ass on my roof or go home. And for fuck's sake, take a shower. You're starting to smell like roadkill."

I hurl one of the couch pillows at his head, but he smacks it away. I scratch at a week's worth of not shaving. He has a point.

"Give me twenty minutes and I'll be up." Dare shoots me a look I don't care to decipher. If I didn't know any better, I'd think he was disappointed with my answer.

"What?" I ask, irritated.

"Nothing," he says, holding his hands up in mock surrender. "I just never took you for a pussy."

"Fuck off."

I know I need to go back. I need to bury my dad and put Cactus Heights and everyone in it behind me —once and for all.

And I will.

Just not today.

BRIAR

TWO WEEKS.

Two weeks have gone by, and it feels like an eternity. I called the funeral home yesterday, and they said John wasn't having a service, but they did get the green light to proceed with the burial. If Asher's back, or planning on attending, I haven't heard anything about it. My brother only knew John as the guy who beat the shit out of his best friend. Not the guy who was so over-whelmed with grief that he couldn't function. Not the man who became a pseudo friend to me when I didn't have anyone else. So, it's safe to say he's not going. Not to mention the fact that Dash still isn't happy about us. I see it in the way his jaw hardens when Asher's name comes up, and the hurt in his eyes when he's faced with the reality that we both lied to him, repeatedly. Two selfish hearts, hiding and lying and sneaking, with blatant disregard to anyone else.

I thought about not going. Why should I? I barely knew John in the grand scheme of things, and it's not like he was the best person in the world. Would Asher be upset by my presence? Is it appropriate for me to attend? All of these questions ran through my mind, but my gut kept telling me that none of that mattered. All morning, I've been thinking about that pigeon—the one Asher buried for me when I was a kid—and I had my answer.

With one last glance into the mirror, I take in my old black combat boots and matching knee-high stockings. My face mostly devoid of makeup. This is a day for mourning, after all. Mourning the death of the grieving father who hasn't really been alive in years. Mourning the boy who lost both parents too soon. But most of all, I'm mourning the death of Asher and me. He abandoned me in that hospital. He broke his promise. Today is the day I bury the idea of us for good.

I tuck my wavy hair behind my ear, smooth the skirt of my simple black dress, and take a fortifying breath. The house is empty and strangely silent when I step out of my room. Dad went to stay at a hotel the first night before catching a flight back to California the next day, while Mom opted to stay with me for a few days. It was weird, but...*nice*, having her around. And I have a feeling I'll be seeing more of her.

Dash, Adrian, and Nat have been taking turns handling me with kid gloves. I've told them repeatedly that I'm fine, and I am. I think. Nat had to do inventory for her mom's shop today, and I talked my brother and Adrian into going to letting me breathe for five minutes, so I'm alone for the first time since *the incident*. That's what I'm calling it now. It easier than saying, "That night when everyone's secrets came to light, I got a concussion, Asher's dad died, and then he left me without a word. Again."

I walk outside, and the heat chokes me, even though it's gloomy and overcast. The sky mimics my somber mood as I make my way to my car. I pause, halfway down the walkway when I see them. Mom's succulents. I bend over, plucking two of them from their place in the garden. The excess dirt crumbles to the pavers at my feet. I'm reminded of the pigeon once again and how Asher risked crossing my mother by picking one of her precious succulents to give it a proper burial.

I'm on autopilot as I turn the ignition and drive to the All Souls Cemetery. I carefully place the plants into the bag in my passenger seat, thinking about how everything has changed in just a couple of short months. It's been messy and emotional and awful and wonderful. People say it's better to have loved and lost than to never have loved at all, but those people have never been in love with Asher Kelley. He doesn't dole out his love freely. He's stingy with it, and when you're on the receiving end, it feels like you've been awarded this extremely rare gift. Being loved by him is magic, but being left by him is tragic.

It's surreal. I've driven past this cemetery more times than I can count. But it was never anything more than scenery, until now. I never thought about what was actually behind those gates. Inching past them, I find myself looking for Asher, without making a conscious decision to do so. I give myself a mental slap to the face. He's not coming. He's doing what he does best. Running.

The parking lot is crowded, so it takes me a few minutes before I find an open space. I follow the signs for tier nine, and plot forty-two, stopping to let a mob of grieving men, women, and children make their way to their loved one's gravesite. Funny how people die every day, but the world keeps spinning, blissfully unaware. It makes me feel small and insignificant in this big world.

When I finally find plot forty-two, there's one, single man standing with his head bowed, hands crossed in front of him with a Bible clasped in his fingers.

"Excuse me," I say, pulling out my phone to double-check the information I was given. "Am I late?" The elderly bald man looks up, shock written all over his face.

"No," he says, clearing his throat. "You're the first one."

I nod as I check the time—five after noon. He stands near the double headstone that reads *Kelley* in all capitals, with Isabel's name on the left and John's on the right. The dates aren't carved in on his side yet, and I think of how incredibly bizarre and depressing it must be to plan your own funeral.

We wait in silence for another ten minutes before it's clear that no one else is coming.

"Shall we proceed?"

I'm tempted to tell him not to bother. That it's just me, and he doesn't need to go through the trouble. But that doesn't feel right, so I bow my head politely, while he makes his speech and says his prayers. When he asks if I want to say a few words, I'm caught off guard.

But, I'm the only person here, after all. I approach the oak casket with hesitant steps.

I don't know what to say. I feel like it's a betrayal to say anything good about him, but I also feel that it would be a disservice to send him off without a kind word.

"I once read that true redemption is when guilt leads to good," I whisper, scooping up a handful of dirt from the bucket in the officiant's outstretched hands. "And you've done good, John. You healed a piece of Asher's soul." I sprinkle the dirt onto the casket before thanking the man. I start to walk away, but then I stop short and pivot back around.

"Almost forgot," I say, kneeling next to the head-stone. I fish the succulents out of my bag and place them both in the middle—one for each.

I stand, dusting off my stockings, take a deep breath, and walk away.

CHAPTER 18

ASHER

My father didn't want a service. Maybe he didn't want to be a burden, or maybe he was afraid no one would show—which wouldn't be off-base. Even I struggled with the decision. I wasn't going to come. In my mind, attending his burial meant excusing every single shitty thing he's ever done. Every mistake. Every bad decision. I was too full of rage and resentment to have any room for reason or rationale.

After I sobered up for the first time since that fucked-up night, I realized I didn't want to become my father. I didn't want to be on my deathbed, wishing I could go back and change it all. Dare insisted on driving me, and we hauled ass to get back into town at the crack of dawn. I was late, but I made it before I was forced to add yet another regret to my list. Two men were in the process of lowering him into the earth. Once they saw me approach, they stopped turning the handle to the device that lowered the casket. Silently, they walked away, one of them dipping his head as if to say *take your time*.

So, here I am, peering down at the box that holds what's left of my father. The man who raised me. He never took me fishing or camping. He wasn't the type. But he never missed a swim meet, and I knew he loved me underneath that tough exterior. It's also the man who later neglected me, abused me, and blamed me for my mom's death. I didn't fault him for the last one back then. I blamed me, too. But, fuck. I was just a kid. A kid who needed his fucking dad.

I look over to the left, seeing my mother's grave, and my throat gets tight. Every year, it gets harder to hold on to the memories, but I can still recall the way she smelled, like vanilla and coffee. And how she'd stay up until all hours of the night to help me beat Donkey Kong or Zelda—or whatever video game I was into at the time—but in reality, she was just as hooked as I was.

Even then, people had something to say about our family. We never fit in. My parents weren't perfect. I remember being in third grade when I heard one of the other moms talking about my parents. She said she was too young, dressed too provocatively, and wanted too much attention. My dad didn't make enough money, drank too much, and didn't care to rub elbows with the right people. We were branded as being white trash, but back then, we were happy.

I think about how I would've reacted if I were in my dad's shoes. How would I cope if the love of my life died in such a sudden, tragic way? Briar pops into my head, unbidden, with her long, blonde hair and the face of a fucking angel. I know without a doubt, if anything ever happened to her, I'd burn the fucking world down. I'm not excusing him or the things he's done. It simply means I can understand him.

I'm truly alone now, I think to myself. I don't have any family left, except my piece of shit uncle who's either lying low or sitting in jail, judging by the fact that I haven't seen or heard from him since he tried to act tough at my dad's house. And I've managed to fuck up my relationships with the only two other people I considered family—three if you count Adrian. I'm sure I'm on his shit list by default.

A hand claps down on my shoulder, reminding me of Dare's presence. He doesn't say anything, just offers his silent support. His way of reassuring me that maybe I'm not completely alone. He knows better than anyone how scary a place your own head can be. Everyone has regrets, but some people are consumed by the mistakes of their past. Dare is one of those people.

"I'll wait in the truck," Dare says before walking away.

I pinch the bridge of my nose, unsure of what to say, what to do. I feel like I should have some epic last words. Something deep and life-changing. But I don't. So, I say the only thing that feels right. The only thing that's true.

"I forgive you."

And I do. Not for him, but for me. Because I don't want this shit to define me or control me. I look up to their shared headstone, and something catches my eye that I didn't see before.

Succulents. Purple fucking succulents.

Everyone deserves to be buried by something pretty.

I step forward and squat down to inspect them closer, turning one with my fingertips. Fresh dirt still clings to the roots as if they've just been plucked. She came, even though she hates me—even though I abandoned her. She was most likely the one person to show up for my dad's burial.

God, that girl. Could she be any more perfect? Could I be any more undeserving? Through it all, it's always been Briar. Even when she was just a shy, yet curious kid, she cared for me. Defended me. Cried for me. Me, the asshole who took advantage of her childish crush and left her without a word, only to come back and fuck with her head some more. Me, who never gave her the benefit of the doubt, and just assumed she'd be quick to betray me, though she'd never given me any reason to believe she would.

I know I said I'd let her go—that it was for her own

good—but I'm too selfish to stay away. Family isn't just about who shares your blood. It's about who bleeds for you. Needs you. And I'm fucking done allowing anything else to matter. Not her parents or even Dash. Not our age difference. Not the fact that she's the epitome of everything good in this world and that I'm constantly walking the line between right and wrong. *This* is right. *We* are right. Fuck everything else.

I place the succulent back down onto my parents' headstone and stand, filled with purpose for the first time in, well, ever. I need to find Briar.

The minute I see Dash's truck in the drive, I know I'm going to have to prove myself to two people, instead of one. Mentally preparing myself for the fight, I take a deep breath and raise my fist to knock on the door.

"Is this a fucking joke right now?" Dash says upon opening the door. He glances behind him briefly before slipping out the front door and closing it behind him. "The fuck do you want, man?"

"I need to see her."

Dash huffs and turns his back on me.

"Wait," I say as his hand grasps the lever. He pauses. "I know I fucked up, but give me the chance to make it right with her."

It's awkward, talking to him like this. About his

sister, no less. But Briar has a way of kicking my pride to the back seat. Dash turns around, and the eyes that match Briar's are filled with contempt.

"There is no *making it right*," he says through gritted teeth. "You betrayed our friendship. You took advantage of her, and then you left her when she needed you. There's nothing else to say."

"You have no fucking idea what you're talking about," I say, trying to rein in my temper. I'm doing my best to play nice. I know I'm in the wrong here, but he doesn't know what Briar and I have. He doesn't know how deep my feelings for her run. He doesn't know that it's always been her. I just need a chance to fix it.

"If you care about her, let her go. Stop dicking her around. She's having a hard enough time as it is."

"Is she okay?" I ask, immediately concerned.

"Just let her go," he says, shaking his head and stepping inside.

And then I'm left staring at the closed door. But I can't let her go. I don't know how.

CHAPTER 19

BRIAR

I power off my phone and toss it into the drawer of my nightstand. Asher has texted and called more times than I can count. I can't bring myself to read the messages. It's hard enough to stay away. I'm afraid I'll cave after a few carefully plucked words, and then I'll be in the same position once more, a couple of months down the line. Empty. Lost. Broken.

It took every ounce of strength I had not to at least hear Asher out when he came to my door yesterday. Everything inside me was screaming to love him and nurture him and just *be there* for him. To see how he was coping after his loss. But it's all so convoluted now, and some addictions can only be overcome by quitting cold turkey. The withdrawals won't last forever; you just have to be strong enough to survive them.

When Dash came back inside, he tiptoed around me, like I was some fragile creature, waiting to see if I was aware of Asher's presence. I didn't say a word. I let him think I was oblivious. What difference does it make, anyway?

"You good?" Natalia asks, zipping my suitcase. Natalia's mom offered me a job at her boutique, and Nat just signed a lease on a condo and extended me an open invitation to stay for a week or forever—her words, not mine. I decided to take her up on it and get out of Dodge for a while.

Standing up to my parents and informing them of my plans to take a year off seemed like nothing in comparison to recent revelations. Mom took the news pretty well. I still haven't spoken to my father, but I know he's unhappy with the news, if the voicemails he left on my phone are anything to go by. Dashiell's at least working on a degree from *somewhere*, even if it's not Dad's school of choice. Not going straight to college at all is unacceptable in his eyes. The pressure and weight of indecision and uncertainty were lifted, only to be replaced by the crushing weight of Asher's absence.

"Yep," I say, forcing a smile, but she sees through it, giving me a sad one in return.

"You're not curious about what he had to say?" Nat asks skeptically, with a nod of her chin toward the drawer.

"Of course, I am," I say bluntly. "But that's how

you fall into old habits." She chews on her bottom lip, and I can tell she's trying desperately not to say something.

"Spit it out." I sigh, stretching out on my stomach on the bed next to her. "Don't hurt yourself."

"You didn't see his face, Bry," she starts. "He was climbing the fucking walls at the hospital, and he blamed himself for your fall. Dash didn't help matters," she mumbles the last part.

"What do you mean? I told you guys—it was Whitley." She's the one who caused my fall, in more ways than one.

"Dash insists Asher pushed you, and honestly, I think it's easier for him to blame Ash for everything."

"He pushed me *out of the way*. It was my brother who almost hit me," I argue.

"Either way," she shrugs, "they both blame him. Then once he got the news about his dad, I think it was just too much for him."

"Whose side are you on?" I try to joke, but it falls flat. "You guys don't even like each other."

"Yeah, well. Things change. And I wouldn't be your best friend if I didn't give it to you straight."

"I just hope they can figure it out," I admit sadly. Even though I know he's no good for me, I don't want him to be alone in this world.

"It'll all work out," she says reassuringly.

"Hey, whatever happened with Adrian?" I ask,

suddenly remembering her mission to make him want her.

"Ugh." She sighs, rolling her eyes, playing with the tips of her scarlet hair. "That was nothing. Just a game we were playing."

She's avoiding eye contact, and something in the sound of her voice makes me wonder if there's more to it than she's letting on. But, Nat doesn't keep secrets. She tells me everything.

Suddenly, there's a knock on my bedroom door, and we both turn in the direction.

"We're dressed, Dash. You can come in." Nat giggles, snapping out of whatever that was. She's been staying with me a lot, and Dash walked in on her undressing the other day. He still hasn't recovered. That, coupled with the fact that I now know way more about his sex life than any sister should, he's been extra skittish lately.

But it's not Dashiell that walks through my door. It's Whitley. Her black hair that's usually sleek and flat ironed to perfection is in a frizzy ponytail, and her face is devoid of makeup. She twists her hands in front of her nervously. Once the initial shock of her standing in my bedroom wears off, Nat springs into action and stands in front of me, blocking Whitley's view of me.

"You have two seconds to walk your Emo-Barbie lookin' ass out of this house."

"Your brother let me in," she says over Nat's shoulder in a meek voice that sounds completely foreign coming from her. I make a mental note to punch Dash. Why in the hell would he let her anywhere near us?

I want to throttle her. To cause her physical, bodily harm for causing Asher more pain than he already had to endure. For setting this whole fucked-up thing into motion. How can one person be the root of so many problems? But something in Whitley's tired, defeated expression has me listening to what she has to say.

"What do you want?" I ask through my teeth, and Nat still doesn't move.

"I'm sorry."

"For what? For having Asher sent away? For lying about sleeping with him? Or is it for sending me to the hospital with a concussion?"

"All of it," she cries, swiping tears off her pale cheeks. "I know, I'm fucking awful. I don't know why. I've always been this way. I've never had friends," she says, and I roll my eyes, shaking my head.

"This is not the time to play the victim," I inform her.

"I'm not," she snaps, mindlessly scratching her forearm in a nervous gesture. "I'm just trying to explain. I see myself doing these horrible things—feeling this intense jealousy that consumes me—and I can't stop. But when you wouldn't wake up..." She leaves the sentence hanging in the air.

"You could have killed her," Nat seethes. A little dramatic, maybe, but not technically false.

"I know. You just have everything. Asher, Dash, Adrian. People are drawn to you, want to protect you, take care of you. You have friends and people who love you. I had Asher for a minute, but then you took him from me. And then, I had nothing. It's just so easy for you."

"Easy?" I scoff. "Yeah, life has been a real treat these past few months."

"I didn't mean it like that. I just couldn't understand why it couldn't be like that for me. Is there something in me that makes me unlovable?" Whitley's scratching intensifies, and she doesn't even seem to be aware that she's doing it. Her forearm is red and raw, and I'm realizing that Whitley's issues are probably much more involved than I ever knew. "I just snapped. And I'm so sorry, Briar. For everything. I just needed to tell you."

"Don't be sorry for me, Whitley. Be sorry for you. I may not have Ash, but I can sleep just fine at night with the things I've done. Can you?"

It's a lie, a flat-out fucking lie, that I sleep well. I've probably only slept a handful of hours total since that night, but she doesn't need to know that. I go through the *what-ifs* night after night. What if I never went to that party? What if I tried harder to convince Ash to leave with me? But more than anything, what if I never kissed him in front of the window that night three years ago? But I can live with myself knowing I've never intentionally hurt anyone, and that's more than Whitley can say.

"No," she admits, with an edge in her voice. "But I'm trying to fix that." Honestly, the fact that she still has an attitude—that she hasn't had a complete personality transplant—gives me hope that maybe she will be better in the future. That this is genuine. Maybe it makes me a fool, but I believe her.

"Well, good luck," I say, a little snidely, but genuine nonetheless. She nods before turning to leave, but pauses in the doorway, looking back at me over her shoulder.

"He's always loved you, you know. I think I knew it before he did. I knew it because he looked at you the way I looked at him."

My throat gets tight, and my eyes burn. But I won't cry. Not in front of her.

"Bye, Whitley."

CHAPTER 20

ASHER

A nother week has passed. Another seven days of not talking to Briar. Another one hundred sixty-eight hours of sitting around my dad's house, taking care of everything he left behind. I've trashed most of the stuff that was salvageable, only keeping things of sentimental value. I've put off his room for as long as I could, saving it for last. I haven't so much as set foot in it since I've been back, unprepared to face the memories of my mother.

I twist the cheap gold doorknob and push. I'm relieved to find that it's nearly empty, save for a bed, their tall maple-colored dresser, and one small wooden box that lies in the middle of the floor. Curiosity gets the best of me, and I squat down to get a closer look.

It's a keepsake box that my mom used to stash

random things in, like jewelry, birth certificates, social security cards, family photos, and the like. It's about the size of a hardback book with a tree carved into the top. I open it, expecting to find the aforementioned things, but instead, I find a manila envelope with my name on it.

Dread. It creeps into me slowly, occupying every part of my being, as my shaky hands reach out to pick it up. It's heavier than I would have thought. I peel it open, dumping the contents onto the floor, and the first thing that spills out is money. A lot of it. I don't count it, but it has to at least be a few thousand dollars. *What the fuck, Dad?*

The next thing I notice is a folded-up piece of paper. I unfold it to find a letter written in my Dad's handwriting.

Asher,

If you're reading this, that means I'm gone. I've known it was coming for a while now. Expected it, and accepted it, even. I never thought I'd get the chance to make amends with you before my time was up, and maybe we didn't, but I want you to know that I died happy, having had somewhat of a second chance with you.

I didn't do much right as a father or a human, and I know I can't take credit for the man you've become, but you've made me proud nonetheless. I failed you in so many ways, and I'll never forgive myself for that. Know that it was never your fault, even when I couldn't see it myself.

The cash enclosed is what Alexander Vale offered me to have you sent away. I knew I couldn't say no. He would have had you thrown in jail, or worse. I thought by making you leave, I was doing the right thing by you. But I've never been good at making the right calls; that was your mother's department.

I never spent a dime of this money and always intended for this to be yours. Same with the house. Burn it, sell it, keep it, whatever you want, because it's yours.

I guess this is the part in the letter where I should impart some words of wisdom. The truth is, I've never been very wise, but I'll give it a try.

I hope that when love finds you, and I suspect that it already has, you're able to hold on to it forever. And if, for some god-forsaken reason you lose it, you don't end up like me. Don't let it break you. You're stronger than that. Stronger than me.

Second chances don't come around very often. Third chances are even more rare. If you're lucky enough to get one, don't waste it.

I hope that when you become a father, you forget everything you learned from me. Love like your mother. Love like Briar. Love like you.

And most importantly, never piss in the wind.

Love, Dad

I drop the letter and attempt to sort out the emotions that slam into me all at once, fighting for the spotlight. I feel sad and angry and relieved and hopeful and...at peace. Closure. That's what this must be. I feel like I can finally let go of it all. All of the loss, all the grief, all the bad.

For the first time in my adult life, I decide to take my father's advice. I'm not letting my chance with Briar slip away. But first, I have some things I need to take care of.

CHAPTER 21

BRIAR

He's gone. For good. I know this is what I wanted, or what I need to happen, rather, but it doesn't make it hurt any less. Adrian admitted to me the other day that he'd been in contact with Asher. I wasn't mad. I was curious. Maybe a little jealous, but not mad. My brother, on the other hand, has been a bit more stubborn. I can't pretend to know what it would feel like to have my best friend lie to me, but I'd like to think that if the roles were reversed and Nat and Dash wanted to be together, I wouldn't stand in their way. It would be weird and a completely different dynamic, but who am I to tell them what they can and can't do? Dash argues that it's different.

Adrian told Dash that Asher had gone back to River's Edge a few days ago. I don't know what I expected. For him to fight for me and pine for me forever? To stay in this town where he has almost no one? Of course not. But it stings.

I'm listening to "Glycerine" on repeat, feeling sorry for myself, when Adrian calls, interrupting my song.

"Hey, pretty girl," he says, using his nickname for me.

"Hey, Ade."

"What are you up to today?"

"I have the day off, so I'm just hanging out at Nat's."

"What do I have to do to get you to come have lunch with your favorite brother-slash-lover?"

I laugh, despite the morose mood I've been in for the last few weeks.

"Never say that again and you've got yourself a deal. Where do you want to meet?"

"I'll text you the address. See you in an hour?"

"Sounds good."

"Wear something sexy!" he shouts into the phone right before I hang up, and I catch myself laughing once again. Adrian is just good for the soul. Just like everyone should have a Natalia, everyone should also have an Adrian.

My phone says it takes forty-five minutes to get there, back in the direction of my house, so I pluck an olive-green T-shirt dress out of my suitcase and slip on my black boots before walking out the door.

Once I'm close, I pull out my phone to double-check the address. I'm led into a residential area, and I wonder if this is a shortcut or something, but as I turn the corner, it says my destination is on the left.

What the hell?

I'm most definitely parked in front of a house, not a restaurant, and I pull off to the side to call Adrian. But then I see him. Not Adrian. *Asher.* He's standing in the driveway, his thick eyebrows pulled together, hands behind his back. Signature black jeans, a black V-neck, and black boots.

I'm not prepared for this. For seeing him again. For the way my stomach flips in response to him. I should drive away. I almost do, but something in his pleading eyes has me turning off the ignition and slowly opening the door.

I take a deep breath, trying to keep my emotions in check, as I walk up to him. We meet in the middle, and the look of relief on his face almost cracks my heart in two.

"What's going on? Where's Adrian?" I ask, knowing this is some kind of setup.

"I need five minutes. That's it." His dark hair hangs over one eye, and I want to brush it out of his face. To hug him. To be held by him. To nuzzle into his warm neck and take in the scent that belongs only to him. But I don't do any of that. Taking my silence as permission, he licks his lips and exhales deeply before continuing.

"Sometimes, when you're hurting so deeply for so long, you don't feel anything at all anymore. And then something or someone comes along that gets under your skin, inside your blood, and makes you feel fucking everything again. And all of that pain that you never felt? It all comes flooding back. I didn't know *how* to feel, Briar. Until you, with your big blue eyes and your heart on your sleeve. You made me feel everything, and I both loved and hated you for it. I wasn't blessed with a perfect life, but I had you."

"Ash," I whisper, taking a step forward, but he stops me with a raised palm.

"Please," he says brokenly. "Just let me finish."

I nod, waiting for him to continue.

"When your dad confronted me with a picture of us together and the drugs he knew I had, I should've known you'd never have any part in that. I convinced myself that you were like everyone else, shallow, and conniving, and self-serving. It was almost easier, because that way, I didn't have to worry about those fucking *feelings*.

"And then when you hit your head, all I saw was my mom. I couldn't save her, and I couldn't save you. I prayed—fucking *prayed*—for the first time in my life. I bartered with God. I told Him if He let you be okay, that I'd leave you alone. And you *were* okay, but then my dad died, and it was clearer than ever. I needed to run, and this time I wasn't going to come back. I knew you'd be better off without me, and I planned on letting you go..." He pauses, running a hand through his hair in a nervous gesture. "Until I saw the succulent you left at my parents' grave."

I suck in a breath, taking in everything he's saying. He's cutting himself open and bleeding before me. He's breaking my heart and making me whole all at once. Tears are streaming down my face at his words, and I don't even try to wipe them away.

"I think I've loved you since you cried for that pigeon. There you were, privileged and beautiful and had everything most people can only dream of, yet you still cared about a fucking bird. And you cared for *me*. You showed me your pure soul that day, and you showed it again when you went to my dad's funeral, and every day in between. And I'm too fucking selfish to give you up."

"What are you saying?" I ask skeptically, afraid to get my hopes up again.

"I'm saying I'm not running anymore, Briar. I'm staying here. With you. And fuck anyone who has a problem with it."

He grabs my hand and leads me inside the house. It's not fully furnished, but it has a few things, like a plush rug in front of a fireplace that's probably never been used and a simple white couch. It looks like it's a stage home for sale, and I wonder what exactly we're doing here. He keeps walking us through a tiled hallway, past some stairs, and into a kitchen.

"What is all this?" I ask, taking in the stainless steel refrigerator and empty marble counters.

"I bought it."

"You *what?*"

"I bought it," he says again. "Or, I'm about to. I told you, I'm here for good. For always. And I want you to be with me here, too."

"Ash," I breathe, tempted to pinch myself. This is all I've ever wanted. And there was a time when I would have blindly said yes to anything he asked of me, but if there's one thing I've learned, it's that if something seems too good to be true, it probably is.

"Isn't this a little fast?"

"Fast? This has been six years in the making. We were always meant for each other. We just did it wrong."

"How do I know that this is real? I can't do this again. I can't lose you again."

"I'm not going anywhere, baby. Even if you don't move in. If you want to stay at home, or in a dorm, or move to another state, we can figure that out, too."

"You're serious," I ask, but it comes out more like a statement. Asher pushes off the counter and strides toward me, his multi-colored eyes blazing into mine. He threads a hand through my hair at the nape of my neck and ducks down so his mouth is level with mine. I keep my hands clenched at my sides. I know if I let myself touch him, I'm done for. I'll stand absolutely no chance.

"I love you," he says against my lips before pressing them to mine. I close my eyes at hearing those words spoken to me for the first time. He told Dash that he loved me, but hearing it like this is so much *more*. "I love every fucking thing about you," he says, pressing another kiss to my jaw, my neck. "I love the way you smell, the way you taste." He nips at the skin on my shoulder. "I love the way you love, recklessly and unconditionally. I love this body..." Ash's hands smooth down my back to rub my ass through the thin T-shirt dress, and my breath hitches. A tear slips free, and he licks it up, bending to grab me by the back of my thighs. He lifts me into his arms, and my legs wrap around him, like they were meant to be there. "And how it was made for me. I loved you even when I hated you. And that's how I knew I didn't hate you at all."

I swallow past the lump in my throat, looking into the whiskey and jade eyes of the boy that I've always loved. They search mine, begging for me to put him out of his misery.

"I love you, too. I've loved you forever."

At my confession, he props me up onto the counter. He holds my face in both hands before devouring my mouth with his. His tongue pushes inside, and I suck on it, eliciting a groan from the back of his throat. We pour everything into this kiss. Every ounce of pain and love and longing and lust and betrayal. Every secret, stolen moment. Every tear, every orgasm, every touch.

Asher pulls back and lifts the hem of my dress as he sinks to his knees in front of me. Starting at the soft skin below my belly button, he peppers kisses, dragging my dress up along the way. Right before he exposes my braless chest, his eyes lock with mine. I can't breathe, can't speak, can't do anything other than focus on the sensations consuming me. Still holding my gaze, he bites the ample, fleshy underside of my breast, and I shudder, goose bumps assaulting everywhere from my stomach to my ears. My nipples tighten almost painfully, and he closes his mouth around one, biting it through the fabric of my dress.

The ache in my core intensifies, and I'm so wet I can feel it between my thighs. Slowly, he peels the dress over my tight pink nipples and sucks one into his mouth while kneading the other. He alternates kissing and sucking and biting, giving them equal attention.

Needing more, I rip my dress over my head, letting it fall somewhere behind me, and pull him in for another soul-shattering kiss. When he pulls away, we're both breathing raggedly. Hooking his fingers into the sides of my underwear, he tugs them down, leaving me in nothing but my black combat boots.

Asher drops to his knees once more. He peels my panties down, letting them drop to the floor, before spreading my legs with his shoulders. He pushes on my lower stomach, forcing me to lean back on my elbows. His tongue parts my lower lips, and I gasp at the contact. Lightly, he flicks his tongue against my swollen clit, and I jerk off the counter in response.

"Stay still, baby. I want to taste you."

Trying my best to obey, I lie flat against the countertop. Ash wraps his hand around my right ankle and pulls my boot off. He kisses the arch of my foot before placing it on the edge, doing the same to the other one. He presses against my knees, opening me to him. I'm completely exposed, and he stands, taking his sweet time to study my most vulnerable place.

He bites on that plump bottom lip and slides two fingers over my clit, rubbing and swirling. He speeds up his movements, and soon, he's rubbing everywhere from my clit to my ass and everything in between as I desperately rock into his touch.

"Please, Ash. I need you."

"I want to take my time with you," he says in a strained voice, and I realize he's scared, too. He's afraid this will be our last time together.

"Baby," I say, sitting up, my fingers going straight for the button of his jeans. "We have all the time in the world." I undo his pants and use my feet to push them off his hips, not even bothering to take the time to rid him of his shirt. I take his length in my hand, directing him to my entrance. Hot and hard meets warm and wet as he thrusts inside me.

Asher holds my gaze as he slowly drives into me, and it's the best kind of torture. I drop my eyes to see his length disappearing inside of me, and I feel myself clench around him at the sight. He groans and buries himself to the hilt, controlling my movements with his hands on my hips.

"I love you," I say again, and those words must unleash something inside of him, because then he's leaning me backward, covering my body with his own, as he thrusts into me like a madman. He takes my nipple into his mouth and sucks, while his hand snakes down my body to rub my clit.

"I'm going to come, Ash. Fuck me, please. I'm going to come." My words run together, almost unintelligible, but the meaning is clear.

"Say it again," he says raggedly. His hair is damp with sweat, and his eyes are glazed over with lust.

"I love you," I cry out. "I love you so fucking much."

Asher brings his big hands to grip my hips, his thumbs touching as he drives into me punishingly. I throw my head back and my body locks up, my mouth dropping open in a silent scream as he fucks me through my orgasm. My legs shake uncontrollably, and I think I might lose consciousness. Ash grabs me by the jaw, forcing my gaze back to him. He presses his thumb against my bottom lip before I suck it into my mouth, swirling my tongue around it.

"Fuck, baby."

He tenses up, and his mouth parts in ecstasy. The veins on his neck and arms are bulging as he spills inside of me. He collapses onto my chest, and I love the feeling of his weight on top of me.

"Don't ever take this away from me," he says, his voice barely above a whisper, as he circles his hips, giving soft, tiny thrusts. His head is nuzzled in between my breasts, and his face sticks to my skin. I run my fingers through his damp hair as I come back down to earth.

After our breathing has returned to normal, he pulls out, slowly, and both of us groan at the loss. I feel our wetness pooling, and he pulls his black tee over his head and brings it between my legs. With more tenderness than I knew he was capable of, he cleans me up. When I bring my knees back together, he stops me, pushing them back open to make sure he got every last drop.

I sit up, and the first thing I notice is Asher's freshly inked side.

"Asher," I gasp, carefully tracing the design with my fingertips. It's the drawing from his drawer. The skull with the succulents and roses covering one eye. And this time, I have no doubt in my mind that it's for me.

"Dare did it," he supplies.

"It's beautiful." And it is.

"It's us," he says simply.

Ash scoops me up, wrapping my legs around his waist. I tuck my head into the space between his neck and his shoulder. Our sticky, love-drunk bodies fusing as one as he carries me back toward the living room.

He lowers us onto the plush carpet in front of the fireplace, and we lie there, tangled together, unspeaking for who knows how long, before he finally succumbs to sleep. He looks so innocent like this. Thick, dark eyelashes fanned against cheeks with the faintest of freckles scattered across them. His lips are slightly parted, and the worry lines between his eyebrows no longer exist.

Because he's at peace. And so am I.

EPILOGUE

BRIAR

ONE YEAR AND TWO MONTHS LATER.

"You can come home any time now," Nat says into my ear. I'm on the phone with her, driving the tree-lined, windy roads in River's Edge. Two months after Asher vowed to never leave me again, I turned eighteen and moved in with him. He stayed at his dad's house while he was waiting for it to sell, and I stayed at my parents' home. I knew those remaining two months of still being seventeen weren't going to make any kind of difference, but I think it was my way of making sure it was going to stick this time. But, I didn't let Asher buy that house he showed me, even after we christened every surface.

One night when we were driving to meet my brother for dinner, I told him that I fell in love with River's Edge and asked what he thought about starting our new beginning there. He promptly showed me exactly how he felt by swinging his truck into a crowded parking lot, pulling me onto his lap, and fucking me right there in the open. It's kind of our thing—sex in semi-public places.

Speaking of my brother, Dashiell and Asher somehow managed to become even closer than they were before. I worried for a while, because it was a rough adjustment period. Dash finally realized that it was really that different at all. Dash, Asher, Adrian, and I... We're all still best friends. The dynamic hadn't changed much in that sense. The only difference is that two of us also liked to fuck each other. A lot. Every chance we got.

Dash completed his bachelor's degree, and next year he'll start law school. In the meantime, he likes to drag Adrian up to River's Edge every chance he gets. They get to see us, and they get to prey on the pretty tourists. *Win-win.*

Adrian likes to claim that he's the reason we're together in the first place and has demanded that we name our firstborn after him to show our everlasting gratitude.

Nat is balancing college and working at the boutique, so we don't get to see each other all that much, but we still talk daily.

As for Whitley and Jackson? I haven't heard from either one of them. I'm pretty sure Jackson went on living as nothing happened. The jury's still out on Whitley. I hope she got the help she so clearly needs.

My phone beeps, signaling my mom calling on the other line, and I make a mental note to call her later. The biggest surprise of the last year was when she announced she was divorcing my dad. Apparently, their issues ran deeper than I ever knew. In a rare, candid moment, my mom informed me that my father had been having affairs behind her back. Yes, plural. As in, *multiple* affairs.

I was floored, but Dashiell didn't seem too surprised. It made me wonder if he knew more than he let on. She admitted that she didn't leave him sooner because she didn't want to disrupt our lives. My mom made a lot of unseen sacrifices over the years, and though I wish she had put herself first, it makes me see her in a different light. It's comforting to know that she cared all along. She's living back at home, trying to figure out who she is without my dad. And of course, my dad stayed in California. We've talked a few times, but except for the occasional birthday call or text asking me if I'd like to come visit him, we don't really speak. He did apologize for the effect his decision had on Ash, but stands firm that he made the right choice as a father. I understand it, but I don't agree with it.

"Or, you could just come live here. You'd love it in

the wintertime, Nat. It's like a magnet for hot guys. *Foreign* hot guys. With accents."

Asher was right; this place really does look like a snow globe in the winter. I don't know if it's because I'm not used to seeing snow, having lived in Arizona my whole life, but everything just feels magical here. People come to River's Edge from all over the world. In the winter, we have snowboarding and skiing. In the summer, everyone comes for the lake.

"I'll come visit soon. I promise."

"Good. Hey, I have to go. I'm about to lose service," I say as I approach the narrow road that leads to our little cabin in paradise. When you live as deep into the woods as we do, you can forget finding a signal.

"Okay. I love you, B. And I'm really happy for you."

"I love you, too," I say, laughing at her random display of emotion.

I pout when I pull into the driveway to see that Ash isn't home from work yet. With Dare focusing most of his attention on the new shop, Bad Intentions, Ash has been working six, sometimes seven, days a week during peak season. Between that and the fact that I have to make the forty-five-minute journey to nursing school five times a week, we haven't seen each other as much as we'd like in the past month or so.

I grab my purse before I make my way to our modest, but beautiful little cabin. The entire front is made up of tall windows, with a deck that wraps around on one side. It's beyond perfect.

I'm looking down at my phone as I twist the knob and walk inside. My head snaps up, taking in the dozens of twinkling lights hanging from the ceiling, and I see Asher, standing in front of me with a bouquet of flowers.

"What is all this?" I laugh. "Where's your truck?"

"Happy birthday, baby girl," he says, handing me the flowers. Only, they aren't just flowers. It's a succulent bouquet, and it's the prettiest thing I've ever seen.

"Thank you," I say, throwing one arm around his neck, the flowers sandwiched between us.

His hands rub up and down my back before gripping my hips.

"They're beautiful." I press my mouth to his and suck on his bottom lip, which earns me a groan.

"Are you happy?" Asher asks, and I realize for the first time since walking in that he looks nervous or unsure.

"Are you kidding me? I have everything I've ever wanted. With *you*."

"I sure as fuck am glad you feel that way," he says, before dropping to one knee.

Oh my God.

My purse and flowers fall to the floor, and I bring my hands to cover my shocked expression.

"Briar," he starts, looking up at me with a mix of love and hopefulness and fear. "I don't know how to do this shit," he admits. "All I know is that my best side is your worst creation. Everything good in me is because of *you*. I'll never deserve the kind of love and loyalty that you've given me since you were just a kid, but I promise to spend every fucking day trying, if you'll let me. Will you marry me?"

Tears are streaming down my face, and swallowing past the lump in my throat, I say, "I will marry the shit out of you."

He laughs, flashing that perfect smile of his, before producing a ring from his pocket and sliding it onto my finger. It's a gorgeous, pear-shaped diamond. It's nothing too ostentatious. It's perfect. I'm about to tell him how much I love it, when cheers and screams and applause coming from my right have me spinning around, my hand flying to my heart. My mouth drops open in shock to find my brother, Nat, Adrian, my mom, and Dare. They're all here, in my living room. I look back at Ash, and he simply shrugs in response.

"I told you I'd visit soon!" Nat shouts, tears shimmering in her big brown eyes.

"How did everyone get here?" I ask, swiping away the tears from my cheeks. There weren't any cars in the driveway.

"Dare's friends brought us. Left our vehicles at his house, so you'd be surprised."

"Well, mission accomplished." I laugh.

We spend the next hour or so hugging, gushing,

crying, and catching up, before Ash kicks everyone out and leads me to our bed.

"Are you ready to be Mrs. Kelley?" Ash asks, kissing up my thighs. I squirm under his touch, biting my lip and nodding my head. My heart feels so full in this moment. He continues peppering kisses up my stomach, chest, neck, and lips, before placing the last one on the scar on my temple. The one that serves as a constant reminder of what we almost lost.

"I love you, Bry," he says, settling in between my thighs. I feel him hard at my entrance, and I shift my hips, trying to take him into my body.

"I love you, too."

"Now shut up, so I can fuck my fiancée."

I laugh out loud, but it morphs into a moan as he pushes inside me, proving that sometimes, bad habits lead to good endings.

And beginnings.

The End

ACKNOWLEDGMENTS

First, I have to thank my husband who fed kids, cleaned house, went grocery shopping, and cooked meals, all while essentially being ignored for, like, an entire month. I love you more than you'll ever know.

A huge thank you to Paige, my editor, who is always ridiculously accommodating. I don't know what I would do without you. No, seriously. Don't leave me. I'd find you.

Thank you to Leigh for being there every step of the way. You're the Serena to my Blair. The Jared to my Tate. I love you even when you're crazy, which is a solid 90% of the time.

Thank you to Ella, for always keeping it real, and for pushing me when I needed it. I'm so thankful for your friendship. "Put a flower on it!"

Mary, you're my favorite. Thank you for being alive. I love you.

Serena, thank you for all your help. Your excitement and enthusiasm for books is something that cannot be faked or replicated.

Melissa, thank you for your special brand of encouragement, usually consisting of, "Stop being a pussy and write the book!" Also, you don't have bad eyebrows, so shut up, Donald.

Clarissa and Julie, thank you for being the kind of women I want my daughter to grow up to be. You're my people.

Shout out to Bex. You're always willing to drop everything to help me, and having your feedback is vital. Thank you!

Sash! Thank you for being an amazing admin and an even better friend.

Thank you to my group, Charleigh's Angels. You guys are my happy place. Straight up. I love you all.

Thank you to all my author friends who helped me in more ways than I can count. I'm truly lucky to have so many amazing women in my corner.

Lastly, to my readers and bloggers, thank you. Thank you, thank you, thank you. I appreciate all your messages, teasers, reviews, shares, posts, and the countless ways you show your support. You're invaluable.

MISBEHAVED BY CHARLEIGH ROSE

CHECK OUT THE FIRST CHAPTER OF
MISBEHAVED, MY STUDENT/TEACHER
ROMANCE!

~

CHAPTER ONE
REMI

Let me start off by saying I don't hate my life. To someone from the outside, it might look like a *bad* life, but I don't care. I know the truth. I have a roof over my head. I'm frying juicy steaks in the kitchen. My dad, Dan, isn't abusive or in prison, which basically puts me at a huge advantage in comparison to the rest of the kids in my neighborhood. I have Ryan, who looks out for me, and, for the most part—albeit in an unconventional, fucked-up way—I feel loved.

Mostly.

But feeling loved doesn't mean that I'm happy with my circumstances. It doesn't mean I'm content with the street I live on that manages to taint every man, woman, and child that is unlucky enough to land here. It doesn't mean that I won't try to run away.

I live in Las Vegas, the city that sucks out your soul and spits out whatever's left of you. Your job is to pick up the pieces and find out who you are.

I'm about to. Planning to. *Soon.*

I flip the steak, and the searing pan hisses in delight. Take two steps to my right. Stir the boiling pasta. *Al dente,* just like Ryan likes it. Walk over to the sink. Wash my hands. Look out the window, the screen is hole-ridden and the frame rusty and eaten by the scorching heat and age. Then I smile. I see Ryan kneeling on our yellow overgrown grass, in front of the cracked, bruised asphalt of the road, working on his Harley. As if he senses me, he lifts his gaze to mine.

Stern. Severe. A little on the psycho side. But, he's my family nonetheless.

Ryan is not my biological brother. My mom, Mary, died in a car accident when I was two. I don't remember her, and although I'm sad that I never got to know her, it's my dad I truly hurt for. All I have left of

Mary Julia Stringer is an old, beat-up camera from the nineties, and I hold on to it like it's my lifeline.

I used to use my high school's dark room to develop the film myself, but now, I'll have to figure something else out. I'm autodidactic. Self-taught, if you will. That doesn't come without a price, because I'm probably no good, but taking photos is what I love. Dad says Mom always had a camera in her hand. Funny how those things can be passed down without even knowing her or having her influence. It makes me feel connected to her.

A few years after she passed, my dad took another stab at dating. Enter Darla and ten-year-old Ryan. I knew Darla was bad for Pops, even at the tender age of five. She smelled like smoke and cheap perfume and always went out of her way to make me feel like a burden. But Pops seemed happy—at first, anyway—and I got Ryan. So, it wasn't all bad. Over the next five years, however, things deteriorated, along with their relationship. Darla started skipping out on us for days at a time, and even flaunted other men in front of my dad. After more than a few knock-down, drag-out fights, Darla had finally bailed for good. When my dad found Ryan, who was only fifteen, packing his things up, he told him to unpack his shit and go set the table for dinner, and that was that. Darla was out, and Ryan was staying. When I asked my dad why she left, his response was something along the lines of, "Darla's a whore. Don't be like Darla."

Duly noted, Dad.

The night Darla left was the first night I snuck into Ryan's room. It was innocent, of course. I wanted to comfort him, even though he showed no signs of being particularly saddened by his mom's absence. At first, he stiffened when he felt the bed dip under my weight. But my intuition had been right, because that night, Ryan held me and cried himself to sleep while I rubbed his arm and sniffled quietly. He never cried again, and we never spoke about it, but he still sleeps with me on occasion. Except now, it's Ryan who sneaks into my room.

And it's not innocent. Not anymore.

The years passed, as they always do, while Ryan still lives at home, neither my dad nor I want to see him leave. Maybe it's because Dad is rarely at home. He makes the Las Vegas-Los Angeles route twice a week, and occasionally takes longer trips that have him on the road for weeks at a time, which leaves him very little time for actual parenting. Since sleeping by myself in this rundown house, in this horrific neighborhood is pretty much a death wish, I'm happy to have Ryan by my side. With his tall frame, bulging tattooed muscles, uniform of wifebeater and don't-fuck-with-me expression plastered to his face, you'd have to be stupid to break into our house.

And it's not the only reason I am happy to have him around. We need each other. It's always been us against the world. Not that the world was particularly against us. It just didn't care.

I start making the sauce for the pasta. Tomato. Basil. Olive oil. A shit-ton of garlic. I read the recipe somewhere on the internet after Ryan and I saw it on some cooking show that aired on one of the few channels we have.

Maybe it will make him crack a goddamn smile for once. He's always been a bit of a ticking time bomb. The homemade, highly unpredictable type. But lately, I feel like he's seconds away from exploding.

Tick, tick, tick.

For the rest of the meal prep, I'm on autopilot. I chop, stir, drain, flip, arrange everything on the plates, take out two bottles of Bud Light from the fridge, and set the table. Then I proceed to kick the whiny door and bang my fist against the screen a few times to draw his attention.

"Dinner's ready," I yell.

"Two secs." I hear the clink of heavy tools dropping onto the concrete near the yellow grass he is kneeling on. His bike's been fucked for two weeks now, and he can't take it to the shop because he spent his last few bucks on bailing out his best friend, Reed. Not that having a broken-down bike has slowed him down any. The guy is never home anymore.

"Steak's getting cold. Get your ass inside or I'm eating without you," I mutter and slam the screen door with a bang.

I wait for him, slouched on my chair in front of our plates, scrolling my thumb along the touch-screen of my phone—one of the three things that my dad makes sure we always budget for: the rent, the food, and my phone. Most kids would be pissed to have an older model, but I'm just happy this thing has internet capabilities. Ryan saunters in and collapses on the chair opposite me, not bothering to wash his dirtied, greasy hands.

I chance a glance at him. Ryan looks like a man. He's looked that way for a long time now. His arms are ripped—not in the gym rat way, just in the way of a guy who does manual labor—and his body is big, wide, and commanding. Long, dirty blond hair that almost touches his shoulders, brown eyes, cut bone structure— the only good thing he inherited from his deadbeat real dad. Every time we hang outside the house together— which, admittedly, is not often these days—girls I went to school with throw themselves at him. He's screwed half of them, I know, even though they're underage. If I'm being honest, it seems to be half the charm about this guy. Other than the fact that he is inked from head-to-toe. It's that slightly unstable, dangerous vibe he gives off. Every girl wants to be good until a bad boy whisks her off her feet and corrupts her.

And every girl hated the one who stood in their way. That'd be me. At least in their mind. Sure, Ryan would fuck them, but that's all they ever got. He always stood a little too close to me, stared a little too long. They noticed. And they were ruthless. So, I was deemed the brother fucker. I didn't really care. Ryan didn't help matters by forbidding the entire male population of Riverdale to stay far away from me. He was out of high school before I even began, but he's somewhat of a legend around here. No one in their right mind would willingly cross him.

"How's the steak?" I ask, keeping my eyes on my own piece of meat as I slice it carefully.

"Juicy." He laughs, his mouth full. From my peripheral, I see a trail of bloody liquid traveling from the corner of his lip to his chin, but he doesn't make any move to wipe it. He takes another bite, his eyes honing in on me. "So, when are you going to turn eighteen?"

"You're my brother," I grind out. "Shouldn't you at least pretend to know this kind of crap?"

"I'm a shit brother," he retorts, his voice as dry as his steak is juicy. "And when asked a question, you fucking answer. It's really that simple, Rem."

That's the part where I should probably mention— he calls me Rem. My name is Remington, and my friends call me Remi, but Ryan, much to my dismay, has been calling me Rem since day one.

"August sixteenth," I groan. Ryan moves his eyes up and down my body as much as he can with the barrier that's the table between us.

"What's two more weeks?" he mumbles as he rubs his lower lip with his thumb, and it's glistening with the olive oil from the pasta and the juice of the steak.

"Until what?" I ask, playing dumb. He knows I'm not dumb. In fact, he resents the fact that I want more out of life than my high school diploma. But his comments have become increasingly inappropriate over the past few months, and even though it's flattering, sometimes alarm bells go off in my head.

"Until your big brother can show you just how much he loves you." Ryan chuckles sinisterly. I let loose a nervous smile. I know Ryan wants to get me into bed, but more than that, he wants to own me. Own my thoughts, my actions, my body. He *thinks* he already does. In his twisted mind, he calls it love. Why wouldn't he? It's not like Ryan has ever seen a good example of it. Hell, neither have I. In his mind, he protects me, takes care of me, and he *needs* me. In a way, I need him, too. But, I just can't ever see us happening. This—what we're doing right this moment —is what the rest of my life would look like. Me cooking dinner, wishing I were anywhere else, and Ryan being perfectly content to work on his bike and get tanked with his shitty friends every night. *No, thank you.*

It's not like the attraction is not there. I had a major crush on him when I was younger. I thought he hung the moon and the stars, making everything brighter in my dull universe, and I think I did the same for him. But if he were the one, it wouldn't feel so freaking wrong every time his throbbing dick "accidentally" presses against my ass at night.

Getting up from my seat, I take our plates to the sink and saunter back with a new beer, cracking it open in front of him. When I do, he snakes one arm around my waist and grabs me in one swift movement so that I'm straddling him on his lap. I can feel the seam of his zipper grinding into my crotch. Not gonna lie—it feels nice.

"Hey," he breathes into my mouth, always a whisper from a kiss, but never there. Where he wants to be.

"Hi." I swallow visibly.

"So." His hand travels into my inner thigh, and I feel something stiffen underneath me. I take a deep breath. The room is dark and dingy and small, cluttered with our old furniture, *with our pasts*. It's not exactly romantic, but I can't deny the heady feeling coursing through me.

"You a virgin, Rem?" he whispers into my lips again, and this time it could qualify as a kiss. A part of me wants it to. The other part begs me not to go over that invisible, fragile line that I'm straddling just now. "You saved yourself for me? Kept this untouched?" His fingers hover over my groin, barely touching.

"No." The word comes out more like a groan. Never mind the fact that I've only done it twice. I don't need to tell him who it was. He knows. Zach Williamson. Eleventh grade. The only guy I dated for more than two months before I got bored. We actually made it through a whole semester before I dumped his ass. I didn't care that I'd given him my virginity. I wasn't waiting for "the one". To be honest, I've never really thought that one person putting their body part into another person was that big of a deal. It's probably a good thing I didn't have high hopes, because both times were pretty anticlimactic.

There's something in Ryan's already-hooded expression that becomes even darker and more severe, and for a minute, my heart beats faster for the wrong reason. Not because I'm excited, but because I'm unnerved. I wait, studying his expression carefully, before his hard stare turns into a half-assed, placid smile.

"Good," he says and squeezes my butt a little too hard, indicating that he doesn't think it's good at all. "I don't think you could handle me without a little practice, anyway."

Then his lips are not hovering anymore—they're kissing—not slowly either. He doesn't ask for permission. He is not tentative or unsure. His tongue invades my mouth in an instant, and it catches me off-guard. As I suck in some air, he takes the opportunity to deepen our kiss. I place both hands on his cheeks to ease him away, and he throws my hands off.

Possessive. Hungry. Angry.

"You taste like heaven, little sister," he hisses into my mouth. Nothing about this feels right. People know us as brother and sister. The fact that we're not blood-related is only somewhat consoling. Hell, even the kiss doesn't feel right. Like we're doing it all wrong. I feel him squeezing my ass harder, digging his dirty finger-nails into my flesh, and wince.

"I've been waiting so long for this." His words not only pierce—they penetrate me—along with his fingers that are now dragging themselves slowly, roughly toward my sex. I breathe out harshly.

"Ryan," I drop my forehead to his, "you're hurting me."

"I know." His tongue continues attacking my mouth, his hands even more aggressive on me than before.

Panic. It trickles into me slowly. I know Ryan. Know him well. He is not a bad guy—definitely not a good guy, but not a rapist either—and he knows damn well my dad would kill him if he ever seriously wronged me.

"You're starting school tomorrow," he says, licking his way down to my chin and neck. I let him, and even though I don't want this, I can't help my body's reac-tion to his touch. It's humming, singing, asking for more. And why not give in to feeling good with someone I know and trust with my life? Still, some-thing holds me back.

"How you gonna get all the way to Henderson every day?"

"Take the bus," I answer flatly. I'm not giving up on

this opportunity. My dad somehow came up with my tuition to one of the best high schools in Nevada. Private. Top-notch. Said he's been saving for years, and only just now—my senior year—saved enough to send me. Not that I'm complaining. I think Dad secretly feels guilty about being gone so often. That, and he's heard what the kids at school say about me. That I'm a whore. A brother fucker.

After my best friend, Ella, moved away, they got worse. I was a lone ranger. An easy target. The boys were all afraid to interact with me—pussies—but the girls? Girls are vicious and sneaky. Like the boys, they're also afraid of Ryan, but they did shit on the down low. Stashing shit—literal shit—in my locker. Stealing my clothes when I was in the shower after P.E. Stuff that couldn't be directly traced back to them, even though we all knew who did it. And while I honestly never really cared what other people thought of me, I was being offered a golden ticket out of this shithole town, and I'm not giving it up. Especially not for something as miniscule as transportation.

"The buses don't run that early, baby girl." Ryan laughs, and why did I think he was that attractive in the first place? His smile is too big, his teeth too pointy, like a wolf's, and the scent of his sweat is too sour.

"Nice try. I checked, Ryan. They're twenty-four hours."

"You can walk, my ass." He pulls his head back,

laughing. "You're not taking the bus alone. I'm giving you a ride back and forth, got it?"

I hate depending on anyone for anything. I may not have a car, but I've worked since the day I turned fourteen. My dad signed a waiver, much to Ryan's dismay, and I got a job at the Dairy Queen around the corner—where I reluctantly quit once I found out I wouldn't have time to work when school started. When I need to be somewhere, I walk or ride my bike. Like I said, I despise being dependent on anyone, but if there's one thing I hate more, it's mornings. Specifically, early mornings. And to get to school on time, I'd have to wake up at an ungodly hour.

I want to say no.

I should say no.

But as his rock-hard erection grinds into me violently, I say something else entirely.

"Fine."

Read *Misbehaved* today for FREE on Kindle Unlimited!